EXILE

BLAKE NELSON

SCRIBNER PAPERBACK FICTION
PUBLISHED BY SIMON & SCHUSTER

SCRIBNER PAPERBACK FICTION
Simon & Schuster Inc.
Rockefeller Center
1230 Avenue of the Americas
New York, NY 10020

Manufactured in the United States of America

1   3   5   7   9   10   8   6   4   2

Library of Congress Cataloging-in-Publication Data
Nelson, Blake, date.
Exile / Blake Nelson.
p.   cm.
I. Title.
PS3564.E44E95   1997
813'.54—dc21   96-53106
CIP

ISBN 0-684-83838-9

CONTENTS

Wherever there is genius, there is a man trying to escape.

SARTRE

PART ONE

winter

I

"Who the fuck is Fred Bragg?" says Mark West to no one in particular. He's standing in the dressing room of Arena, a nightclub in New York City. He's looking at the chalkboard that lists the evening's spoken-word performers.

"He's from MTV," says Cynthia, passing behind him.

"What, he's the MC?"

"He's a poet."

"So why's he on top?"

"He must be headlining," says Cynthia.

"What are you talking about? *I'm* headlining."

"He must have been added. How would I know? He has a video on MTV."

"What, he's a musician?"

"He's a poet. He reads a poem. It's good."

"How many books does he have?" Mark asks her, though Cynthia has nothing to do with it. She's here to take pictures.

Mark walks directly upstairs. He finds Ed in his office in the back of the club.

"Ed!" says Mark, pushing open the door.

Ed is on the phone.

"Ed, who the fuck is this Fred Bragg and why is he above me on the goddamn list?"

Ed finishes his conversation and hangs up. "He's a poet."

"No, Ed, I'm a poet. He's a fucking MTV guy."

"Right. He's a poet. Who's on MTV."

"How many books does he have?"

"How many books do *you* have?"

"Three. And they've been reviewed. And they've sold."

"How many?"

"Lots. I don't know. Lots."

"MTV goes to 250 million households."

"What the fuck are you talking about, Ed? This is supposed to be my show. This is my gig. If this guy's so hot let him have his own show."

"Come on, Mark, this'll be great for you. He'll pack the place. People will see you. Maybe MTV will be here. Maybe you could do a video."

"I don't do videos. I do books. That's what poets do. Jesus Christ." Mark flops down in the chair across from Ed's desk. "You got any pot?"

"No I don't." He picks up the phone. "And listen. Don't go over fifteen minutes tonight. Keep it quick. Don't do that one about the subway, or whatever that was. The long one."

"How about drink tickets?" says Mark, distracted now, looking around the room.

"I can't help you."

"Got a cigarette?"

Ed gives him one. "I gotta make some calls, Mark."

"So make them," says Mark. He lights the cigarette and blows a stream of smoke up into the ceiling.

"Listen, Mark," says Ed, the phone tucked between his shoulder and ear, "they don't like us to smoke up here. Why don't you go down to the dressing room?"

Downstairs nobody wants Mark to smoke either. Cynthia waves at the air and scowls. Mark lets her scowl. He sits on the counter with his back to the lighted mirrors. He watches Cynthia load film into her camera. They used to go out. Now they're just friends. "So what are you doing here anyway?" Mark asks her.

"Just shooting some stuff."

"For who?"

"The *East Village Eye*."

"Who do they want? Me or this Fred guy?"

"Just the show in general . . . Fred."

"Fucking MTV," says Mark. He smokes. "You haven't seen Alex, have you?"

"Did he say he was coming?"

"He's supposed to be doing an article about me for *Flash*."

Cynthia says nothing. Mark stubs out his cigarette. Above them the ceiling creaks with the weight of the audience.

Ed is right about the club being packed. When it's Mark's turn, the main floor is so full he has trouble getting through the crowd to the stage. But even with all the people the room feels cold and inhospitable. As Mark nears the front a huge teenager won't let him by. Mark tries to push around him but the boy blocks his way. It's like a rock concert. He's staked out his spot.

"Uhm, excuse me!" says Mark, jabbing him in the back. "I'm *reading*. Would you mind getting out of the way?"

The boy turns and looks down at Mark, who tries to push by him. He grabs Mark's coat. Mark looks up at his face. It's a grotesque, idiot face. Too young. Not smart. What's he doing at a spoken-word event?

"Excuse me but I'm *reading?*" says Mark, trying to pry the kid's hand off his coat. "I'm supposed to be *onstage* now?"

"Oh," says the boy. He releases Mark, shrugs, reassumes his stance.

Mark climbs onto the stage. There are drums there. And amplifiers. Fred's got a band. Which will make the audience even less patient with him, a single, music-less reader. Mark breathes deeply and takes his place in front of the lone mike on stage. His papers are bent and mangled from his trek through the crowd. He straightens them, tries to shrug himself back into his coat, which the teenager pulled to one side. He doesn't feel right. The crowd is weird. Mark doesn't know who they are or what they want. He reads his first poem. When he's done there's no response, then a smattering of clapping from the back. Probably Cynthia.

"Dude," says someone in the front.

"What?" says Mark without looking up. Another person in the front laughs.

"Dude, read another poem."

"I am, dumbass," says Mark, grinning in the glare of the lights. More laughter. But it's strange laughter. They're not with him. Mark reads another poem. This time with more force. When he's done there's more strained silence. Mark, an experienced reader, does what he always does when he gets off to a bad start: he stops. He sets his papers on one of the amplifiers and reaches into his pocket for a cigarette. He lights it slowly, deliberately, waves out the match and stares for a moment into the crowd.

"Cool dude, smoke that cigarette!"

"I am, dumbass," says Mark again. This time he gets a real laugh. From more than the heckler and his friend in the front. That makes him feel better. He picks up his papers, biting the cigarette in his teeth. Then he grabs the mike and snarls out his poem "Monster," doing his best rock star pose. It's the poem he was going to do last, it's one of his best, he does it now to swing the audience . . . but it doesn't work. No one claps when he stops.

"Hey, dude," comes that same voice from the front. "Are you Jim Morrison?"

"No, I'm Mark West," he says. He intends it to be funny but it isn't. He's losing the crowd. People in the back are beginning to talk. The big kid on his left, the one who was so determined to hold his spot, starts pushing his way back toward the bar.

"Dude," says that same voice in the front.

Mark ignores him. He pulls his first book, *Exile,* out of his pocket. He'll read a couple short pieces from that and get off.

"Hey, dude."

"What?" says Mark through his gritted teeth and cigarette.

"You suck."

Mark squints into the glare of the lights. "What did you say?"

"I said you suck."

"Oh, yeah?" says Mark, dropping his cigarette. "You wanna try? You wanna come up here?"

"Sure. Can I?" says the voice. His friends clap and push him forward.

"Come on up," says Mark.

The kid crawls onto the stage. Mark waits until he's fully upright but not quite balanced. Then Mark charges forward and body-slams him back into the crowd. There's a stunned silence from the audience. Then cheers. Now Mark's got their attention.

"Hey! Hey fuck you!" says the guy's friend.

"Fuck yourself," Mark snarls at the friend. "Come up here, you little fuck."

"You suck, you asshole," says the original heckler, from wherever it was he landed.

"Yeah, sure I suck. Come up here, I'll rip your fucking throat out!"

The crowd loves this. They begin to hoot and clap. Mark picks his cigarette up and takes a long drag, staring long and hard into the room. The applause continues, builds, someone whistles. But Mark isn't responsible for this. The applause is for the violence. Mark is struck for a moment by the crudity and ugliness of the people, of the room, of his own participation in this event. He had intended to be a real poet, a literary artist. How did he end up here?

Mark gathers his papers and slips off the stage. He pushes his way to the dressing room stairs. One of the bouncers is guarding the entrance. He laughs as Mark sweeps by. "Way to knock 'em dead!" he says.

Downstairs Fred Bragg and his band are preparing to go on. They're dressed in bell bottoms and floppy hats. They must be doing a seventies disco parody thing. Or maybe not. Mark doesn't know and he doesn't care. He gets his coat and shoulder bag.

"Hey, man, what happened out there?" says the guy nearest him, one of Fred's band members.

"Nothing," says Mark, hurriedly packing his stuff.

"Did you punch somebody?"

"I didn't do anything." Mark lifts his eyes to look at the guy. He's wearing yellow pants, platform shoes. His face is made up. He looks like a clown.

"I guess they're not into poetry so much," says the guy.

Mark doesn't know if this is an insult or just an observation. "Yeah, maybe not," he says, "maybe they're into clowns."

The guy laughs nervously. "Yeah, maybe," he says. Mark thinks he hears the word *asshole* as he leaves but he can't be sure.

Outside it's winter. Mark steps through the snow on the sidewalk and crosses the street. He walks across town to the East Village, to his apartment building. He lets himself in and climbs the four flights of stairs to his room. Once inside he pours whiskey into a glass. He collapses in the chair at his desk and takes several quick sips. He lights a cigarette. His hands are shaking. Also his shoulder hurts where he hit the heckler. He massages the spot. He's thirty-one years old, too old for body slams. He drinks more whiskey. He smokes. His hands shake. And then the rest of his body. Violently.

So he goes to his closet. He digs through his manuscript box for a small, tightly rolled baggie. He was saving this for a special occasion and apparently this is it. He finds the baggie and brings it back to his desk. Carefully he opens it. He spreads a bit of the brown powder on the front of a magazine. He chops at it with his pocketknife and then separates a thin line. He gets a dollar bill out of his wallet and rolls it into a straw. He carefully exhales and then snorts up half the line. He puts the dollar into the other nostril and snorts up the rest.

He sits back in his chair and takes another drag off his cigarette. Carefully he moves the magazine to one side of his desk so he can put his feet up. But there's still snow on his shoes; dirty, wet snow. He brushes the slush off his desk. Then he reaches for the radio on the windowsill and turns it on. He turns on his desk lamp and gets up to switch off the overhead light. This is when he first feels the heroin. The weakness in his legs. The swimming sensation as he walks the four steps to the light switch. He turns off the light and then stays there, one hand on the plastic switch, the other hand caressing the wall as the drug and the freshly dimmed room resonate warmly through his spine and skull. He goes back to his chair. He takes out a new cigarette but then can't find his lighter. He gives up and is finally forced to rest his head on his desk. The radio plays. The radiator hisses. Outside white snow falls against the black sky.

2

"You really shouldn't be disturbed by it," says Howard Fisch, Mark's editor and the publisher of Free City Press. "The club scene is about spectacle. It's not about real art. Of course MTV is there, that's their territory."

Mark stares out the window of the restaurant.

"Cheer up," says Howard. "Grant season is right around the corner. We'll get you some money this time. We're way overdue."

"Those people aren't going to give me money."

"Of course they will. It just takes time."

"They won't. You watch."

"A little publicity wouldn't hurt. What about Alex? What did he think of the show?"

"He didn't come."

"Why not?"

"His *Flash* editors nixed it. They decided spoken word is over."

"Well, good. Spoken word *is* over," says Howard, drinking his tea.

Mark lights a cigarette.

"Listen, Mark, I talked to a guy in Colorado the other day, and I was telling him about you and we talked about teaching—"

"I'm not going to teach. I hate people who teach."

"Just listen. He told me about a student of his who got a fellowship at the University of Texas. He got a stipend, free room and board . . ."

"I can make more money working at Steel."

"Yeah, but Steel is a nightclub. You want to be a bartender all your life? You've done that. It gets old. *You* get old."

"I'm not that old."

"I'm telling you, Mark, sooner or later you're going to have to think about these kinds of options."

Mark sighs. "How am I going to teach? I barely graduated from high school. What am I supposed to say to a bunch of college brats?"

"What did you say to the people at Arena?" says Howard. "And how much did you get paid for saying it?"

That night Mark is reading at an AIDS benefit at the Confluence Gallery in SoHo. Admission is ten dollars but a quick head count reveals that all but five or six people are either performing or friends of performers. Fifty dollars raised for AIDS, thinks Mark. That'll pay for the lunch they had to plan the event.

Cynthia is there. She's sitting with her folk singer friend Virginia Taylor. There's been a buzz about Virginia recently. She's supposedly the next big thing. Not that Mark is impressed. In the seven years he's lived in New York, Mark has seen several next big things come and go. Two years before, he was the next big thing according to

New York magazine's "Top Ten People to Watch." They called him a "Downtown Baudelaire of the Nineties." He sent the clipping home to his mother in Baltimore. Howard sold a few more copies of his books and that was that.

"There's nobody here," says Mark, taking the seat next to Cynthia's.

"It's still early."

"Hi, Virginia," he says.

"Hi, Mark," says Virginia, not looking at him. She's replacing a string on her guitar.

"Jesus," Mark whispers to Cynthia, "I hate benefits where nobody shows."

"It's for a good cause," she whispers back.

"It's fucking depressing."

"Oh, Mark!" says Natalie, one of the organizers of the event. "Cynthia! Virginia! Thanks so much for coming!" She hands them a printed schedule of the evening's performances and moves through the sparsely filled chairs to hand out schedules to the other performers. Virginia lifts her guitar and tunes the new string with the others. Cynthia looks through her journals. She's a photographer by trade but she also writes and occasionally reads from her photography journals at spoken-word events. Mark should probably go through his own stuff but goes outside to smoke instead. As he stands in the cold several more groups of people show up and pay full admission. This should improve his mood but doesn't. He begins to pace on the sidewalk and then walks around the block. There's a restaurant around the corner. Without thinking he goes in. He goes to the men's room in back. He locks himself in the stall, lowers the seat cover and sits. Quickly, efficiently, he pulls the baggie out of his coat. With his pocketknife he scoops out a modest amount of the brownish powder. He holds it to his nose and snorts it up. He does the same in the other nostril. Then he stands up, flushes the toilet and hurries back to the benefit.

Cynthia is onstage. She's reading a funny story about an encounter with a bum she photographed on Forty-second Street. The bum proposed to her. This brings a titter of amusement from the concerned, benefit-minded crowd. Mark slips quietly into his seat and arranges his first book and the several unpublished poems he's going to read. When he feels settled he looks around the room. It's nearly full. In fact, there are people standing in the back. One guy in the corner he recognizes from the *Village Voice*. And there's Ann Powers. And another free-lance guy he's seen around. Why are they here? To see him? But then he remembers: Virginia is playing. The critics are here to see the next big thing.

Cynthia finishes to warm applause. Mark is next. He shuffles through his papers one last time, finding his hands and general motor skills to be pleasantly impaired. He exchanges warm smiles with Cynthia as she comes back and he goes forward. At the podium Mark can see that the gallery is quite full, and even as he's standing there, more people are coming in.

"Hi," he says to the rows of people. His mouth is a little slow. Also there is a tingling sensation in his lower back, in his butt, all the way down the back of his legs. He begins with a long poem from his second book. He stumbles a bit at first but then finds the groove of it, rediscovers it. He reads it better than he's ever read it in his life. His two middle poems go equally well. He finishes with the title poem from his first book, *Exile*:

God
It'll be
Easy to go
Easy to hate you
Easy to leave
This city
Wish I could
Hurt you more
Get at that
Haircut
Those shoes
That sway in your
Shoulders
Wish I had
Money
Something the world
Wanted something
You need
Wish I could
Do more than
Stay away
Not come to
Bed walk these
Streets in
Permanent
Exile

The audience must think this has something to do with AIDS. They give him a surprising gush of applause. Or maybe it's the way he read it. Mark looks into the darkened room, his head pleasantly fogged. Something about the strange joy in his face incites the audience to clap more. For a moment Mark loses himself in this wash of approval. But then the applause fades. A beat too late he remembers where he is. He says a quick "Thanks" and glides gracefully back to his seat, where Cynthia is the last person clapping. "That was great!" she whispers to him. Mark glances over at Virginia. But she is less excited. In fact she's glaring at him. She's supposed to be the next big thing. She can't be upstaged by a mere poet. She looks away from Mark and adjusts the capo on her guitar.

But Virginia does fine. Whatever chord Mark struck with the benefit audience, Virginia strikes it too. After her four-song set, she returns to her seat, flush with excitement. She chatters nervously as the house lights come on and the three of them prepare to leave. Then she wants to know about the journalists, who are still standing along the back wall.

"Do you think I should introduce myself?" Virginia asks Cynthia.

"No. Let them come to you."

"But they're just talking. To each other."

"So let them talk," says Mark, casually. But then he sees that Virginia is staring at him. It occurs to him that Virginia has never taken him seriously before. She's only been around a year or so, she doesn't know that he was once the Downtown Baudelaire of the Nineties.

"Do *you* know them?" Virginia asks Mark.

Mark looks behind him at the back wall. "That guy's from the *Voice.* That's Ann Powers. That guy on the right is somebody too, from *Spin,* I think."

"Could you introduce me?" says Virginia.

Mark looks at her. He looks at Cynthia. "No. Cynthia's right, let them come to you."

After that, the three of them eat at a nearby diner. Virginia asks Mark more questions about journalists in general and the ones at the benefit in particular. In the course of the conversation Cynthia tells Virginia about Mark's *New York* article and its various repercussions. By the time they're all in a cab, Virginia seems to think Mark is some sort of publicity whiz. When they drop off Cynthia, she still has more questions. And so Mark accepts her offer to come over.

Virginia's apartment is big, clean, and expensively decorated. She opens a bottle of white wine and joins Mark on the couch. Virginia does most of the talking. She went to Oberlin College, double-majored in music and communications. This is her sister's apartment, her sister who is married to a corporate tax lawyer who lives in London. Naturally, Virginia disapproves of the corporate world. She's always loved music. She's wanted to be a performer for as long as she can remember. Her first six months in New York have been a struggle but now an independent record company is seriously interested in her. But she needs some publicity, not just previews but a feature article, a profile, a big review in the *Voice*.

Mark listens patiently to all this. It's been hours since the dope but since he never expends any energy, since he just sits there with his glass of wine, the pleasant heroin numbness seems to linger in his system.

By the end of the night, it is Mark who has made the best use of Cynthia's advice: *Let them come to you.* He doesn't do anything to encourage Virginia and yet she gladly scoots closer to him, touches his neck, kisses him.

The large apartment has a large bed. Mark enjoys the feel of the flannel sheets as he slides under the soft covers.

The two of them are clumsy together but they manage to have sex. Afterward Mark sprawls on his back, breathes, feels his heart beating smoothly in his chest. But then Virginia moves her head onto his chest. She wraps one leg over his body, suffocating his blissful sense of postsexual expansion. Even worse, she continues to talk. She's still worried about getting into the right magazines. Also she wants to know more about Mark's *New York* article, what happened afterward, did he get calls from publishers? And why didn't it last, how come he's not famous? Did Mark blow it somehow?

But she gets no answers. Mark is asleep.

3

As happens every time he sleeps with someone else, Mark spends the rest of the week wanting Cynthia back. It's February now and bitter cold. Mark broods on this subject, spending his nights wandering the frigid East Village. At the end of the week Mark bartends at Steel. He works Thursday, Friday and Saturday nights and is momentarily flush with cash. He talks Cynthia into going to a movie and then buys her dinner, all the while hoping for an invitation back to her apartment.

But Virginia has told Cynthia about her evening with Mark.

"So what are you going to do with her?" Cynthia asks him, as they eat.

"I don't know. What am I supposed to *do with her?*"

"Calling her would be nice."

"Why? It was her idea."

"What was?"

"Having sex."

"And since it was her idea, you feel no responsibility toward the situation?"

"She wanted to have sex and I went along with it," says Mark. But he doesn't want to talk about this. It was these kinds of arguments that turned Cynthia away from him.

"You could at least go see her play on Sunday."

"Where's she playing?"

"No Se No," says Cynthia.

"Really? Is it open?" says Mark. No Se No, the notorious Lower East Side performance space, was the center of the scene a few years before, during Mark's Baudelaire of the Nineties days. It's where he and Cynthia first met.

"I guess they're doing acoustic shows on Sundays."

"Are you going?" Mark asks her.

"I think I have to work."

"No Se No," says Mark. He thinks about it, remembers it, but then shakes his head. "It's probably not the same."

He walks Cynthia home. There's snow and ice on the sidewalk and at several points they slip and must hold each other up. Mark savors every touch, every brush of their arms. But at Cynthia's apartment building there is no invitation upstairs. He watches her go inside. He watches her go into the elevator. He watches the elevator go up.

He keeps walking. He skids and slides his way to a bar he knows on the next block. It's warm inside. A rap song is thudding out of the jukebox. He walks around the pool tables to the tiny bathroom. The single stall is empty and he quickly shuts and latches the door. He sits on the seat and digs his baggie out of his coat pocket. But then the door to the bathroom opens and loud drunken voices fill the room. There's a jostling in front of the stall door. Mark stares at the flimsy latch. The door shakes but holds. "What the fuck—" says one voice.

"There's someone in there," says another voice.

"Shit."

"Open the fucking door!" laughs a third.

More noise, more commotion, Mark tries to hurry. He gets out his pocketknife and begins to untangle the baggie.

"Somebody's getting fucked up."

"Hey, no drugs in the bathroom!"

"Maybe they're fucking."

"No fucking in the bathroom! And no getting fucked up. Unless you share it with me!"

Laughter.

"Who's that guy with Tina?" says one of them.

"It's *Donald*."

"Fucking *Donald!*" They all laugh.

"Fucking Tina . . ."

"That bitch blows smoke in my face one more time, I swear I'm going to—"

"You're going to what?"

More laughter.

"Yo, gimme a cigarette."

"Get your own."

"Hey, fuck you."

"Fuck *you!*"

"Hey, you in there, I gotta piss, OPEN THE FUCKING DOOR!"

This isn't working. Mark abandons his efforts and starts to wad up the baggie. But then the talking stops. There's an eerie silence and then . . . WACK!!! The door explodes open. The latch flies off, just missing Mark's face. The door slams open and shut and then hangs, vibrating on its hinges. Mark looks up to see the person who just kicked it in. It's a white kid dressed like a black kid. His friends stand behind him. Mark stares up at them from where he sits.

"What the fuck . . . ," says the first kid, looking down at the baggie.

"No drugs in the bathroom," says his friend quietly.

"Whatcha got there?" says the first kid. He steps forward, tries to snatch it out of Mark's lap.

Mark stabs him in the arm with his pocketknife.

He jumps back. "What the . . . ? You just *stabbed* me."

Mark is as stunned as he is. Everyone freezes for a moment. The kid clutches his arm. He turns to his friend. "He just *stabbed* me."

"Is it bleeding?" says the friend.

"I don't know." The stabbed kid backs out of the stall, backs out of the bathroom, still clutching his arm. The other two follow. When they're gone Mark stuffs the baggie in one coat pocket, the knife in the other. He pulls his coat closed and peeks out of the bathroom door. He can see the three of them at the sink behind the bar. They're inspecting the wound. Mark sneaks out of the bathroom and makes his way around the pool tables. He accelerates toward the door. But then a girl steps into his way. He knocks into her, spilling her beer.

"Hey!" she says. Mark knocks into her friend too but keeps driving toward the door.

"Hey!" comes a different voice, a masculine voice, from behind the bar. "That's him. Stop that guy!"

Mark is on the street. He runs around the corner and then breaks into a full sprint down Fourth Street. But the street is slick with ice and he takes a nasty crunching fall on the frozen cement. As he's getting up he sees two pursuers, running and slipping just like he is.

Mark does not panic. He gets up carefully. Then he begins to run again, more slowly this time. It's not so important that he run fast as long as he stays upright and keeps moving. This strategy works. When he gets to the next block one of the guys has fallen and the other has not gained ground. He turns and runs up Avenue B, making good time on one stretch of iceless pavement. But at Sixth Street he's still being followed. Mark runs toward Tompkins Square Park. It's closed for the night, he'll dare them to follow him over the fence and into the dark maze of trees and bushes. Mark vaults the iron fence. He bursts through a line of shrubs. He sprints up a snow-covered hill and down the other side. Then he runs into a tree branch. It catches him in the face, knocks him off his feet, he lands backward in the ice-crusted snow. For a moment he lies stunned but then he rolls over and scans the park around him. His pursuers didn't follow. The park is quiet. Mark feels a growing sting on his face around his chin and lower lip. He dabs at it with his fingers. He's bleeding. He scoops up some snow and holds it against his mouth. He waits, watches, until he's sure he's alone. Then he stands up, brushes himself off, begins the walk home.

Back in his apartment Mark inspects the damage. His lip is cut. He's got a scrape on his right cheekbone and another along his jaw. Also his right wrist is aching horribly, he must have landed on it when he first fell down. With his left hand, as best he can, he gets the baggie out of his coat pocket only to find he didn't close it properly. The last of his heroin has spilled into his pocket. Mark doesn't hesitate to cut the pocket out. The coat was old already and one of the sleeves is now partially torn off the shoulder. Carefully, and cringing with the pain in his wrist, Mark begins to brush the brown powder out of the pocket and onto a clean sheet of typing paper. Then he has to separate the powder from the grime, the grit, the bits of hair and thread. When he gets it reasonably clean he forms two large lines and snorts them both.

The dope hits him hard. He becomes nauseous and lurches to the sink. He throws up once, twice and then leans against the wall, slides down to a sitting position. He cradles his wrist in his lap and lets his head tip forward as he momentarily loses himself. But hours later, when the drug wears off, Mark wakes up in his bed, his right wrist aching so severely that tears of pain roll down his bruised cheek.

"Hello? Mark? It's Virginia," says the voice on the phone three days later.

Mark, still sore, still bruised, takes a silent breath. "Hi, Virginia."

"I just wanted to invite you to my show tomorrow."

"Oh, right. Where's it going to be again?"

"No Se No."

"Oh, yeah. I heard they started that up again."

"It's been pretty good so far."

"I'll try to come by." Mark adjusts the phone on his shoulder. He's trying to make a sandwich one-handed. "You know, I was going to call you . . ."

Virginia says nothing.

". . . But I didn't get your number the other night."

"I didn't give it to you."

"I guess you didn't," says Mark. He's losing the phone.

He struggles to keep it on his shoulder. "Do you want to give it to me?"

"What are you going to do with it?"

"I don't know. Call you maybe?"

"I'm not sure I want you to call me."

"Okay, I won't call you then," says Mark.

"I just don't appreciate that whole *call me* thing, I get really sick of that."

"Yeah, me too," says Mark.

"But if you want to come to the show I'll put you on the guest list."

"That would be great."

"Do you know Ann Powers?"

"No, I don't."

"Cynthia said you know her."

"I know who she is. It's not like I'm friends with her though," says Mark. "I couldn't really introduce you."

"No, I wasn't thinking that. I was thinking of who at the *Voice* I should talk to about folk stuff."

"I really don't know. I could ask around."

"Cynthia said you're friends with Alex Wright."

"Alex, yeah, we used to do spoken-word stuff."

"Are you still friends with him?"

"I see him around. I don't know if he can help you though. He writes for *Flash* now. They only do big rock stars."

"Well, I know I'm not a big rock star but it just seems like the folk scene shouldn't be totally ignored."

"To be honest I don't talk to him that much. He's more into the magazine crowd now."

"Oh," says Virginia.

"Sorry."

"Do you know Garcia Sanchez?"

"I don't think so."

"He's a journalist. I'm having dinner with him tonight. He wants to put me in *Downbeat*."

"Never heard of him," says Mark.

"Well, whatever, like I said, if you want to come on Sunday I'll try to put you on the list. I'm not really sure how many spots I get. But I'll see what I can do."

"All right, you do that."

"Bye."

"Bye," says Mark. But she's already hung up.

4

The next afternoon Mark has a lunch date with Howard at the Union Square Bar and Grill. Mark gets there first and fidgets at his table while he waits. Around him the room buzzes with intent conversations. Everyone is well-dressed, professional looking. At least some of these people must be big-time publishers, authors, editors, since this is reportedly where those people hang out. Mark scans the room and watches the entrance for Howard. A young businesswoman smiles at him from the bar. Mark tries to smile back but it's a weak smile, he can't really meet her eye. Mark feels out of his league here. His heart jumps when Howard finally appears.

Howard's in his mid-forties. He wears his grey hair in a ponytail. "An old hippy" is how he was first described to Mark. A gay, rich, Harvard-educated old hippy. The gay part seemed to help Mark's cause initially. Mark being the cocky young star of the downtown scene, Howard gravitated toward him naturally. But since then, Mark wonders if the tables haven't been turned. Howard has not only become his all-purpose editor, agent and publicist, he's also become Mark's closest confidant and in an odd way, his best male friend. Which would be fine except that Howard has lots of other friends. Mark has only Howard.

But Mark forgets all of this when Howard sits down. They are not just having lunch. Howard has something for him.

"Hello, Mark, how are you?"

"Great," says Mark.

Howard settles himself in his chair. They sit for a moment in silence, grinning at each other.

"So where is it?" says Mark.

"Oh, the book," says Howard. He reaches into his bag and produces what is up to now Mark's crowning achievement: the proofs of a British edition of *Exile*.

"Wow," says Mark. The cover shows a lone figure walking across a bridge, on a dark foggy night. "That's so cool!"

"And there's more." says Howard. "Nigel wants to do your second book."

"Oh, man!"

"But there's a reason why he wants to now," says Howard, pausing for dramatic effect. "*Exile*'s going to be reviewed in the London *Times*."

"No shit!" says Mark.

"And here's where it gets really good," says Howard. "Nigel spoke with a Japanese woman he works with and he said something about *Exile* and the upcoming review and I guess there's some interest there."

"I could be big in Japan," says Mark dreamily.

"Well, you're going to be big in England, or at least bigger than you are here."

"Fuck America. Who cares about America anyway?"

The waitress comes and Howard orders a sandwich. Mark orders a cheeseburger.

"The thing about this is," explains Howard, "it feeds on itself. I mean, this can change the whole complexion of your career. Especially for grants."

"The Japanese book, would that be in Japanese?" says Mark.

"Of course."

"Wow. I'd be *translated*."

Mark looks back to the bar but the young businesswoman is with a businessman. Too late to smile at her now.

The cheeseburger comes. Mark tries to squirt ketchup on it but his right wrist is still so sore he can't grip the ketchup container. He rests his hurt hand in his lap and goes about his meal left-handed.

"So are you writing? What have you been doing?" asks Howard.

"Working at Steel mostly."

"Did you look at that Yevtushenko book I gave you?"

"I haven't had time. But I did an AIDS benefit thing."

"How was that?"

"Okay."

"How's Cynthia?" says Howard.

Mark shrugs.

"How's Alex?"

"Who knows? Who cares?" says Mark, admiring his book again.

"Maybe Alex could write something about the British edition."

"He doesn't care about this stuff anymore."

As Mark's burger gets smaller it becomes more difficult to handle. He tries to stabilize it with his aching right hand but a pickle drops out of it and lands in his lap.

"Fuck," whispers Mark. He puts the burger down on his plate and drinks his water. "Did you read Alex's last *Flash* piece? It was some crap about blind dates. What a sellout."

Howard watches with concern when Mark attempts to take another bite left-handed.

"What's wrong with your hand?"

"Nothing. I slipped on the ice. I think I sprained it."

"Did you go to the doctor?"

"Nah. It's all right," says Mark, dropping another pickle in his lap. "I don't have insurance anyway."

Howard frowns at his young poet. And takes a bite of his own sandwich.

On Sunday Mark makes a firm decision not to go to Virginia's show. Then he goes out. It's a cold cloudy day. He stops at a thrift shop on Avenue A to look for a new coat. But he can't move his wrist enough to try anything on. So he kills the rest of the afternoon at the big cineplex on Nineteenth Street. After that he picks the *New York Times Book Review* out of a trash can and reads it in a coffee shop.

But when seven-thirty rolls around he's thinking about No Se No. There's nothing else to do. And there'll be other people there besides Virginia, other women, maybe someone will have pot. He puts on his hat, pulls his ripped, pocketless overcoat tight and heads toward the Lower East Side.

The beginning of the bad news at No Se No is the person working the door. It's the guy from Fred Bragg's band. The guy Mark thought looked like a clown.

"Uh, hi," says Mark, standing casually inside the doorway, where it's warm.

"It's five bucks cover," says the guy. He doesn't appear to recognize Mark.

"Actually, I think I'm on the list. Virginia Taylor's."

The guy digs a piece of paper out of his coat pocket and looks at it. "What's your name?"

"Mark. Mark West." Mark blows into his frozen left hand. He watches the guy scan the paper.

"I don't see it."

Two people come in behind Mark. He moves out of the way. They pay their five bucks and go in. The guy looks back at Mark. "Hey, aren't you that poet?"

"Yeah," says Mark, hopefully.

"I thought I recognized you," says the guy.

Someone else goes out and the blast of cold air reminds Mark what's waiting for him outside. He smiles at the clown guy. "She said I'd be on the list. I just did an AIDS benefit with her. Can't you just let me in?"

The guy shakes his head. He's now looking inside, avoiding Mark.

Mark looks inside too. It's pretty crowded but he doesn't see anyone he knows. The sad thing is, if this was a few years ago he'd be in for free, no problem. Alex would be there, Cynthia, the whole gang. Now there's no one inside that Mark recognizes. The downtown world turns over fast. And the new people don't give a shit who came before.

On the other hand, he's freezing. He could get a coffee and sit in the back. It might be fun. And there's nothing else to do. But then he remembers Virginia. She fucked him, tried to use him, and now she's jerked him off on this guest list thing. Why did he even come here? He turns and goes out. He crosses the street and calls Cynthia from a pay phone. He gets her machine. He hangs up but stays in the phonebooth, where, in place of heroin, he clumsily snorts up half an old capsule of Benzedrine he found in his manuscript box. It's bitter, stinging stuff. And it hits him wrong, jangles his nerves. Fortunately there's an open liquor store on the corner. He buys a pint bottle of cheap whiskey and sneaks a quick swig of it on the sidewalk. That feels better. But now he's restless. He wants to walk.

The wind has picked up but he hikes westward, all the way to West Broadway where he turns south toward the twin towers of the World Trade Center. The whiskey keeps him warm, the speed keeps him moving. He crosses Canal Street, passes through Tribeca, arrives finally at the exposed esplanade of Battery Park. Here he braces himself against the wind off the Hudson River. The freezing black water churns and sprays, so much so that when Mark ducks into the Battery Park Mall he's got ice stuck in his stocking cap. He brushes it off, shakes out his scarf, warms himself under the Mall's bright lights. Then he sneaks a drink from his pint bottle and lights a cigarette. But it's a no-smoking area. He can only get a couple drags before the guards arrive.

Kicked out of the Mall, Mark continues southward, through the old Battery Park, the paved curve of the southernmost tip of Manhattan. Here it is darker, colder, the freezing wind is coming from behind him, it pushes him along. He continues around, beneath the Staten Island Ferry Port, and then along the East River to the South Street Seaport. He tries to go in but a security guard meets him at the door. The Seaport is closed.

Mark is too tired to walk anymore. He finds the subway, pays, goes in. The platform is quiet and cold. He lowers his numb body onto a bench. But his brain is still racing from the speed. His thoughts turn to Virginia, No Se No, how stupid he must have looked, begging to be let in. He digs a pen out of his breast pocket and finds a dirty piece of paper on the ground. Through the grit of the paper, he tries to write:

> Scammer bitch
> Ha ha I can't wait to watch
> You get what you want
>
> Burn under the
> Spotlight
> Fry
>
> Call Ann Powers
> And use my name
>
> (See what it gets you!)
>
> In the event of your death
> Please be advised
> Total oblivion awaits you
> No one cares about your stupid songs
> Your stupid friends
> Your stupid life
> And you can look me up
> In the Library of Congress
> Under "Japan, Translations"

But something's happening to his sore wrist as he writes this. It's thawing. The numbness is giving way to a very sharp and intense pain. In fact, the pain feels like it's alive, like it's a separate being inside his arm, fighting to get out. "Ah, ah . . . fuck!" says Mark out loud. He drops his pen and cradles his wrist in his lap. He doubles over it. "Ahhhh . . . shit!" Just then an express train comes roaring through the station. An icy wind blows along the platform, but the noise of the train provides a welcome cover for Mark's cries. "Fuck, oh fuck, oh man, oh man . . . oh, *God!*" he wails. When the train is gone he lowers his voice. He looks down the station platform. There's a black woman at the far end. She promptly looks away. "Oh, God," says Mark, rocking himself now. His pen is on the ground. The paper falls there too. "Oh, Jesus. . . ."

5

Cynthia doesn't recognize Mark's voice when he calls on Monday.

"You don't sound like yourself," she tells him.

Mark clears his throat. "I was just wondering if you, uhm . . . if you want to go to a movie."

"Tonight? I don't think so. I was just out all day. It's so cold."

"It is," says Mark.

"I'm sorry."

"No, it's all right. I was just looking for something to do. What are you doing?"

"Nothing. Watching this photography thing on PBS."

"Huh," says Mark.

"What are you doing?"

"Nothing."

"Didn't you have lunch with Howard last week?"

"Yeah. We hung out."

"How is he?"

"He's still gay," jokes Mark. Cynthia doesn't laugh.

"No, he's fine. It was good. I guess my books are coming out in England. *Exile* and maybe *City of Situations*."

"That's great, Mark," says Cynthia.

"Yeah, it's cool. I'd be more excited but I'm sort of having a problem."

"Which is?"

Mark clears his throat again. "I think I broke my wrist."

"You broke your wrist?"

"I fell on the ice."

"Did you go to the doctor?"

"I don't have insurance."

"You don't need insurance. Go to the emergency room."

"I just . . . I don't want to deal with it."

"You could have some sort of permanent damage. If it's really broken."

"Do you think?"

"I don't know. Probably you could. You might as well go. Why wouldn't you go?"

"They'll want money. Roger Channing broke his leg that time. When he got hit by that car. And he's still dodging credit people. And it wasn't even his fault."

"Well, lie. Or do something."

"Won't it just heal though? I mean, there's no bones sticking out or anything."

"There don't have to be bones sticking out."

"What did people do before doctors? They just healed."

"They just *died*. Jesus, Mark, your books are coming out in England. Go to the damn doctor."

"It's not really that bad. It feels better today."

"Listen, Mark, I don't want to argue about it. I think you should go to the doctor. And if you won't, don't talk to me about it because it's just going to frustrate me."

"I know. You're right."

Cynthia sighs audibly.

"So what did you do on Sunday?" asks Mark.

"I had dinner with Damian."

"Yeah?" says Mark.

"We're sort of, you know, seeing each other."

"You are?"

"Didn't you know? I'm sorry. I should have mentioned it."

"No, that's all right. It doesn't matter."

"He's pretty serious about it. It's a little weird."

"Damian . . ."

"What did you do? Did you go to Virginia's show?"

"I went by. It didn't look that great."

"Really? I heard it was fantastic. Suzanne Vega was there. Everyone went to Virginia's afterward."

"Yeah?"

"I asked her if you were there. I figured you would be."

"No, I had stuff to do."

"So nothing's happening with you and her?"

"Nah. She's too ambitious."

"I know what you mean."

"Actually, Damian's sort of the same way."

Silence.

"I mean, not like her," says Mark. "But he has that same college sensibility, like he's just entitled to things. You know?"

"I don't think we should talk about Damian."

"No, I totally like him. I'm happy for you. It's just these college types . . . like Virginia, it's like she doesn't understand that New York isn't the campus coffee shop. It's like they haven't got their ass kicked yet."

"Damian's had a very difficult year. His mother died of cancer."

"No, I think he's great. But it's just like, with Virginia, she has the blinders on, she has one goal, she doesn't care about . . . I mean Damian isn't like that. It must have been terrible about his mom."

"I should go. I want to watch this thing on TV."

"Okay. You're probably right about the doctor. Maybe I'll go tomorrow."

"Goodbye, Mark."

"All right, goodbye."

Mark hangs up the phone and in the same motion turns and heads for his manuscript box.

Howard is up early. He sits in his Brooklyn Heights apartment, at his large oak desk. Classical music plays quietly from the stereo. In the soft light of a desk lamp he drinks tea and reads through a collection of essays by D. R. Andersen, a Dutch poet and intellectual. The phone rings. Howard looks at the time. It's six-thirty in the morning. He looks at the phone, hesitates, then picks it up.

"Mr. Howard Fisch?" says a female voice.

"Yes?"

"This is Sergeant Hendrix at the Fifth Precinct. Do you employ a Mr. Mark West?"

"Yes, in a manner of speaking."

"Sir, we have Mr. West in custody. He was found intoxicated in a subway station. We would like to release him into your custody."

"I have to come now?"

"Yes, sir."

Howard rubs his eyes. "All right. Where are you?"

The woman tells him and Howard hangs up. He turns off his stereo and puts on his shoes. He washes his hands in the bathroom, smooths the mass of greying hair behind his head and ties it in a ponytail. There's a conversation he's been meaning to have with Mark. This will make it easy.

Three hours later, he's sitting across from his poet in a downtown coffee shop.

"I wasn't even that drunk," says Mark loudly. "Ask them. Ask them what my blood alcohol level was."

"Well, what were you then?"

"I was asleep. I was tired."

Howard shakes his head.

"I was trying to go home," says Mark.

"It was the Astor Place station. That *is* your home."

"I was walking around. Fuck. I hate my apartment."

Howard stirs his coffee. "How's your arm?"

"It fucking hurts."

Howard puts his spoon down and sips his coffee. Mark's coffee sits untouched in front of him.

"I got a phone call the other day," says Howard. "I was going to wait to tell you, but maybe this is the best time."

"Why? What is it?"

"Well, before I tell you that, let me tell you something else. The Japanese thing. It's not happening."

"It's not?" Mark says, his eyes drooping for a moment.

Howard looks at his coffee. "And Nigel's changed his mind. He's going to wait on *City of Situations*. There's some money problem. He's doing a Leonard Cohen book and they're redirecting their money into that."

"Fuck," says Mark.

"Okay," says Howard. "Now the phone call. It was a guy out west."

Mark's head begins to sink.

"Listen!" says Howard. He reaches across the table and shakes Mark's good arm. "This is important."

"I'm listening."

"This guy. He's an old friend of Michael's at Naropa."

"Uh-huh," says Mark, looking at Howard's hand where it's touching his wrist.

"His name is Bill Masters. He's head of the English Department at a small college in Oregon. In Portland. They have an artist-in-residency program. It's not like Naropa. It's just a normal college. It's small. But they've got some money. And they like your work. Or at least they trust Michael's taste. They want to talk to you."

"Oh, Jesus," says Mark. He pats his pockets for his cigarettes.

"Mark, think of what this is. You get out of the city. You live out west for a year. Oregon's like Colorado. There's trees and grass. You can clear out your system—" he lowers his voice "—of whatever you've got in it."

Mark remains silent, he's out of cigarettes.

"It'll be a new environment, new experiences. It'll be great for your work."

"How do you know?"

"Because I've seen what's happening to you happen to other people."

"Nothing's happening to me," says Mark. He grabs at the waitress as she passes. "Excuse me, miss, do you have an extra cigarette?"

The woman turns on him, is going to say no, but when she sees how terrible he looks, she changes her mind. She tosses a lone Marlboro on the table.

Meanwhile, Howard is leaning forward. "Do you know why so many poets become drunks and drug addicts?"

"Why?" says Mark, lighting the cigarette left-handed.

"Because it's an easy out. They don't have to work, they don't have to be productive, all because they're *artists,* they're *tortured,* they're too *sensitive.*"

Mark smokes.

Howard isn't getting through to him. He tries another approach: "Mark, why did you become a poet?"

"Because I'm stupid?"

Howard is losing his patience. "What do you want? To disintegrate? Do you want to be Dylan Thomas and become famous for being a joke? Is that what you want?"

"I'm losing you, Howard."

"Just think about this college thing. Just talk to the guy. Go live in Oregon. This would help your career in every way. I guarantee it."

Mark takes a deep drag of his cigarette. "If I went to this thing, what would I have to do?"

"Nothing!" says Howard. "That's the beauty of it. You'll probably have to teach a class or give a lecture or something."

Mark blows smoke sideways.

"The thing is, Mark," says Howard, changing his tone. "As a businessman. And I know I'm not much of a businessman. But as a person who has a vested interest in this situation. I don't . . ."

Mark watches him through the smoke.

"I think you . . . I think *we,* we've reached the maximum return on the downtown writer thing . . . I'm not sure that your work, or you as a person, are really going to remain interesting . . . remain a viable artistic entity, if you just hang around the East Village passing out in subway stations. And to be perfectly honest, I mean you know how

I've always felt about this . . . well, there's a whole tradition . . . people like Dylan Thomas, the whole mystique of self-destructiveness . . ."

"What are you saying, Howard?"

"What I'm saying is that your second book wasn't as good as your first book. And your third book isn't as good as your second. And there's a pattern there. Not an irreversible pattern but a pattern nevertheless. But it's up to you to break that pattern. And it's up to me, as a businessman, to identify which of my people are on upswings and which are on downswings, and to . . . invest my time and effort accordingly."

Mark takes another drag of his cigarette. He looks for a moment into the eyes of the older man. Then he looks away and exhales.

PART TWO

spring

6

Six weeks later Mark is sitting at Gate 14 at La Guardia Airport. Beside him a Hispanic woman and her three children are squirming in their chairs. The smallest boy crawls into the seat next to Mark and touches his ear. His mother grabs the child. "Julio, stop that!"

"It's all right," says Mark, smiling as she pulls the child away. But the mother doesn't smile back. She avoids making eye contact. Mark doesn't understand. He looks as benevolent, as harmless as humanly possible. He's wearing a button-down shirt, dress pants, a tweed herringbone blazer Howard gave him. He looks respectable, grown up, writerly. He's even got the *New York Times* in his shoulder bag, which he reaches for, unfolds, shakes open and then peruses for book reviews or other news relevant to his profession.

Mark looks like an adult. He's acting like one. It's kind of fun. When the plane loads, Mark enjoys the gesture of pulling his ticket out of his breast pocket. It's like a commercial. He's a *business traveler*. He smiles at the ticket taker and she at him. As he proceeds down the tunnel another woman asks him about the weather in Chicago and then starts talking to him about her trip to New York. It occurs to Mark that he has become an eligible bachelor. Not by his personality necessarily but by his age, his clothing, his demeanor, and now, his profession. Starting today, Mark is officially an Artist-in-Residence.

Mark waits patiently as his fellow passengers find their seats. He has not been in an airplane in years and is excited by the prospect. He takes his seat and flips through the magazine he was handed by a stewardess. It's a business magazine, the articles are about stocks, bonds, money market funds. Mark has never thought about such things before but maybe he should. Howard got him a great deal with Willamette University. Also, with all the free time he'll have he might try a novel, or better yet a screenplay. If his friend Alex could break into the magazine business surely Mark could break into movies.

Mark stops at an article entitled "Where to Invest $1,000 Right Now." He doesn't understand it but he reads along anyway. When a man sits down beside him, Mark smiles at him. The man wears a suit, has a briefcase. He's a businessman. For the first time in his life Mark feels like he could relate to such a person.

"Hi," Mark says.

The man smiles tightly back. He is ten years older than Mark and he looks tired. When he removes his coat there are sweat spots under his arms. Mark goes back to his magazine. He flips to the next article: "Tax Free Bonds: Bottom Line Thinking for the Bottom Line Investor." Mark wonders at that. Aren't all investors "bottom line"? He wonders what sort of investor he would be. Risk-taking? Conservative? Having money must really affect a person, he thinks, you must really learn a lot about yourself.

Mark watches with interest when the stewardess demonstrates the seat-belt mechanism. She's fortyish but attractive. There is something pleasing about the way she slides the metal seat belt lock together. Since Mark is the only person paying attention she lets her eyes rest on him for a moment. It thrills him. He looks away. He smiles to himself and watches out the window as the plane moves across the tarmac.

The flight to Chicago takes no time at all. Mark gets off at O'Hare and waits for the connecting flight that will take him to Portland. He doesn't know exactly what to expect of his destination. He did a poetry slam in Buffalo once and he's guessing Portland will be something like that. A sort of miniature city. A couple main streets, a couple main attractions. On the weekends he imagines he will go on bike rides in the mountains. That's what Howard said. Everything will be healthy and green. The people will be friendly. The streets will be clean. Women will be impressed that he's from New York.

After a few minutes of walking around Mark bums a cigarette from a young man, probably a college student. He's slouched in a chair in the smoking area. Mark lights the cigarette and asks him where he's going.

"San Antonio," is the answer.

"Is that where you're from?" asks Mark, practicing his interpersonal skills.

The boy nods without enthusiasm. Mark takes the hint. He smokes his cigarette and wanders away.

Boarding the plane for Portland Mark gets his first real taste of his new destination. Unlike the group on the New

York–Chicago leg, the Chicago–Portland crowd seems more low-key. There are fewer business suits, a more casual attitude among the people. He waits patiently for an old woman to move down the aisle. The old woman is embarrassed about holding things up. She is a country woman. Mark is impressed by her ruralness and how uncomfortable she is with the crowded airplane. He hopes she'll be sitting near him so he can talk to her. But she's sitting near the front. Mark's seat is in back, next to a young woman about his own age. She's dressed in a fake leather jacket and has poufy moussed hair. She won't look at Mark and he decides not to talk to her. Instead he gets out his notebooks and tries to write.

> Old woman
> From the farm
> From the fields
> What did you see
> In the big city?

But it's absurd. A Hallmark card! He laughs to himself at this pathetic attempt. He wads up the paper and smiles over at his seatmate but she continues to stare forward. Mark decides not to write. He gets out a collection of essays by one of Howard's European philosophers. He kicks his shoes off and settles into his seat. But the book is unreadable. And he's bored. And he forgot to get a magazine from the stewardess. For a brief moment he feels nauseous, already sick of himself, sick of his new life. He watches the ground beneath him blur and then drop away as the plane lifts into the air.

⠿   ⠿   ⠿

Portland is obscured by clouds so that Mark doesn't get a good look at it until the plane breaks into the open air and by that time they're barely fifty feet off the ground. It's a strange meteorological effect. Portland seems to exist in a thin stratospheric slot between the earth and a huge thickness of grey cloud cover. The plane lands and taxis to a stop at the terminal. Mark remains in his seat and waits for the crowd to clear. He looks at the terminal through his window. A representative from the university will be there to meet him. He touches the material of his herringbone coat and feels around with his hand to make sure his collar is straight. Then he gets off the plane.

At the end of the tunnel a middle-aged man approaches him. "Mr. West?"

"Hi," says Mark.

"I'm David Simmons. Bill sent me. Welcome to Portland!"

"Thanks. Thanks a lot," says Mark, shaking his hand.

"This is my wife, Mary Anne," he says, bringing a smiling, heavyset woman forward. "She's also in the English Department."

"Nice to meet you, Mr. West."

"Nice to meet you," says Mark. There's something wrong. Mark looks at the two of them. They're waiting for something. "Oh, uh, call me Mark."

David and his wife laugh with relief. Mark smiles broadly at the two of them. "Well, let's get your bags," says David and they all proceed to the baggage carousel.

In David's Volkswagen, Mark sits in the backseat. They discuss his flight, the climate, how warm it's been in New York. David has a sister who lives in New Jersey so he follows the weather there. Mary Anne is quiet at first but then she tells Mark how happy the Willamette faculty is about his appointment.

"Everyone is so excited to have a younger person," she tells him. "Henry was wonderful and everyone loved him, but he's nearly seventy years old."

Mark doesn't know who Henry is.

"I think it'll be better for the students too, having some-one who has some connection to their world. Poetry can seem so irrelevant to young people."

"That's so true," says Mark. They're driving on a high-way. Cars passing them on the left contain bland-looking white people. White people in cheap American cars. Women with wide faces, broad shoulders. Men in trucks. A man drives by with heavily greased hair, then a woman with flipped-back hair. It's western style. Mark's out west.

"I mean, here especially," says Mary Anne. "Probably in New York it's different. People are so much more cultural there."

"I don't know about that," says Mark.

A rusted station wagon drives by. The male driver is smoking a cigarette. Then a minivan with a pretty teenage girl in the passenger seat. She looks right at Mark. She smiles at him.

"So how far from the ocean are we here?" asks Mark.

"Eighty miles," says David. "We're not exactly on the coast, like some people think. Eighty miles to the ocean but it's wonderful there. It's beautiful. We'll go there."

"Great," says Mark.

"I think you'll find this area in general to be really some-thing. Really beautiful."

"The natural aspects make up for the lack of culture," says Mary Anne.

"Now, honey, don't say that," David tells her. Then he finds Mark in the rearview mirror. "I think you'll be pleasantly surprised by our city, Mark. It's not nearly as provincial as people think. When my sister was here we went to the opera. There's an excellent historical museum . . ."

But Mark's thoughts are beginning to drift. They're on a different highway, and then they're lifting upward, they're on a bridge looking down to the right at what must be downtown Portland. It's a small compact city. Smaller than Mark had imagined. The couple of buildings that stick up are generic. The hills around it are sprinkled with homes. He turns to his left to see the rest of it. But there is no more. That's it.

7

Willamette University is on a hill above downtown Portland. David steers off the freeway and drives a few blocks to a sign that announces the school. The campus is green and lush. David points out the library, which is a new structure of glass and concrete. The Dance and Performing Arts Center is an older, ivy-covered building. Similar looking is the Geology and Earth Sciences Building. Apparently Mark's getting a tour.

"This is the Agriculture Department. One of the best in the state . . . ," David is saying.

"I hear they grow great pot out here," says Mark, tiring of David's voice.

David and Mary Anne exchange looks. "It wouldn't surprise me. If it has to do with the soil it would make sense," says David. Again he seeks out Mark in the rearview mirror: "Bill says you're working with a Japanese translator?"

"Yeah, well—"

"Because I think you'll see there's a strong Asian connection here. A real Pacific Rim feeling. The Japanese especially, they love Oregon."

"They like the environment, honey," says Mary Anne. "I don't think it's a cultural thing."

"Of course it is," David corrects his wife, "the Native American culture. The frontier mentality, the mythic West."

"Well, to some extent," concedes Mary Anne.

The mythic West, thinks Mark, looking in vain for something mythic in the depressing little campus outside his window.

To Mark's great relief they proceed to his new residence. It's an apartment in a modest building a couple blocks from the Willamette sign. David has the keys. He opens the front door and leads them to apartment 7B on the second floor. The apartment is big. It's furnished with bland dorm-style furniture. The floors are hardwood. A large square of grey daylight covers the living room floor.

Mark tries to act pleased. He walks from the living room down the hall to the bedroom. It's also large and blandly furnished. The kitchen is big. There's a small dining room area that is awash with the same grey light. Mark has the sensation of being very far north. The grey dark North.

Mark praises the new apartment as much as he can. David and his wife seem to expect it, seem to need it. But when his bags are moved in and he's commented on every possible detail, David still won't give up the keys. Mark tries asking David about his position at the university. David is an associate professor of English. Mark is unsure what that is and David tells him. Mark nods. He is very tired now. Finally Mary Anne remembers an appointment.

David hands over the keys. The two leave. Mark collapses on his dorm-style couch and quickly lights a cigarette. He smokes and stares out the window at a scraggy tree branch and the dull grey sky beyond it.

In the morning Mark has a meeting with Bill Masters, the head of the English Department. Mark wakes up two hours early. He goes across the street to a convenience store where he buys cigarettes and a jar of instant coffee. He makes a cup back in his kitchen and drinks it, staring at the wall and at a strand of black electric wire outside the window. Like the previous day, the sky is unremittingly grey.

After his coffee Mark takes a shower and shaves. He puts on the same shirt-pants-coat combination he wore on the plane. Dressed and ready he walks across the grassy commons to the Humanities Building that David pointed out the day before. He finds Bill Masters's office and checks the clock at the end of the hall. He is exactly on time. He knocks. A voice tells him to come in. He does.

Bill Masters sits at his desk. He is pretending to look at something but Mark suspects that he's the big event in Bill Masters's schedule this morning. "Mr. West, come in, sit down," he says gesturing to the chair in front of his desk.

"Please," says Mark, taking his seat. "Call me Mark."

"And you call me Bill!" says Bill happily. "It's great to finally meet you. I was just discussing your book *Exile* with some of my colleagues last night. They can't wait to meet you."

"Thank you . . . sir," says Mark, adding this last bit to see how it plays.

"Oh, don't *sir* me," says Bill, so pleased with himself it makes Mark nervous.

Mark is careful to smile. He has a quick flashback to his first meeting with Howard Fisch. He almost blew that by being too smug and sure of himself, by not meeting the older man's enthusiasm. He has to handle this correctly.

"So tell me, is it true, about your success in England?"

"That's what they tell me."

"And you're being translated into Japanese?"

"Last I heard," says Mark.

"That is absolutely fantastic," says Bill. He abruptly picks up his phone and dials three numbers. "Lisa, could you come in here?"

An instant later Lisa arrives. She must be the English Department secretary. She looks slightly confused, like she isn't used to being summoned. "Lisa, this is Mark West," says Bill. "He's our new artist-in-residence. He's a poet from New York City."

"Nice to meet you, Mr. West," says Lisa.

"Call me Mark."

"Mark," interrupts Bill, "would you like some coffee? Some tea?"

"Coffee would be great, Bill."

"Two coffees, Lisa, if you don't mind," and then to Mark, "Cream and sugar?"

Mark nods yes.

"Like they drink it back east!" says Bill. "I'll have cream and sugar in mine too."

Lisa, baffled, goes to get it.

"I won't waste your time here, Mark," says Bill, turning suddenly serious. Mark immediately switches gears with him, affecting a similar facial seriousness. "Now I know you're not here to start an academic career . . ."

Mark nods seriously.

"Obviously your publisher has big plans for you and

this is part of an overall grooming process. I just want to say that we here at Willamette are thrilled to be part of that process. A lot of people underrate this college in terms of sophistication or being out in the boonies or whatever. But I think you'll find that we are very aware of what your time here means to you and your career. We want to help you. We want to be part of the development of one of America's most promising young talents."

"I really appreciate that," says Mark.

The coffee arrives. Bill continues to talk as Lisa distributes the cups, the cream, the sugar cubes. Mark is grateful for something to do with his hands. He stirs his coffee, all the while maintaining eye contact with his new boss.

". . . If there's anything you need," Bill is saying. "Even informally. If you want to have a beer, relax a bit, talk about problems you're having with your work."

Mark nods.

"Or, if that's not your style, that's fine too. The point is, I'm here. We're all here. And we're at your disposal."

"That's great," says Mark. "Thank you."

But Bill isn't finished. "Having Henry here. It was a wonderful experience. But he was at the end of his career. And I'm not so sure that a man in his later years . . ." A concerned look comes over Bill's face. But then he brightens: "You, on the other hand, you're just starting! I can't tell you how exciting it is for us to have that sort of energy here. A young talent like yourself, that's just what we need here at Willamette."

"You're too kind," says Mark. He's never said that before; it sounds weird coming out of his mouth.

Bill looks at his watch. "All right then. I've got to run," he says, standing up to shake Mark's hand.

Mark stands to accept it. Bill's handshake is firm. Mark

is careful to look directly into his face. But the earnest expression he finds there worries him. He doesn't quite know how to respond to it. He smiles awkwardly, trying to simulate Bill's sincerity, but he doesn't quite get it right. His face doesn't know how to do it.

Mark leaves the English Department in a daze. The grey-ness of the sky seems to press down on him as he walks aimlessly for a few minutes. Then he regains his senses and asks a student where the college bookstore is. He has to figure out who this "Henry" person is, especially since he is replacing him. At the bookstore, Mark follows the signs to the English Department shelves. He finds a large inventory of Hemingway, Fitzgerald, Faulkner. Beyond that is a section of Shakespeare's *Sonnets,* followed by small stacks of Maya Angelou and Elizabeth Bishop. He's getting close. Then he sees it: three slim volumes of a book by Henry Tillman. It's a poetry book. It's called *Conversations with Nature.* There's a picture of Henry Tillman on the back. He's a big-shouldered man, in a lumberjack shirt, his thin white hair combed neatly across his large head. Mark looks at the shelf where he found the book but it's unmarked. He looks over the remaining shelves for copies of his own books. There are none. But Howard will take care of that. He opens *Conversations* to a poem about trees. Or maybe it's a conversation with a tree. Mark skims a couple lines but can't get the sense of it. He tries a different one but gets lost instantly. He's not much of a poetry reader. But it doesn't matter. Tillman is the man's name. And he knows what he looks like. And the book is called *Conversations with Nature.* He repeats the title three times and puts the book back on the shelf.

8

Back in his apartment Mark lies down on his couch and falls asleep. He dreams he's back in New York, bartending at Steel. He goes into the back room. There are people there he doesn't know. It's dark, smoky, something's happening, something bad . . . Mark wakes with a start. He's sweating. He looks at the clock. It's five-thirty. He's got an English Department cocktail party to attend.

There aren't many people in the third-floor lounge when Mark arrives. And except for a few bottles of wine, there's not much in the way of cocktails either. Bill is not there yet, nor are David or Mary Anne. Mark helps himself to a glass of wine and stands next to an older woman. He smiles at her but doesn't speak. He surveys the room and the sprinkling of neat, well-dressed people. It's odd that he's so much younger than everyone else. He wonders if he's thinking about this artist-in-residence thing all wrong. Maybe he shouldn't worry so much about appearances, about being polite and diplomatic. Maybe he should show up late, drunk, with his shirt untucked. He's been hired to be an artist-in-residence; maybe they want a little drama, a little artistic license.

"So are you a student here?" the older woman asks Mark.

"No, are you?" asks Mark.

"Oh, no," says the woman cheerfully, "I teach. I'm Irene Fletcher."

"I'm Mark West. I'm the new artist-in-residence."

"You're the Japanese boy. Oh—" She looks at him. "You're not Japanese."

"No."

"I thought the new artist-in-residence was Japanese."

"Nope."

"Well, Henry was such a dear man. I think he'll enjoy retirement. The students loved him so."

"That's what I hear," says Mark, as he watches Mary Anne enter the room. He is relieved by the sight of her smiling face. Following her comes David. Mark is less excited to see him. But so far they are Mark's only friends. He is careful to smile at them both.

Mary Anne approaches the two of them. She speaks to the older woman first. "Mrs. Fletcher, what a lovely dress!"

"Oh, thank you, dear. You look wonderful yourself."

"And have you met Mark, our new poet-in-residence?"

"We were just talking," says Irene.

David joins the three of them. "Hello, Mark," he says, shaking hands.

"Hello," says Mark, mimicking the formal tone of David's voice.

"Well!" says David. The four of them stand in an awkward square. Mark looks at Mary Anne, then at Mrs. Fletcher, then back at Mary Anne. He likes her face.

Another man approaches their group and speaks to

Mrs. Fletcher. David takes the opportunity to talk to Mark. "So how was your meeting with Bill this morning?"

"It was great. It went really well," says Mark. Though he's never been much of a schmoozer Mark sees that he is going to become one. Starting now everything is going to be "great," "wonderful" or "terrific."

"Bill likes Mark, you knew that," says Mary Anne. Mark is glad to have her in the conversation. He wishes he could say something to her personally. But what do you say to somebody's wife? Mark has no idea.

Suddenly everyone's attention turns toward the door. Bill Masters has arrived with Henry Tillman in tow. People continue with their conversations, but all eyes are on Bill and Henry. Mark quietly drains his glass of wine and reaches behind him for the wine bottle. He refills his glass and watches Bill and Henry across the room. He is not looking forward to this.

David is the one who suggests going over. Mark nods in agreement. He tries to smile but it's been a long day and his face is tired of smiling. As David leads the way, Mark falls in behind Mary Anne. He gets a whiff of her, a soothing feminine smell. He follows in her wake as they cross the room.

David gets to Bill first, who is laughing with two professors. Henry Tillman is not laughing. He has a firm, grim look on his face. He is not part of the conversation. He reminds Mark of a sculptor he knew at Steel, a mean, tough, impossible man.

David seems intent on being involved in this passing-of-the-torch thing they are about to do. He interrupts Bill's conversation a little too forcefully, as if his prize, Mark West, will justify any sort of social awkwardness. For his part, Bill handles it well, spotting Mark and casually introducing him to the two men he's talking to. Mark shakes their hands and is happy to meet them. "And this," continues Bill smoothly, "is Henry Tillman."

Mary Anne, whom Mark has been partially hiding behind, moves out of the way. Bill steps back. Everyone falls quiet for a moment while Mark extends his hand to the white-haired man whose face is set in a tight grimace. But the older man's hand does not come forward. For a painful moment the old naturalist poet stares hard at his young urban replacement. Mark sees immediately that the man is insane. Not clinically but artistically. He is not quite of this world. He's the real deal.

"Nice to meet you, Mr. Tillman," says Mark. He understands people like this. It is really his only pleasure in life: meeting people crazier than he is.

The old poet makes a low grumbling noise. Bill remains silent. David rocks nervously on the balls of his feet. One of the two professors starts to say something, then changes it to a cough.

Mark lets his hand drop. But he's not offended. "I saw your book today in the bookstore," he says calmly. "*Conversations with Nature.*"

"Oh, I love that one," says Mrs. Fletcher. She's forced her way into the circle. "Henry, I thought you told me our new poet was Japanese. He's not Japanese. And look how young he is!"

Everyone bursts into nervous laughter. Everyone except Henry, who continues to grumble to himself. Mark smiles with the others as they all share a laugh. Then he sneaks a look at the old man. The stern expression is gone. Now he just looks confused. And old. Mark drinks his wine. He is suddenly deeply tired. He forces the smile back on his face and listens to the chatter around him. Then Mary Anne saves him. She's getting more wine, does Mark want some? He does. He goes with her back across the room.

Mark holds his wineglass while she fills it. Quietly, gracefully she begins to apologize for the old poet. "Don't think anything bad about Henry. He comes on rather gruff but he's one of the most generous men—"

"No, no, I'm fine with it."

"He really is one of the most giving men I've ever known. He is absolutely full of love."

"No, I liked him. He's kind of . . . crazy."

She sighs deeply and puts down the wine bottle. "I really wonder why that happened. That was very odd." She looks at Mark. For the first time she looks closely. She seems to study him.

"No, I'm used to it," says Mark. "People have egos. It's hard. In New York, it happens all the time."

Mark would be happy to spend the rest of the evening with Mary Anne but of course David has to come over. "Listen, Mark—" starts David. He's going to apologize for Henry. But Mary Anne stops him. "He's fine," she says. "There's no problem." Soon Bill is there too, and Mark must explain to him that he has taken no offense, that he liked Henry, that he's used to awkward meetings with other poets. "It happens all the time in New York," he tells the semi-circle that has formed around him. Meanwhile, Henry Tillman has left the party.

"It's not entirely out of character," says Bill and there follows a recounting of an incident years before when Henry punched a critic at a conference in Montana. It's an old story, everyone has heard it before, but it calms the group. Mark is grateful for that. When the story is over and everyone has laughed, Mark asks Mary Anne where the restroom is.

Exile

▦   ▦   ▦

Mark breathes easier when he's out of the lounge. He takes his time finding the bathroom. He wanders the bright empty hallways looking at the cartoons and other personal items taped to the office doors. In the men's room, he washes his face and looks at himself in the mirror. He has a faded tired look about him. It's been a long winter.

Back in the hallway he passes a young woman. She's digging a pack of cigarettes out of her purse. Mark watches her go by and then spins around on his heel. "Hey, are you going to smoke?" he asks.

"Uh-huh," she says without looking at him.

He hurries to catch up. "Hey, uh, could I . . . where can you smoke here?"

"On the stairwell."

"Could I bum a cigarette?"

She hands him one.

Mark falls in beside her. "Were you at the English Department party?"

"Uh-huh," she says, pushing through the doors into the chilly night air. Mark follows. He puts the cigarette in his mouth and stands beside her while she lights hers. Her face is small, delicate. She must be a student.

Mark leans over to let her light his cigarette. He takes a deep drag and blows it straight up into the night sky. The nicotine seems to release something in his chest. He takes a seat on the cement stair steps. He rests his elbows on his knees and takes another deep drag of his cigarette. The girl turns to say something and finds him there, beneath her, deep in a nicotine reverie. "Hard day at the office?" she says, looking down at him curiously.

"You know it," he answers.

69

"My name's Samantha. But people call me Sam."

"My name's Mark. But please, by all means, call me Mr. West."

She stares at him for a moment. Then turns back around and finishes her cigarette without saying another word.

9

Besides smiling a lot at cocktail parties, Mark is also supposed to run one poetry workshop. This workshop of six advanced English students meets every Friday at two. Bill has explained how this works. The students will read each other's work and talk about it. Mark doesn't have to "teach" anything. His primary role is to mediate the discussions. And to serve as evidence that living, breathing poets actually exist.

On the first day of class Mark arrives early. He finds the room, it's small, a large table fills most of the space. Mark takes a seat and waits. People come in. He says hi to them. When there are six people sitting around the table, Mark asks one of them what time it is. It's ten after. "Okay," he says. "I guess we should start."

They all stare at him. "Who are you?" says a middle-aged woman.

"I'm the teacher," says Mark.

But after that things proceed smoothly. They spend the first half of the class introducing themselves. They are a mixed group, two men, four women. One of the men is an English graduate student, complete with wire-rim glasses, skinny arms, curly thinning hair. The other is on the basketball team. The middle-aged woman turns out to be fifty-two years old. She's a housewife and a Christian. One of the younger women belongs to a sorority. Another is Vietnamese. Mark guesses she's about sixteen but she's actually twenty-five. The most noticeable student, visually at least, is named Vanessa. She won't say much about herself. She has long stringy black hair, a pale face, a slight greasiness to her complexion. But when they pass around the first round of poems, hers is the only one that is interesting. It begins with something about her cat but ends in a deserted laundry room, late at night, the narrator hypnotized by the spin cycle, the dryer's "harsh whisper" and the "razor frost" of the winter night outside.

At first Mark can't imagine what they will talk about for the remaining hour, but once each poem is read aloud the discussions seem to sustain themselves. The students have no problem finding details to discuss and small points of rhythm or style to critique. They've done this before. Mark finds it pleasant and occasionally interesting, like when the graduate student talks about decontextualization, or when Vanessa grows impatient with the sorority girl's literal interpretation of her metaphors. Only occasionally does Mark get so bored as to lose track of the discussion. Otherwise he's happy to sit there, occasionally nodding or agreeing or smiling at Vanessa, who tends not to smile back.

When his first class is over, Mark is relieved and excited that this, the potentially worst part of his new job, isn't so bad after all. He ventures into the big cafeteria where he gets coffee and sits at a booth with *The Oregonian*. It is here that Mary Anne finds him. She's loaded with papers, books, teacher stuff.

"So how'd it go?" she asks, stopping at his table.

"Pretty good," nods Mark.

"I saw Bill earlier and he said he was nervous for you and then I started getting nervous for you."

"No, it was easy, they did all the talking."

"That's usually how it is."

"Do you want to sit down?" says Mark, gesturing to the other seat.

Mary Anne hesitates.

"Please, I need the company."

Mary Anne unloads her arms onto the table and sits across from him. Mark is happy to have her. "No, I was so nervous, I feel relieved. It was easy."

"How was the work?"

"The poetry? I don't know. Fine."

"It's so uneven at that level. You might get one or two people who are actually talented and then the rest can be just terrible."

"It wasn't terrible. It was fun. It was just bad poetry. I've been around it all my life. I've produced it."

Mary Anne smiles at him.

"So what are you doing?" Mark asks.

"I'm on my way to freshman comp."

"How's that?"

"It's all right."

"Man, the teaching thing," says Mark. "I always thought it would be so boring. I mean it is. It was totally boring. But it was easy. You just talk. You just sit around and talk."

Mary Anne doesn't quite agree with this assessment.

Maybe Mark is insulting the teaching profession. "I don't mean it would be easy to be a real teacher, you know, like you."

She smiles.

Mark smiles. He looks around the cafeteria and then back at Mary Anne. She has a nice face. Smooth adult skin. He likes the day-old lipstick on her plump lips. The bit of blue along the top of her eyes.

But he's staring. He looks away.

"Well, I should go," says Mary Anne. She scoots out of the booth.

"All right, I'll see you around," says Mark. He admires her red sweater, the shape of her stout shoulders and breasts. But she looks embarrassed as she stands up. They smile awkwardly at each other and then she leaves.

Mark goes back to his apartment. He eats and reads a magazine and listens to a basketball game on the radio. Then it's nine o'clock. On a Friday night. He decides to go out. He puts on the heavy black overcoat he bought to replace his old one. He walks from the campus into downtown Portland. It's strange to walk the streets. Mark feels oddly visible and exposed. People notice each other. People look at each other.

"Hey, dude, you got any change?" says a dirty teenager standing in a phone booth.

"Sorry," says Mark quietly.

He turns down Broadway. Portland reminds him of Baltimore, his hometown. There's that same quiet stillness in the air. Mark passes two women looking in a store window. They both wear denim jackets, denim jeans. There's a pinched quality to their faces that makes him think of frontier life, of pioneers in covered wagons. He gets the same feeling when he passes a man with an oily baseball cap and a large walrus mustache. The Wild West, or in this case the remote forest outpost. Mark wonders if there will be anybody here, anybody to talk to, what's he going to do with himself for the next year.

But just then he spots a young couple across the street. The girl wears a blue leather jacket, the guy has bright orange hair. Cool kids. Mark follows them. Sure enough they lead him to a small brewpub, full of relatively hip-looking younger people. It's called the Alchemy Bar. Mark goes in and sits at the bar. He orders a beer. He watches a music video on the TV above the cash register. When his beer comes he lights a cigarette and looks around the room.

He sees Samantha. She's in a booth against the far wall. She's facing away from him so Mark watches the girl she's with. This other girl wears a cute retro dress and has a lunchbox for a purse. She's doing all the talking, they're both smoking and nursing pints of the thick yellowish microbrew everyone is drinking.

Mark watches the TV. He blows smoke at the ceiling and drinks his own beer. He looks back at Samantha. The other girl looks in his direction but doesn't notice him. But then Samantha gets up. She walks around the room, circling the bar, passing right behind Mark.

"Hey, Sam!" says Mark, turning toward her.

She's startled at the sight of him.

"You're still called Sam aren't you?"

"Yeah," she says. She looks at him. "What's your name again?"

"Mark."

"That's right."

"What are you doing?" asks Mark.

"Nothing, talking to my friend."

"Uh-huh."

She continues to look at him. Mark lets her look. He flicks ashes into the ashtray.

"Are you here by yourself?" she asks.

"Yeah. I just moved here. I don't really know anyone yet."

"I thought you went to Willamette?"

"I do. I mean . . . I sort of work there."

"Oh," says Samantha. "Well, I have to call someone."

"All right," says Mark.

She smiles.

Mark smiles. He watches her walk away. Then he goes back to his beer. When Sam comes back he doesn't try to talk to her again. He sits facing the bar while she rejoins her friend in the booth. He watches the TV and drinks. After a few minutes he sneaks a look at the booth. The other girl is watching him. She looks away. The two of them are talking intently. Mark waits. He drinks.

A few minutes later he feels a tap on the back. It's Sam. "Mark?"

"Hi," he says.

"This is my friend Jill."

Mark nods to Jill. Jill ignores him.

"We're going to a party," says Sam. "And we were thinking, if you want, you could come with us."

Mark nods.

"Since you don't know anyone yet."

Mark looks at Jill. "You sure? You got room and everything?"

"Yeah, come on," says Sam. "It'll be fun."

Mark looks once more at Jill. Then he drains his glass and follows them out the door.

10

Sam drives. Jill sits in front. Mark sits in the back, smokes, watches the dark city pass outside his window. The party is in a house, just out of town. Sam parks and they get out. People are milling around the front. Mark follows the two girls up the steps. Jill leads, until a young gay guy on the porch says her name. Jill greets him, hugs him, kisses him on the cheek. Sam stands awkwardly on the steps for a moment, then proceeds through the crowded doorway. Mark follows. The two of them push through the hall and into the kitchen, which is also crowded. Mark stands behind Sam but then has to move to let a dreadlocked teenager get to the refrigerator. There are beers in the refrigerator. Mark helps himself to one. He opens it with his pocketknife and takes a long drink. Sam, meanwhile, has moved toward the back door. There are people in the backyard. Sam disappears down the back steps.

Mark stays where he is. He drinks his beer. He lights a cigarette. The people around him are younger than he is, student age, early twenties. They look different enough from their New York counterparts that Mark is content just to stand there a moment and observe. A cute girl across from him is wearing corduroy pants with the cuffs cut off. The pants are dirty and stained. She's also wearing Kmart tennis shoes. The guy she's talking to has platinum-dyed hair and an ugly orange sweater. Another woman is wearing a threadbare T-shirt with some sort of auto parts logo on it. She's fat and her stomach is hanging out the bottom of it. Which, Mark notices, seems to be intentional. Mark drinks his beer. He's in Portland. This is the grunge look. Or the postgrunge look. Whichever, it's not like anything he's seen in New York.

But the strangeness is working both ways. Mark is still wearing his heavy black overcoat. Also, he's the only one wearing real shoes. He catches a girl staring at him as he moves toward the back door. When he doesn't see Samantha he finds himself stuck in a small pantry room. Here too he is stared at. Probably these people all know each other. Or at least have seen each other before. Mark isn't sure how to proceed so he steps over a person on the back steps and ends up in the backyard. It's dark out here. As best he can tell, Samantha is not among the dozen or so people scattered around the yard. There's a couch though. Off to the side. It's unoccupied. Mark tests it to see if it's wet, it's not, he sits.

He settles himself. He drinks his beer. A few minutes later Sam appears. She's got a sweatshirt on over her dress. She sees Mark. She starts to walk toward him, then stops to talk to someone. Mark tries not to stare at her. Jill has just come down the steps so he watches her instead. She leads a female friend out onto the grass, out of earshot of the other people. He can't tell what Jill says but she looks pissed.

"No!" says the friend. "I didn't say anything. I swear!"

"Then who told him?"

"I don't know. But it wasn't me!"

But Jill sees Mark watching her. She glares at him and drags her friend farther away.

Mark drinks.

"Hello," says a voice. It's Samantha, she's snuck up on him in the dark.

"Hello," he says.

"Are you having fun sitting here by yourself?"

Mark nods, shrugs.

"Don't you want to meet people?"

"I'm meeting people."

"Who?"

"You. Your friend Jill. That woman inside, with the auto parts shirt."

Sam looks at him. Then she looks around the yard. "These are mostly Jill's friends. I don't know anyone either."

Mark drinks.

Sam decides to sit. She settles herself against the far armrest. "So you said you work at Willamette?" she says.

"Yeah. I'm the poet-in-residence."

"You're what?"

"I'm the poet-in-residence."

"What's that?"

"It's a . . . it means that I'm a poet and I live there and I get paid."

"By who?"

"By the English Department."

Sam pulls her sweatshirt tightly around her shoulders. "I'm an English major."

"I figured you were."

"From when you ignored me on the stairwell that night?"

Mark feels around in his coat for his cigarettes. "Did I ignore you?"

"Sort of," she looks at him. "It's okay though."

Mark finds his cigarettes. He opens the hardpack and pulls one out. He offers one to Sam. "Cigarette?"

Sam reaches out and takes one. "So why do you get paid to write poetry?"

"It's just something they do."

"But I mean why do *you* get to do it? Instead of someone else?"

Mark lights his cigarette. "I guess they think I'm a big shot."

She bends forward so he can light hers. She puffs at it and sits back. "Are you?"

Mark flicks an ash into the yard. "Sure. I'm the Baudelaire of the Nineties."

"What's that?" says Sam.

"Nothing," says Mark. He looks over at her. Her dress has hiked up a bit. He looks at her thighs, her knees, her white socks. She's small. She has cute hair. Her face: it's youthful, pretty. But it's a fleeting kind of pretty. It reminds him of girls he knew in high school. Girls who weren't very smart.

He stares into the yard. He drinks his beer. "So, do you have a boyfriend?"

Sam laughs. "Where did *that* come from?"

"Just making conversation," says Mark. He waits the appropriate amount of time and then, "Well, do you?"

"Not exactly."

"What does that mean?"

"That means I don't have a boyfriend."

"I see," says Mark.

"Do you have a girlfriend?"

"No."

"Why not?"

"I don't know."

"You want one though, don't you?" she says.

"Do I look like I want one?"

"Sort of."

"Don't you want a boyfriend?"

She looks away. She smokes.

"Or did somebody fuck with you?" says Mark.

"Nobody's fucked with me," says Sam quietly.

Mark looks into the yard. "I used to have a girlfriend."

"Yeah?"

"In New York. We broke up though."

"How come?"

"She was too good for me."

"Was she really or did you just think she was?"

"Actually I never thought of that. Does that happen? Do you think people are too good for you, even when they're not?"

"Of course. If you really like them."

"Wow. So maybe she wasn't too good for me."

"If you broke up with her over that, there was probably something else wrong with the relationship."

"Yeah, it's true. I think she thought I was immature."

"That's probably the real reason you broke up."

Mark flicks his cigarette into the yard.

"So you're from New York?" asks Sam.

Mark shrugs. "I'm from Baltimore originally."

"What's in Baltimore?"

"Not much."

"New York must be cool."

"It's all right," says Mark. He looks over at her. She smiles at him. "Did I really ignore you that night on the stairwell—"

But then some other people want to sit on the couch. Sam hesitates but then gets up and moves over to Mark's side. At first Mark tries to move to give her more room. But she seems excited by the closeness. And by the new topic of conversation. "What about that night?" she says.

"I was going to ask you," says Mark.

"You're the one who just sat there."

"You turned your back on me."

"I was trying to talk to you."

"You weren't trying very hard."

"Well, how hard am I supposed to try?" says Sam. "A strange man, following me out there like that."

"Well, what am I supposed to do? I've hardly got off the plane and this amazing girl lands in my lap. . . ."

11

Samantha has a small mouth but it's addicting, like eating a tiny piece of delicious candy. Mark can't separate himself from it. They're in his room, on his bed, he's trying to get his pants off without leaving the immediate proximity of Sam's face. Finally, without getting off her, he manages to get them below his knees where he tries to kick free of them. Meanwhile he's got her dress up and one hand inside her underwear. But that's not really working. He finally sits up and pulls her panties off.

"Do you have any condoms?" she asks.

"Somewhere," he says. In the dark he feels around for his coat.

While Mark bites into the condom packet, Samantha untangles herself from her underwear. Mark's pants aren't completely off either, he's still caught in one of the legs. He rolls the condom on and then yanks his foot free.

When the clothes are finally gone they find each other in the dark. Mark kisses her. Then he lifts himself onto her and eases himself inside. For a moment then he does nothing, just settles into her, holds her head in his hands and breathes in the smell of her face and hair.

But she wants to fuck. So they do. First Mark is on top, then Sam, then Mark again. Sam is amazing. At every change it gets better and more intense. Finally Mark has had enough. He wants to come. He gets on top of her, props himself on his elbows. He kisses her mouth, sucks on her lips, inhales her nicotine breath. She begins to hum quietly beneath him, it's a beautiful, sexy sound that makes him come so hard he nearly blacks out. But even then, even semi-conscious, he wants her more. He begins to smear his sweaty face against the tangy wetness of her neck and chest. He chews on her neck, her ear, her hair. Then he moves down her face, to that delicate mouth which is so small and wet and warm.

In the morning the room fills with grey light. Sam lies with her back to him. Mark curls up behind her. He touches her back, runs his hand along the side of her torso, into the valley of her waist and up the soft slope of her hip. He scoots closer. His dick swells. He begins to kiss the back of her neck and then he can't help himself, he turns her onto her stomach, rolling on top of her as he goes. His weight seems to flatten her. Her thin shoulder blades press into the mattress. It arouses him all the more: her head turned sideways, her eyes closed, her hair falling across her face. Condomless this time he finds the place and moves himself into her. She sighs, hums. He finds the wrists of both of her arms and pulls them to her sides. He grips them there, so that she is completely pinned, she is totally possessed. And yet with her eyes closed she is somehow dead to him. He tries licking her ear, biting her neck.

"What are you doing?" she whispers, her eyes still closed.

"I'm fucking you," says Mark.

"Do you have a condom?"

Mark slips out. "I'll get one."

It's midday when they finally get up. Mark pulls on his pants and puts water on the stove to make instant coffee. Samantha follows him into the kitchen.

She sees the heating water. "I don't need anything, I should probably just go," she says.

"Are you sure? How about some juice?"

"No, I'm fine."

Mark stands over her chair while she puts on her shoes and socks.

"Thanks though," she says smiling up at him. Her face is so young, so sweet. Mark scratches at his hair. He touches the slight beard that's growing on his chin and cheeks.

"That was fun," says Mark, looking directly at her shoe.

"It was," says Samantha, also looking at the shoe.

"Thanks for taking me to that party."

Sam smiles. She looks sleepy, soft, fresh. "You'll probably get so bored here."

"I'm not bored so far."

But that's not true. As soon as Samantha is gone he is bored out of his mind. But in the best possible way. He stumbles around his apartment, looking for clean socks, heating water for coffee, trying to remember what he was going to do today. He flips through *Portland Weekly*, starts water for a bath, then turns it off and looks at himself in the mirror. He goes into his closet, into the kitchen, into his bedroom. He stands by his bed, trying to imagine Sam's take on it, on him. The room needs something: posters, a bookshelf. He's a poet, he should have some books around. He flips on his radio and tunes in the alternative rock station. Meanwhile the water's boiling, he makes instant coffee, takes a couple sips, puts on his shoes, then decides to go out for coffee and pours out the instant. He puts on his coat, looks for his pocketknife and then crawls under his bed when he thinks he's spotted Sam's underwear. But it's just one of his own socks, he sniffs it anyway. That's what he needs, something that smells like her. He crawls across the bed and begins sniffing around for her, where she slept, where her head was. He finds her scent on the pillow and presses his face into it, breathing long and deep.

Outside the grey skies seem brighter than usual. He walks into downtown Portland, heading at first toward Newberry's, the local discount department store. He needs a lamp and a shower curtain for his apartment. But on the way he stops at an old-style magazine-tobacco shop. There's a *New York Post* sticker on the window. Could they actually have it? He goes in. They have it. They have all the New York papers. Even the *East Village Eye*, which Mark checks for photos by Cynthia. They also have a large literary journal section that includes the *Quarterly Review* and has several old issues, including one that he's in. He should show this to Sam.

Sam. Once she enters his mind he doesn't really see what he's looking at. Instead he remembers the two of them leaving the party, Mark walking behind Sam, the terse conversation with Jill at the front door. Then Sam driving to his house. The awkward moments in his kitchen before he kissed her. But after that, everything falling into place. The ultimate grace of human sexuality, that moment when both parties have made up their minds and then everything just flows, everything comes together. And then this morning: The smell of her breath. The smell of her hair. The smell of her sex. Pretty little Samantha oozing the bitter tang of the female sex. Mark can practically taste it in his mouth.

"Can I help you with something?"

Mark snaps out of his trance. It's the cashier girl. "Oh. No. I was just . . ."

"Looking?"

"Exactly," says Mark. "I was looking."

"Well, if there's anything I can help you find," she says. She's cute and Mark likes the openness, the friendliness of her face. But the minute she's gone he's back to Sam. Her body. Her face. How old was she? And where did she learn to fuck like that? Mark's got to handle this right. He can't appear too eager. He'll wait a couple days and then call her. He didn't get her number though. He'll get it.

Mark puts down the *Quarterly Review*. He walks around to the glossy magazine rack. There's a new issue of *Flash* out. He picks it up and finds Alex's latest article: "Her CD Collection: What Your Girlfriend's Musical Tastes Say About Her—and You!" Mark tries to read it but he can't really focus. And the smell of tobacco is making him want to smoke. He goes outside and lights a cigarette. He looks at the vintage magazine covers in the window. The nicotine gives him a pleasant moment of vertigo. Also he can see himself reflected in the window. He looks good with his cigarette. He imagines Samantha can see him like this, poised, cool, smoking.

Being a poet, what a life. Fucking beautiful women all night and then walking around, dreaming about it all day.

12

But poets don't get paid to dream, they get paid to write. And when Monday comes and the rest of the world goes back to work, Mark prepares to do the same. He walks downtown to Newberry's. He buys a new notebook, a packet of pens, and goes across the street to Coffee Star. He gets a coffee and sits at a table by the window. He rips open his bag of ballpoints but the first two pens he tries don't work.

"You have to light them," says a male voice.

"Huh?" says Mark, not looking up from where he is scribbling on the page, a horrible scratching scribble, since there is no ink coming out.

"You have to light it," says the guy at the next table. A kid. He has a thrift-store suit on. A strange wispy mustache. His hair is dyed black. He holds out a lighter. "Just heat the end of it a bit."

Mark stares at him.

"Here," says the kid. He takes the pen from Mark and

holds the lighter flame underneath the tip. Then he hands it back to Mark. "Try it now."

Mark takes back his pen and tries scribbling on the top of his first blank page. At first it just scratches but then it loosens up, a blotch of ink comes out, smears. Mark uses a napkin to clean the pen tip, then tries again. It works.

"All right," Mark tells him. "Thanks."

"No problem," says the kid.

Mark continues to draw loops and circles across the top of the page. Then he writes:

> Okay
> Pen is
> Working

He takes a sip of his coffee which is fast cooling. Also the plastic lid is leaking. Or something. The paper coffee cup is leaving a coffee ring on the table. He wipes it with his coat sleeve, wipes off the whole table which is damp and sticky. Then he writes.

> New pens
> New notebook
> New life

Cigarettes. He pats his pockets for his hardpack. He gets out a Marlboro and the kid beside him whips out his lighter and lights it for him.

"Thanks," says Mark.

The kid nods. "Hey, you don't got another one, do you?"

"Sure," says Mark, giving him one. Mark looks back at his notebook.

"Whatcha writing?" asks the guy.

"A letter." This is Mark's stock response to unwanted inquiries.

"A letter," says the kid.

"To my girlfriend," says Mark.

"To your girlfriend."

Mark tries to go back to his notebook but the kid is now staring at him mercilessly. "Where does your girlfriend live?"

"New York," says Mark. A mistake.

An hour and all of his cigarettes later, Mark says goodbye to Brendon, who wants to be a writer himself and who, because of his conversation with Mark, is now going to move to New York City to begin his career. It's getting dark now. Mark has accomplished nothing. He leaves Coffee Star and walks the streets trying to recharge himself with thoughts of Sam. But now there is something tired and sad in his thoughts of her. What he really needs is a good night's sleep. He stops at a liquor store and buys a pint of Jack Daniel's. Then on a whim——and because he still can't believe he's getting paid thousands of dollars to hang around a college campus——he walks back into Newberry's and buys a small color television. He's never bought a TV before. It's bigger in the box than it was on the shelf. And heavier too. Two blocks out of Newberry's he has to set it down and rest. He smokes a cigarette and, as inconspicuously as he can, opens and sips his whiskey. That feels better. He walks most of the way back to the university, then stops again on a park bench. He sits. Again he smokes and samples the Jack Daniel's. He wishes he had pot. What he'd really love is a little taste of heroin.

A raindrop hits his wrist. Another hits his forehead when he looks up at the grey sky. The TV box is already stained with two large drops and makes a drumlike *thock* when it's hit a third time. Mark looks around. He bites his cigarette between his teeth and grabs the box. He lugs it across the street into the doorway of a church. Here he drops it roughly on the stairs, out of the rain, and immediately takes another long shot of whiskey. He smokes his cigarette and watches as the rain gets worse, becomes a regular spring downpour. It's been three days since he's seen Sam.

It's been five days since he's seen her when he passes Mary Anne in the hall by the cafeteria. He stops and chats with her and then pops his odd question. "I need to find a student."

"Do you know her last name?"

"I don't. It's Samantha something."

"Samantha Rigby?"

Mark watches her face carefully. "Yeah, I think so. Light brown hair. Sort of skinny."

"That's her," says Mary Anne.

"Do you know her?"

"No. I think David had her in one of his classes. How do you know her?"

"I just chatted with her at that faculty thing. She asked me about some stuff and I was going to call her."

"Oh."

"Yeah, I just thought I might give her a call," but here Mark gives himself away. Something strains in his face, Mary Anne sees it instantly.

"She's cute," says Mary Anne, continuing in the direction she was going.

"Yeah, she is," says Mark, following.

"But you just want to tell her something?"

"Uhm, well," Mark looks around the hall, and then quietly, "Well, no, not exactly, we sort of hit it off. I was thinking of maybe seeing her. Would that be cool? I mean, it's not against the rules or anything, is it?"

Mary Anne says nothing.

"I don't know," says Mark. "She's probably too young. I should probably just blow it off."

Mary Anne sighs. "I don't think anyone would really mind. I wouldn't be that public about it though. I mean if you sincerely like her. I don't think anyone's going to file a formal complaint."

"Rigby," says Mark. "Samantha Rigby."

"I would be careful though. I don't know anything about her but I hear her name a lot. Probably that doesn't mean anything or maybe it does."

Mark nods respectfully. He can guess what it means. "So how's David? How's freshman comp?"

"Actually that reminds me. We're having some people over Friday evening. People just come by after their last class. It's not official. You don't have to come. But stop by if you feel like it."

"All right," says Mark, nodding. "That sounds fun."

Samantha Rigby is listed in last term's student directory but there's no address or phone number. She's not in the phone book either. Mark takes every opportunity he can to walk through the campus. He spends three hours on Thursday afternoon reading the paper and drinking coffee at a central table in the cafeteria. But no Sam. On Friday he hangs around the English Department lounge in the afternoon, pretending to read the *New York Review of Books*. No Sam. Then it's ten after two. Mark is late for his workshop.

He arrives in the classroom distracted and then realizes he forgot to bring his copies of the poems they were supposed to critique today. But it doesn't matter. Because *Exile* has arrived at the student bookstore. Vanessa has a copy of it. So do the Christian housewife woman and the graduate student. Mark chuckles nervously at the sight of it. Then, when he suggests they begin, Vanessa wants to talk about *Exile* first. Again he smiles nervously. "Sure, go ahead."

"I just wanted to say I think this is the worst misogynist shit I have ever read. I can't believe you got this published."

Mark swallows and looks across the table at her.

"And I especially can't believe they're letting you teach here," she says directly into his face.

Mark looks down at his folder. The one that's supposed to have the student poems in it. "Well," he looks around at the other students, "does anybody else have any thoughts?"

The older woman raises her hand. "In the first part. Of the 'Exile' poem. When it says:

> God
> It'll be
> Easy to hate you

My question is: Do you really hate God?"

"Oh, no," says Mark. "I just meant . . . the thing about God . . . that's just an expression."

"Because . . ." The woman hesitates, looks at Vanessa. "Because I agree with Vanessa about your view of women. I think you're obviously very bitter and negative. But if you hate God. I mean to me, as a Christian, that's much worse. Because that's hating everything. That's hating life itself."

"No, I didn't mean the poem to be talking to God. I just started with that because—"

"I can't believe they want us to *learn* from you," says Vanessa. "That you're supposed to be *educating* us."

Mark looks at her. Then back at the Christian woman, who says, "I just don't see how you can say you hate God. Even if you don't mean to. In a way that's even worse. If you didn't know what you were saying. That's just . . . pure evil."

Mark stares down at his notebook. "Don't you ever say *God, it sure is a nice day out today?*"

"I don't care about God," says Vanessa wildly. "I care about men just throwing their hatred around like it has no effect. Writing stuff like this as if no one is going to read it and feel how much of a creep you are."

"We're not supposed to take stuff personally," says the sorority girl. The dumbest person in the class is coming to Mark's rescue. "He's just expressing himself. And you're not supposed to judge. We all agreed at the beginning that we weren't going to judge people on a personal level."

Mark doesn't look at the sorority girl but her presence rallies his confidence. "I understand what you're saying, Vanessa," he says quietly. "I mean there is some anger in that poem. Actually, what happened was . . ." But even as he talks, even as he calms everybody down, he feels a strange sense of internal collapse. He is breaking the first rule of poetry, of all artistic endeavor: *Never apologize, never explain.*

13

Mark wasn't going to go to David and Mary Anne's after class, but now he is. He lets himself in. David and Mary Anne are on the back porch with some students. A teacher he doesn't know is in the kitchen with some other people he doesn't know. He moves around them to pour himself a large vodka and grapefruit juice. He drinks half of it and refills it with vodka.

Mary Anne comes into the kitchen. She sees Mark and slides in beside him. "Glad you could make it. How was your class?"

"Terrible," he says.

"What happened?"

Mark takes a big sip of his drink. "They got my book."

"They didn't like it?"

"They hated it. This one girl hated it. And this Christian woman thinks I'm Satan. That was sort of funny actually."

Bill Masters appears in the doorway.

"But this girl Vanessa," continues Mark. "She was the only interesting one in the class. And now . . ."

"Hey, Mark!" says Bill Masters. The hallway is filling up with Willamette faculty.

"Hi, Bill," says Mark.

Bill moves closer to him. Mary Anne moves away. "Mark, could you step out here for a moment?" says Bill.

Mark does. He follows Bill, not to the back where everyone else is, but to the front where they can sit by themselves on the steps.

"Do you mind sitting out here?" says Bill.

"Not at all," says Mark, still sipping at his drink.

"Listen, Mark, Vanessa came to see me today."

Mark nods. What if he gets fired? What will Howard say? But it's Howard's fault. He sent the books.

"I know you don't have a lot of experience in these situations but I need you to help me with this."

"Sure."

"We've all had to listen to this sort of gender bias stuff for years now and it gets old, I know, but the thing to keep in mind is that this is a young woman and she's just starting. That's why she's here. And this stuff is new to her. Maybe she hasn't thought about it too much. You know, she's taking her first women's studies course, she's just starting to see how things are. Are you with me?"

"Yeah."

"So what you need to do is let her work through it, maybe even help her along. Admit that the work that bothers her is problematic and that she has a valid point."

"I kind of already did that."

"Well, that's great. That's exactly what you need to do. Isn't she right? Isn't there some anger there? So give her that. Grant her that. Let her work it out for herself."

"Act sensitive," says Mark, nodding.

"No, no. Nothing like that. What I'm saying is . . . well,

let me put it this way: what we can't have is a confrontation, a big blowup, or anything that goes beyond your particular classroom situation. *Containment* might be a good way to think about it."

Mark nods. "We did manage to get through the class."

"You're halfway there then. She'll calm down. She'll probably fall in love with you by the end. She'll probably be stalking you by the time you leave." He laughs.

Mark doesn't laugh. He stirs his drink with his finger.

"So listen, how's the writing?" says Bill.

"To be honest, I haven't done much."

"Well, that's all right. It'll come. You know, I've been working on some stuff myself. Maybe you'd like to take a look?"

Mark would rather not. But he remembers where he is, who he is, who Bill is. He thinks for a moment and then comes up with the correct answer. "Sure Bill, I'd love to."

Later that night Mark watches his new TV in his living room. It only gets one station, though, so he's forced to sit through several tabloid news shows and then a terrible situation comedy. He flicks it off. It's Friday night again and he has no idea where Sam is. There seems only one thing to do: go back to the Alchemy Bar.

When he gets there it's even more crowded than last week. He orders a beer and lights a cigarette. He scans the booths. No Sam. He watches the bartender work. He watches a guy in a leather trenchcoat talk into the pay phone. The group on his left is talking loudly about going to a club called Sanctuary to see a band. Then some other people come over, two women in miniskirts, they're going too. As they begin to leave, Mark asks them where Sanctuary is. They tell him.

Mark lets them leave. He smokes another cigarette, finishes his beer. Then he follows their directions into a rough-looking neighborhood. At first he doesn't see the club, the front is nondescript and there's no sign. But then a door opens and two punk kids come out, followed by the noise of bass and drums. Mark catches the door behind them and goes inside. Immediately he sees that Sanctuary is the CBGB's of Portland: dark, cavernous, druggy. Mark buys a beer and watches the band. They're not very good. Then he smells pot. He'd love to get stoned. He scans the room for possible dealers. The guy he picks isn't one, but he refers Mark to someone named Chuck. Chuck isn't there but if Mark will wait . . .

Mark will. He goes to the bar. A half hour later a small pockmarked kid tugs on his sleeve. "Hey, dude, what's up?"

"Not much. Are you Chuck?"

"I sure am. What can I do you for?"

"Just a little pot if you got it."

"I've got eighths for forty."

"Do you have anything smaller?"

"No man, eighths is the smallest."

"Okay. What do we do?"

"Follow me." They go back toward the stage and slip into a small storage room behind the sound board. "You just want pot, right?" says Chuck.

"Why? What else do you have?"

"What do you want?"

"God, I'd love a . . ." Mark lowers his voice. "A little dime bag of heroin."

"A little dime bag of heroin?" laughs Chuck. "Dude, where are you from?"

"Back east," says Mark.

Chuck leans against the wall and digs in his pockets.

"Here, check out this pot." He hands Mark a small plastic pouch.

"That's an eighth?"

"Yeah. Forty bucks."

It looks all right. Mark opens the seal and smells it. It smells all right. Not great. But it's real. And it's not like he can't afford it. "All right," says Mark.

"Hey listen, man," says Chuck. "You really want smack?"

"I don't want forty bucks' worth."

"I can get you a bag. For twenty."

"Is it powder?"

"Yeah, sure, I can get powder."

"Right now?"

"Right now," says Chuck. "Come on." Mark follows him back out to the bar.

Chuck leaves him there and disappears for ten minutes. When he returns he comes straight to Mark at the bar. "Come on," says Chuck. Mark feels uneasy now. Chuck's moving too fast. The guy working the door is noticing all this.

For some reason they go outside. A light mist has begun to fall. Chuck leads him across the street and into a gravel parking lot. "We gotta do this fast," he whispers to Mark. "There's cops all over the place."

Mark watches Chuck's face. In the dark it looks even skinnier and uglier than before.

"Here you go, man," says Chuck, standing semi-hidden between a truck and a van.

It's a miniature Ziploc bag full of white powder.

"It looks like coke," says Mark.

"It's China White," says Chuck. "This stuff rocks."

"Mind if I taste it?" asks Mark.

"Man, you gotta hurry. There's cops everywhere around here."

Mark opens his pocketknife, touches his tongue to the tip and touches the tip to the white powder. He tastes it. "Well," says Mark moving his tongue around. "It isn't coke."

"Yeah, it'd be fucking two hundred bucks if it was."

"And it isn't speed," says Mark, tasting it again.

"No shit it's not speed. C'mon man, you want it or what?"

"This isn't anything," says Mark.

"That's fucking China White. That shit will fuck you up."

"China White," says Mark, looking into the bag. "What, they bring it here from China?"

"Yeah, it comes direct from Hong Kong. Straight across the ocean." Chuck is getting antsy. "It's heavy shit, man. Fucking lasts forever."

Mark reseals the Ziploc and hands it back to Chuck. "I think I'll pass. But I'll take the pot."

Chuck reluctantly takes back the white powder. Mark folds up his knife and gets out his wallet. He pulls out two twenties.

Chuck stares at the Ziploc.

"I said I'll take the pot," repeats Mark.

"What's wrong with this?" says Chuck.

"It's not heroin."

"It's not?"

Mark shakes his head. "Somebody must be trying to rip you off, Chuck. Someone must think you're stupid."

Chuck stares at him.

"But I'll take the pot."

BLAKE NELSON

"Yeah, sure." Chuck digs into his pocket. "Hey, I got some better stuff if you want. Same price. It's got some bud in it."

Mark clenches the twenties in his hand and holds them while he inspects this new bag. It's the same size but it's got three large buds. He opens it and holds it to his nose. It does smell better.

"It was my fucking roommate, dude," says Chuck. "It was his stuff. He told me it was China White. I don't normally deal that shit. How was I supposed to know? I ain't no fucking junkie."

Mark hands over the two twenties. Chuck doesn't bother to continue his explanation. As soon as he's got the cash he's gone. Mark is left standing in the parking lot. He slips the pot into his pocket and begins to walk slowly in the opposite direction.

14

That same night, across town, Jill and Samantha sit in a booth at the Kelly Street Pub.

"He was staring at me," says Jill. "At the party. He was sitting on that couch, listening to my conversation."

"He was not."

"I'm telling you, he *was*," says Jill. She drinks her beer and watches two young men at the pool table.

"He *was* sort of strange," says Sam. "You should have seen him the next morning."

"What did he do? Read you some poems?"

"*No,*" says Sam. She thinks about it. "I sort of liked the fact that he was . . . I don't know, have you ever gone out with a poet? From New York?"

"Oh, *please,*" says Jill.

"What?"

"What's worse than a poetry professor hanging around the Alchemy, trying to pick up girls?"

"He wasn't trying to pick me up."

"Oh, no, not at all."

"Well, at least he was nice about it. Not like that creep from Stephanie's party."

"That guy was a total fox."

"He practically raped me."

"He was just young."

"He came on my *dress*."

Jill drinks her beer.

"I think he liked me too much though," says Sam. "The poetry guy, I mean."

Jill sighs.

"He had that look about him. Sort of sad."

"He's *old*," says Jill. "You get your choice: the old ones who worship you and are pathetic. Or the young ones who come on your dress and are pathetic. At least the young ones are cute."

Sam lights a cigarette. "Yeah, but the old ones can at least have a conversation."

Jill isn't listening. "Check out Mr. Levi's," she says, grinning at the nearest pool player as he lines up a shot.

"Jill, don't."

"Look at this idiot," says Jill, smiling provocatively at the guy as he shoots. He misses.

"Hey! Look what you made me do?" he says to Jill from across the room.

"I didn't make you do it," says Jill, smiling more.

The guys comes over to their table. "I was going to win!" he tells Jill, already captivated by her.

"You still might," says Jill.

Sam rolls her eyes.

"Hey," says the guy, shifting his stance. "You guys want to play doubles or something?"

Jill laughs.

"What?" says the guy.

"Did you ask us if we want to play doubles?" says Jill.

"Yeah," says the guy. "Why? What does that mean? Is that like . . . a sex thing?"

Jill smiles at his cluelessness.

"No," says the guy. "I just mean do you want to play pool. Or whatever."

"I don't play pool," says Jill, "but I do need another beer."

"Oh, man," says the guy, laughing. "I'd buy you a million beers. But I'm totally broke."

Jill smiles sweetly at him: "Then why are we having this conversation?"

The guy laughs. He waits for Jill to laugh. She doesn't. The guy's expression changes. He backs up a couple steps. He goes back to his pool game.

"Jesus, Jill, why do you do that?" says Sam.

"Why do I do what?" says Jill, draining the last of her beer.

That same night, Vanessa sits alone in a booth at the trendy Omega Cafe. She drinks tea and reads from *The Letters of Sylvia Plath.* The smell of clove cigarettes wafts through the room. It's coming from the next table, where three high school girls are discussing their upcoming night at the local underage dance club. Vanessa wishes they'd hurry up and go. The girls are loud and obnoxious. And Vanessa can't stand any smoke, let alone cloves. When one of the girls needs sugar for her coffee she reaches over the booth and grabs Vanessa's. Without asking. Vanessa scowls in their direction, but it's her own fault. It's Friday night, not a good night to try to read at the Omega. She should probably just go home.

"Hey is that you, Vanessa?" says Brendon, coming to her table.

Vanessa recoils at the sight of him.

"Oh, hey, I didn't mean to scare you," says Brendon, smiling. "What are you doing?"

Vanessa shrugs. "Reading."

"Hey, Pete," says Brendon, to one of the guys he's come in with. "Get me a coffee."

Vanessa looks at Brendon. He's wearing his usual thrift-store suit. A tie. His dyed black hair is now dyed blue. She sees him downtown all the time. Him and his weird friends. But they've only really met once, outside the library a couple weeks ago. Brendon just sat down next to her and started talking.

"So what are you doing tonight?" he asks.

"Nothing," says Vanessa. "Later I'm meeting a friend."

"Who?"

"Just somebody."

"We're going see this guy's band," says Brendon, looking around the cafe.

"Yeah?" says Vanessa. But she sounds too eager. She tries to restrain herself. "At Sanctuary?"

"At somebody's house. At some guy's birthday party," says Brendon.

"Here's your coffee," says Pete, setting a cup down on Vanessa's table.

Pete and the other boy automatically pile into Vanessa's booth, but then see Vanessa's shocked look. "Hey, are we sitting here or what?" they ask Brendon.

Brendon smiles at Vanessa.

"There's no other tables," says the other boy.

"You can sit here," says Vanessa, her heart pounding. She slides over.

Brendon sits on Vanessa's side. Pete grabs the Sylvia Plath book.

"So what did those chicks outside want?" the other boy says.

"Who knows," says Brendon. One of the girls at another table sees Brendon and waves. Brendon starts talking to her across the aisle.

"This is that chick that killed herself," says Pete, looking at the book.

"She was a poet," says Vanessa, as casually as she can.

But now a guy has come over to tell Brendon about another party. He too has dyed hair. And the same mismatched clothing style as Brendon's friends. But Vanessa sees that he is not like them. Beneath his artsy surface he's very clean and good-looking. He's from the suburbs. And yet he defers to Brendon.

"Check it out," says the other boy. "Here come those chicks from outside."

"Tell Brendon," says Pete. The other boy kicks Brendon. But it's too late. The girls are already crowding around the table.

"Hi, *Brendon*," says the prettiest of them. Her voice is so gushy and saccharine it makes Vanessa ill. And ever so slightly jealous.

Meanwhile, back at Sanctuary, Mark leaves the parking lot and walks uphill, toward Portland's industrial section. After a few blocks the traffic thins out. There are no bars here, no cops, no people. He walks over railroad tracks, along one unpaved block that is just gravel and potholes. It's Portland's version of Tribeca: dark, silent streets flanked by old loading docks and warehouses. He looks for something to smoke Chuck's pot with. He sees an empty

Coke can in a doorway. He picks it up, it's filthy, he drops it. A block later he finds a 7-Up can, sitting on a loading dock. Not only is it clean, it's still half full. Mark pours it out, shakes out any last drops. He carries it until he finds a section of the loading dock that is relatively hidden from view. He hops onto the platform, seats himself against the brick wall. This is one nice thing about Portland: all the space, all the weird little places to hide out in.

Mark shakes the can out a couple more times. Then he bends it, creasing it across the middle. Using the leather punch on his pocketknife, he pokes six tiny holes on the creased spot. Then he puts a bit of the bud on the spot, lights it and sucks the smoke out through the drinking hole. He gets a sudden, harsh hit. He coughs. Pot smoke drifts out of the can and off the top. He hurries to take another hit, to not waste it. He sucks it down until the pot on the crease is just a small bit of ash.

The light mist that's falling has gotten heavier. Mark watches it from where he sits. The pot is good. He enjoys the light jittery reverie he is prone to when stoned. It's not like the all-engulfing heaviness of heroin. Pot is fun because it makes him think—dumb tangential thoughts but thoughts nevertheless. But he misses the warm hole heroin lowers him into. He misses that sense of melting, of immersion, and then the eventual recovery, the steely tension of his body returning to him.

He stands up and looks around the loading dock. The wood planks of the dock smell good. There's a woodsy, mossy smell to the area in general. Mark lights a cigarette and paces the part of the dock that's covered. The mist is turning to rain which is falling in waves. It looks like snow in the streetlight. When a stray car approaches, he stops and stands motionless. The car drives by, its headlights on, its wipers flapping. Then it's gone. The docks are quiet again. Mark continues to walk, to pace, back and forth along the damp wooden planks.

15

Mark is watching TV. The phone rings. "Hello?"

"Is Mark there?"

"This is Mark."

"This is Samantha."

"*Samantha*," says Mark.

Pause.

"What are you doing?" asks Samantha.

"Trying to watch TV."

Pause.

"I bought this TV and it doesn't even work," says Mark.

"What doesn't work about it?"

"Nothing comes in. I get one channel."

"You don't have cable?"

"I don't want cable. I just want normal TV. But I can't get it. I'm going to take it back."

Pause.

"Where did you buy it?"

"Newberry's."

"They sell TVs at Newberry's?"

"Sure, they sell everythin

"Well, I'm sorry it doesn

"It does work. It just do
reception. I can't get anytl
Alaska or someplace."

Pause.

"It doesn't matter. What a

"Nothing. Homework."

"What sort of homework?'

"I'm reading *The Duchess* (

"How did you get my number?"

"From Information."

"I couldn't get your number."

"I know. It's not listed."

Pause.

"So what did you do all week?" asks Sam.

"Nothing. Thought about you."

"Really?"

"It's kind of hard not to. When I can smell you on my sheets."

"Do I smell?"

"No. You smelled good. It's gone though. I think it's gone. Let me check—" He puts down the phone. "Yeah, it's pretty much gone."

"Are you in bed now?"

"No, I'm in the hall."

Pause.

"I thought about you," says Samantha.

"Yeah?"

"I couldn't smell you though."

"That would make sense."

"I just thought about you in general."

"Good thoughts or bad thoughts?"

thoughts. I guess."

ound too sure."

know you that well. But I did think about you.

nes I don't even do that. Or sometimes I just feel

"How nice."

"With you it's more like a food you've never had so you don't know what it tastes like at first. Even though you're tasting it. You don't really understand the taste of it."

"Huh."

"I don't mean that as an insult. I mean it as a compliment more than anything."

"I take it as a compliment. I guess."

"I thought I wanted to do something with you again."
Pause.

"What kind of thing were you thinking of?" says Mark.

"I don't know. What do people do in New York?"

"Go to a movie?"

"We could. We'd have to hurry though. The last shows are usually at nine forty-five."

"Nah. I don't want to hurry."

"Me neither."

"Do you have a TV?"

"Yeah."

"What channels do you get?"

"All of them. I have cable."

"Maybe I should just come over."

"Okay," says Sam.

"Should I get something to drink?"

"I have wine here."

"I have some pot. Do you like pot?"

"Sometimes."

"I'll bring it. Where do you live?"

She tells him.

"Okay then."

"Okay."

Mark and Sam watch TV. They drink wine and smoke pot. Then they have sex. Then they go to bed where they have sex again.

In the morning they walk downtown. They eat at a small hipster cafe. Sam knows the gay waiter who serves them. They're old friends apparently. They keep up a conversation throughout breakfast. Mark can't help but resent this intrusion, but it's probably for the best. He's having trouble talking to Sam. Without sex as the ultimate goal of conversation, he seems to have nothing to say to her.

When they finish eating, Sam hugs the waiter and promises to call. Mark waits as the goodbyes become a whole new conversation. When they are finally out on the sidewalk Sam doesn't look at Mark. She seems distracted. Then she wants to stop at a vintage clothes store. Mark follows her in. Sam wants saddle shoes. Mark watches while she digs a pair out of a box. But he's hovering. He moves away from her and flips through a rack of coats.

There's a pretty girl across from him at the dress rack. He watches her hold dresses against her chest. He looks back at Sam, who's kneeling on the floor, trying to force the saddle shoes on.

"Those don't fit," Mark tells her.

"I know."

"Don't put them on, you'll fuck up your feet."

"It doesn't hurt to try them on."

"Sure it does. You'll end up like those pygmy women with deformed toes."

"What pygmy women?"

Mark doesn't answer. He picks up a tweed hat off the top of the rack. He puts it on and looks in the mirror. It makes his head look funny.

Sam is still struggling with the shoes.

Mark puts the hat back. He pulls out a black raincoat but several of the buttons are missing.

"Arrrgh!" says Sam, throwing the saddle shoe back in the box.

Mark finds a herringbone blazer that says Harris Tweed on the label. He tries it on. It feels pretty good. "Check this out," he says to Sam.

"Very literary," she says. She's joined him at the coats.

"Do you think it's stupid, being a poet?" says Mark, still watching himself in the mirror.

"Not if you're getting paid," says Sam. She's pulled a beige raincoat out of the rack. Mark watches her try it on. It makes her look older. It changes her face, her posture. She looks like an actress from the sixties. Or a model. Or the sexiest substitute teacher imaginable.

"This is sort of interesting," says Sam.

Mark watches her go to the mirror. The effect is enhanced. Samantha is stunning.

"How's it look?" says Sam.

"It's nice," says Mark.

"You think?" says Sam, turning sideways in the mirror.

Mark nods weakly. He can't take his eyes off her. She's got him now. She owns him totally.

Back at her apartment, Samantha opens a bottle of wine. They stand in her kitchen with wine glasses. Sam is still wearing the raincoat. Mark can't help himself. He leans over and kisses her on the mouth. "So how am I tasting today?"

"Good," she says.

But it was a dumb thing to say. Corny. Mark swirls the wine in his glass.

Samantha looks away.

"Does this feel weird to you?" says Mark.

"What?"

"I don't know. This."

"No," says Sam. "I mean, a little. It's all right though."

Mark drinks.

Sam drinks too. Then she puts down her glass. "You know what I think?" she says, sliding her arms around his neck.

"What?"

"I think you worry too much."

Mark tries to redeem himself in bed. He fucks her hard, using the natural swing of the bedsprings to its fullest advantage. He thinks she's coming when she grabs at his hair, his ears. She does not hum, she grunts. Short sharp exclamations that encourage Mark to rock the bed harder. But that works against him. Before he can stop himself, he's on the brink of orgasm. He stalls as best he can. He lets himself down until his full weight is on Sam. She seems to know what's happening and gently strokes his head, his shoulders, as far down his butt as her hands will reach. He kisses her, then breathes on her forehead and eyebrows. He grinds into her. She hums. "I think I'm going to come," she says.

"I know I am," says Mark.

"Hmmmmmm," says Sam.

Three days later Mark is sitting in a Winchell's donut shop. He sips his coffee and scribbles at the top of the page until the ink begins to flow. He writes:

you get her but
you can't
hold her down

Once the pen is working he stops to light a cigarette. He
stares out the window for a moment.

It's good
to grow up
lose your ego
lose yourself
lose the girl
stand on the corner
in the pouring rain

But the last two lines sound like a song. It is a song. He
heard it on the radio this morning.

oh silent
sam
silent slut
sam
fucking the
boys
again sam
can't
keep your
pants
on sam
when
will you
ever
learn?

"When will you ever learn" is from another song. Maybe he should stop listening to the radio.

> Fucking
> Is a good way
> To get into heaven
> To fill your ego
> Or maybe you just want
> Out like I want
> Out in this way
> We are
> Together

Mark puts down his pen. In the last three days there has been no word from her. He's left one message on her machine but doesn't want to do more. He sips his coffee. He just didn't get the girl. It happens. He closes his notebook. He sips his coffee. He lights another cigarette.

PART THREE

summer

PART THREE

16

Three months later Mark West is sitting on the curb outside a Quiki-Mart in the dusty desert town of Elko, Nevada. He's inspecting the plastic lid of his coffee cup. It doesn't have a slot to drink through. He uses the scissors on his pocketknife to cut one. Bill Masters comes out and finds Mark sitting on the ground. He hesitates but then joins Mark. He's got coffee too. He studies the lid on it.

"It doesn't have a hole," says Mark, reaching into his pocket for his knife. "Here. Use the scissors." He shows Bill the triangle he's cut in the lid of his cup.

Bill cuts his own hole and then, when he's got the lid back on, he inspects Mark's knife.

Mark drinks his coffee. The two of them are driving to Boulder, Colorado. They're going to a summer poetry conference at the Naropa Institute. Howard has arranged for Mark to be on a panel. Bill is going to hang out, he's friends with some of the organizers. A small group of Willamette poetry students might also make the trip, Vanessa among them.

"Man, check out the desert," says Mark, watching the wind blow tumbleweeds across the main road.

Bill looks, nods, goes back to unfolding the various blades of Mark's knife. Mark grins at him: "I stabbed a guy with that once." Bill laughs at Mark's joke. Mark laughs too.

Three hours later they enter Utah. The sun is down. Mark is drinking beer now, from a six-pack stashed under the seat. Bill is still driving, still drinking coffee. But he's sharing Mark's enjoyment at being somewhere new, at being in motion.

"So I was hoping I'd meet Howard at Naropa," says Bill.

Mark shrugs. He was hoping Howard might come too. "He's sick. I think he's got the flu."

"So what's your relationship with him like? It seems like he really pushes you."

"He does everything. He's pretty much my whole career at this point."

"Does he do all the English editions? And the translations and everything?"

"He sets it up. Some guy named Nigel does it in England."

"Huh."

"Yeah, Howard's cool. I wish I could do stuff for him like he does for me. You know? He's loaned me money. He's found me places to live. He's bailed me out of jail."

"He bailed you out of jail?"

"No. He didn't have to actually pay bail. He just had to come get me."

"Wow. What did you go to jail for?"

"I fell asleep in a subway station."

"Jesus Christ," says Bill, looking over at him, trying to see his face in the darkness.

"I was tired. I sort of dozed off. And then this transit cop started poking me with his stick."

This news seems to upset Bill. But it also excites him. Mark watches him shift in his seat.

But Mark is drunk. And he's grown to like Bill. And he's sick of always being polite and diplomatic. "Yeah, the main problem was, I grabbed the stick. Apparently that's the thing. If you grab the stick, you go to jail. The whole thing was stupid, really."

"But isn't jail in New York . . . isn't it . . . terrifying?"

"Naah. What are they going to do? Kill you? Let somebody else kill you? Nah. It was cool. I mean it's not really. It totally sucks. But you know, it's fascinating for a couple hours. You're never going to see shit like that."

Mark pauses to drink. Bill is getting fidgety. He wants Mark to continue.

So he does: "Like the first time. There's these four yuppies. And one of them is totally fucked-up drunk. I mean the guy can't stand up. And whatever they did, it's his fault. So they all come into the holding cell and there's all these bad-ass black guys there and just some really scary-looking types. Except for me of course. So these four yuppies are standing there in the middle of the cell and they're furious at the drunk guy. He fucked up. He's going to pay. I didn't catch what they did. Smashed a car or something. So for the first hour they're arguing about lawyers and telling their drunk friend what a dick he is. They're really loud, really on top of everything. They're like take-charge yuppies. So they do that. Then after a while they start to run out of steam. You know, they stop talking so loud. They start to look around. Their little group begins to contract. And then people start to fuck with them. Like their drunk friend is asleep on this bench but this huge black guy wants to sit there so he just throws him off the bench. And the drunk guy wakes up on the floor and he's going to kick somebody's ass but then he sees who did it."

Mark finishes his beer and goes for another one. He pops the tab and it sprays slightly onto Bill's dashboard. "Sorry," says Mark, wiping it with his coat sleeve.

"It's okay," says Bill. "So then what happened?"

"So now it's getting late. And then this other guy walks up to the drunk yuppie and sort of kicks him. For no reason. So the other yuppies, they're starting to freak. And these guys, you know, they got their little suits, their little pony tails. So after the initial shock wears off, after they've stood there in their little circle for a couple hours, they just start to lose it. And they're all looking over their shoulders and man, do their voices go down. Way down. They're practically whispering. I mean there's four of them. And you know, it's not like the movies or anything. There's no gangs or any real threat. It's just a bunch of fuck-ups. The real dangerous ones are the quietest ones. The ones who really did something are just chilling. But these yuppies, another hour goes by and these guys are fucking terrified. They give up on the bench. And they sit on the floor in this tight little circle against the bars, where the cops can see them the easiest. And they're sitting there and they are just beat. They are just totally fried. All the adrenaline, all the talk about their lawyers and how they're going to sue the police and they're going to sue the drunk guy, they're going to do this and that. By this time, these guys are fucking crying. One of them's sobbing like a baby. And they're all embarrassed and they hate each other and I mean, they just crumbled. I never saw anything like it. These guys were the biggest ass-kickers in the world and they just disintegrated before my eyes."

"What were you doing? Didn't anybody fuck with you?"

"Nah. Why? I didn't have anything."

"Did you sit on the bench?"

"Fuck no. I spent the whole night standing right next to the bars. Just like the yuppies."

"Weren't you scared?"

"Of course I was. But what can you do? You're there. Anyway, it's so fucking interesting. I mean besides the yuppies. Just watching people when they first come in. And just watching how people arrange themselves. Who sits where. The weird little interactions that go on."

"And no one bothered you?"

"There was no reason to bother me. And besides, I was into it. I mean, that was one of the most interesting nights of my life. I was so wired the next day I just walked around Manhattan all day. It was fucking wild. That's why when they found me in the subway, the other time, I was just like, yeah sure, I'll go to jail."

Bill digests this story. He drives. "So you're from Baltimore?"

"Yeah."

"So what does the West family do there in Baltimore?"

"My family's not West. It's O'Donnell. West is my stage name."

"So what's your real name?"

"West. Now it is."

"You had it changed?"

"I had to."

"Jesus," says Bill. "Was that Howard's idea?"

"That was before Howard. You know, Mark O'Donnell, it's not exactly memorable."

"Isn't that kind of weird though? Do other writers do that?"

"I don't know, probably."

"Tobias Wolff," says Bill. "I always wondered if that was made up."

"Could be," says Mark.

"It's just too perfect. It's just such a perfect writer's name."

"When I first got to New York there were all these people with cool names. Jennifer Blowdryer, Jeanne Caffeine. There was this guy Winchester Chimes. I loved that. He died of AIDS though."

"Would you change it again?"

"No. Once you have a book you're pretty much locked in."

Bill nods. He drives. "Did you ever write about being in jail?"

"I tried."

"It didn't work?"

"Things like that, things that are really out there. It doesn't work."

"Yeah, but what an experience!"

"I tried."

"Geez!" says Bill, shaking his head again. After a while he starts to laugh. "Hey you got any more beer under the seat there?"

"Sure," says Mark, pulling one out. He hands it to Bill, watching the highway as he does. Bill is excited now and it worries him.

"Ahh!" says Bill when the beer sprays his lap. But he

takes a big slurpy sip anyway. The car moves off toward the shoulder before Bill corrects it.

"You know what it's like, being in jail?" says Mark.

"What?" says Bill eagerly.

"It's like being on stage."

Bill takes another sloppy sip of his beer.

"Everything you do has significance," says Mark.

"Wow!" says Bill, drinking more. The car moves off toward the shoulder. Bill pulls the car back into the lane and takes another deep drink of his beer. Mark looks over at Bill. He watches the highway. He feels himself sobering up.

17

It's late the next night when Bill and Mark pull into a driveway in Boulder, Colorado. It's a long gravel driveway leading to a beautiful old house that sits tucked beneath two leafy oak trees. When Mark opens the car door he's struck by the pleasant summer heat, the sharp smell of vegetation, of flowers in bloom.

Bill and Mark are going to stay here with a married couple Bill knows. These two appear at the back door as soon as the car is stopped. Mark knows the drill by now. One thing about being an artist-in-residence, he's learned how to meet people. As the car doors slam, Alice and Paul come down the wood steps to greet the weary travelers. Mark shakes their hands and smiles his professional smile. They all go inside.

In the kitchen, Mark sees that he has entered a hippy household. Pots and pans hang from the ceilings, various herbs line the walls, onions and garlic hang in wire baskets; all of which complements the large wood-burning stove that dominates one side of the room.

Alice is the literary one, the one connected to Naropa. She wears a peasant skirt and has long jet-black hair that is greying in streaks. Paul is tall and quiet. He works for a computer company. Alice and Bill do most of the talking. Mark drinks a cup of tea that is too sweet because they don't have sugar and Mark poured too much honey into it.

After an hour of chitchat Mark and Bill are shown their respective rooms. Bill will sleep upstairs and Mark will have the basement all to himself. It's a good arrangement, he's got a Hide-A-Bed and his own toilet and sink. Also there's a heavy back door that Paul is nice enough to open for him. "So you can step outside to smoke," Paul tells Mark.

Mark thanks him profusely and as soon as Paul's gone pushes open the door and steps quietly up the stairs and into the backyard. He stands in the thick green grass and lights a cigarette. He smokes and looks around the yard. It's dark but he can see the unkempt lawn, the old wood fence which surrounds it. He looks back at the house. There are lights on upstairs. But he feels like he's spying so he walks around to the driveway and leans on Bill's car to finish his cigarette. There are no lights on this side of the house so it is here that Mark first looks up and sees the incredible night sky, the blaze of stars in the sharp mountain air. Mark smokes and stares. Behind him, Bill's car is still cooling. It makes ticking, settling sounds.

The next morning Bill comes down to the basement but hesitates at the foot of the stairs. "Mark? Are you awake? Feel like a little breakfast?"

Mark frowns at his boss from beneath the covers. "I just want to sleep."

"That's fine," says Bill. "Alice and I are going into town,

and then I'm going over to Naropa. I'll swing by later and get you."

"Which way is the town?" says Mark, peeking out at him.

"Right over there," points Bill. "Take a left out the driveway and follow the road."

"All right," says Mark.

When Bill is gone Mark gets up to piss. Then he stands in the middle of the room in his T-shirt and underwear. There's a small slit of a window but the summer sunlight is so bright it illuminates the whole basement. He digs through his bag for his sunglasses. He puts them on, gets a cigarette and pushes open the back door. He sits on the stair steps in his underwear and smokes. When he hears the side door open he ducks down, then lifts his head enough to see Paul getting into his car. He drives away. Mark creeps up the stairs a little further, he sees there are no cars in the driveway. Everyone is gone. He comes all the way out. He stretches, stands barefoot in the lawn, his bare white legs bristling in the morning heat.

Mark puts on a pair of cutoffs and sneakers and heads into town. It's hot walking along the road and he's sweating when he finds a small bohemian coffee shop on the edge of town. Penny Lane it's called. Mark orders an iced tea from the nose-ringed teenager at the counter. He pays and sits outside at one of the tables. He lights a cigarette and then gives cigarettes to two girls at the next table. He's hoping maybe they'll talk to him. But they don't. So he drinks his tea and watches the occasional car drive by.

That night Bill takes Mark to a Naropa party. At first Mark is excited but when they get there the Naropa people seem oddly aloof. It's not that Mark expects any special attention, but they must know who he is. They must know Howard. One woman, Sarah Colbert, has a book out on Howard's Free City Press. But when he tries to join into a conversation she's part of, no one will talk to him. But it doesn't matter. Mark drinks vodka and pokes through the host's bookcase. Then he finds a small group of people smoking a joint in the backyard. Here he makes a friend of a strange young man who bums cigarettes from him. His name is Burt and he's East European, though he is unable to explain where exactly he's from.

"You like this party?" asks Burt when they are alone on the back porch.

Mark shrugs. "It's all right."

"I know another party."

"Well, what are we waiting for?"

Mark tells Bill he's going for cigarettes and he and Burt start walking. "It is a long way," apologizes Burt. "I think we must hitchhike." He sticks out his thumb. The first car they see stops. It's a bunch of kids in a pickup truck. They drive Burt and Mark to an intersection within a block of Burt's party. As they approach the house, Mark sees it's a young Deadhead-ish crowd. Mark is overdressed but gamely follows Burt through the front door. But it's crowded inside. "Come!" urges Burt. "We must find Agnes." They make it through the house to the backyard. Here there is a keg, a small fire, people playing guitars. Burt must know someone or else just cuts in line because by the time Mark is oriented he's got a beer in his hand. Mark gives Burt a cigarette. They smoke.

"Good party, yes?" says Burt.

"Yes."

"There is my friend Agnes. Come."

They approach two women standing by the fire. The one named Lori is a typical hippy type but Agnes is wearing silver cat's-eye glasses and a red party dress. She has curly black hair, black lipstick. Burt tells her Mark is from New York.

"New York? Really?" says Agnes, excitedly. "That is so awesome! Where do you live? What street?"

"I lived on East Fourth Street."

"Ohmigod! I lived on Avenue A. When I stayed there last summer. I love the East Village!"

"All right," says Mark, grinning at her enthusiasm.

"Where did you work? What was your job?"

"I, uh . . ."

"He's a poet," says Burt. "He's from Naropa."

"I work as a bartender sometimes," says Mark.

"Where?"

"Steel."

"Ohmigod! I've heard of that. I've heard of Steel."

"All right," say Mark.

"Steel is like this . . . ," Agnes tells Lori. "It's this really cool place."

"What else can we do tonight?" Burt asks Agnes.

"There's a rave over by the university." She looks at Mark. "Do you like raves?"

"Sure. I guess so."

"I used to like them but not anymore. I mean, I'd go to one."

"Do they have LSD?" asks Burt.

"At the rave? Probably."

But that's all the possibility Burt needs. They all get into Agnes's car and drive to the rave. It's in a large concrete building. They pay five dollars and go in but there's not really anybody there.

"It's still early," explains Agnes. Meanwhile Burt has vanished. Mark follows Lori and Agnes to a bar where Mark tries to get a drink. But they don't serve alcohol. Mark buys a "smart drink" and tastes it with his finger.

But then Burt comes back. He needs money to buy acid. Mark and Agnes both give him ten dollars and he leaves and is back again minutes later. He's got it. They all stand in a circle and look at the four small pieces of pink paper. Burt is the first to take one. He pops it in his mouth, maneuvers it under his tongue, laughs at the rest of them. Then Agnes puts hers in her mouth and Lori and Mark do the same. Then Agnes and Burt dance. Mark and Lori follow.

An hour later the rave is filling up. It becomes very hot. The four of them stop dancing and sit on the cement floor along a wall. Burt disappears. Then he reappears and wants the rest of them to follow him. They do. He's found a back exit, a fire door that's propped open. Behind the building a group of teenage ravers are drinking quarts of beer. But that's not why Burt has brought them here. He leads them along the back wall to a place where a fire-escape ladder hangs down from the roof. It's high up but there's a car parked beneath it. Burt scrambles onto the hood of the car and climbs up the ladder. Mark helps Agnes onto the car. She seems to enjoy holding his hand. When she and Lori are both up, Mark grips the rusted ladder. It is then that the acid first hits him. The ladder seems to squirm as he holds it, his fingers seem to meld with the steel rungs. But he knows it's just the LSD so he keeps climbing.

On top of the building, the first thing Mark sees is the incredible canopy of stars overhead. Also, the mountains beyond are suddenly visible. They are huge and looming and incredible to behold. In his more immediate field of vision, there are maybe twenty people on the roof. Most are dancing. One woman is topless . . . no, two women are . . . and a naked man, a skinny bearded guy with a tiny penis buried in pubic hair . . . and people playing bongos . . . and more teen ravers . . . the music is in the floor . . . Mark feels his whole being shiver . . . the scene swims before him . . . he closes his eyes once . . . his whole body is brimming with electricity.

He bumps into Agnes. Or she bumped into him. "Oh!" she says, a strangely confident look on her face. Mark leans on her shoulder for support and her hand slips deftly around his waist . . .

18

Vanessa has been driving for two full days when she pulls into a truckstop just beyond Cheyenne, Wyoming. She did not understand how far away Colorado is. Or how hard the drive would be. She gets out of her mother's station wagon and tries to stretch her legs. Her butt is sore. Her knees don't seem to work. Also it's so hot. Her jeans feel filthy and her shirt is stuck to her back. She's pulling at it when she enters the restaurant but inside the air-conditioning is on full blast. Now she's too cold.

Vanessa sits by herself at a table by the window. Three other students were supposed to come with her. That's why she brought the station wagon. But they all backed out. Vanessa should have known. She pulls the menu out from behind the napkin holder. A scattering of truckers sit at the counter, their backs to her. They talk quietly but a little farther down another man is turned in his seat, he's staring straight at her. He smiles. Vanessa looks down at her menu. The waitress comes. "Coffee?"

"Yes, please," says Vanessa.

The waitress pours her coffee. "Know what you want?"
"A BLT?"
The waitress is a pleasant older woman. "Anything to drink?"
"Just water, please."
The waitress leaves and Vanessa wraps her hands around the coffee cup. It's so cold in here. She looks out the window at her mom's car. Maybe she should get her sweater. She'd be happy for an excuse to wear it. It's a rust-colored cardigan, similar to one she's seen Brendon wear. The problem with artsy clothes is you can only wear them in certain situations. A Wyoming truckstop is probably not one of them. She decides to go without.

She looks back at the counter. The man who smiled at her has turned around. She looks up the empty rows of booth seats. And then outside through her window at her mother's car. She's never been so far from home.

As Mark waits for the panel discussion to begin, he surveys the audience for any sign of Agnes or Burt. He is still hung over from their wild night, even now, two days later. But it's a pleasant hangover, a sort of relaxed stupidness, not like yesterday when his head ached and he barely had the stamina to walk to Penny Lane and get his iced tea. No, today he still feels wasted but it's a good wasted. It's a horny wasted. He wants to see Agnes again, wants to improve on his miserable performance with her in the park by the rave, where he kept shivering and couldn't keep it up and was even too fucked up to respond to her patient blowjob. But now where is she? Where's Burt? Bill didn't know. Bill had never heard of Burt.

"... And Mr. Mark West, a native of New York City,

whose three books on Free City Press have enjoyed considerable interest abroad . . ."

That reminds Mark, he's got to call Howard. Maybe the Japanese thing is back on.

". . . Sarah Colbert, who is also published by Free City, is the author of *Mind Candy*. She's from Los Angeles . . ."

The symposium is on the dearth of nonacademic poetry and what people like Mark and Sarah Colbert and the three other panelists can do about it. The best part: it's outside. Mark is sitting at the end of a cafeteria-style table that is covered with a clean white tablecloth. A large tent shields them from the sun. The audience is about thirty people sitting on chairs in the grass opposite the tables. There was a problem with the microphones so he and Sarah Colbert are going to share the microphone on their side. The other panelists, none of whom Mark has heard of, will share one on their side.

One of the other panelists starts to talk. Mark tries to pay attention. But the man's voice is a dull drone. Mark begins to daydream. He remembers Agnes, her tits, they were small but with taut responsive nipples. He loves that, when women get off on their tits being sucked. Getting down off the roof, that was the tricky part. Mark slipped on the car hood and landed in a heap on the ground, much to the amusement of the teen ravers. And then Agnes in the park, fucking on grass, his knees implanted in the soft earth. And then that first moment of condomless entry: like velvet, but then when he went for the condom, his body suddenly so far away from his acid-sparked brain, fumbling with himself, his alien hands, his alien dick, poor Agnes giggling insanely and then lunging at him, wanting to fill herself and there he is lost, limp, stupid . . .

The audience politely applauds. The first speaker has finished. The second speaker begins. Agnes was a good kisser but her breath was sour. God only knows what Mark's breath was like. That's the thing about getting old. At thirty-one he doesn't smell yet, but he will. All old people do. Rotting from the inside. The terrible breath of teachers, bosses, anyone you have to stand next to in adult life. And Agnes, how old was she? Mid-twenties? She was already a bit sour. Too many raves. Too many drugs. Too many strangers fucked in the dirt. When she couldn't revive his failed dick, he sucked her tits and fucked her with his fingers as best he could. Mark sniffs his fingers, but then remembers where he is and covers it by pretending to scratch his nose. He drinks from his water glass. He can't really remember her face. But he's got a clear picture of her purse, on its side in the grass, her splayed legs, her party dress bunched around her waist. Mark smiles at the image: crazy Agnes, a pudgy white doll, underwear scattered, her bare butt in the mud . . .

A third panelist is talking about the language of poetry. "If we want the reading public to come back to this form, we simply must speak a simpler, more honest language." The audience nods and a few people clap. When the third panelist is done it's Sarah's turn. Mark now has no choice but to sit upright in his seat and listen carefully. He trains his eyes on Sarah's face and gives her a whole minute of his undivided attention. She's hipper than she looks. She talks about the L.A. coffeehouse scene, poetry slams, the various underground zines and presses. But this worries Mark. That's what he was going to talk about. Well, they'll just have to hear it again. He sits back, begins to space out. That's when he sees Bill, standing in the back, chatting quietly with Vanessa.

When Sarah is finished, Mark rambles for ten minutes and then the panel is over. It's lunchtime. He gets his food and joins a table with Vanessa, Bill Masters, Sarah Colbert and a few audience members. Despite their problems, Mark is glad to see Vanessa's familiar face. He takes the seat beside her and welcomes her to Boulder. "Anybody else come?" he asks her.

"No," says Vanessa.

"That's too bad," says Mark. He considers his paper plate. He's got a piece of chicken, some macaroni salad, a slice of watermelon. Vanessa avoids looking at him. But it doesn't matter now, any awkwardness between them. Not that it was so bad in the workshop. After that initial blowup things calmed down. Some sort of mutual respect was established. At least from Mark's side. Vanessa was the best poet in the class and the most entertaining to watch. She was the only one who took it seriously, the only one who actually struggled with her art.

"I went to a rave the other night," Mark tells her between bites of watermelon.

"Yeah?" says Vanessa.

"It was wild," whispers Mark. He feels euphoric for some reason, residual LSD or maybe the rush of public speaking. "People were dancing naked on the roof."

Vanessa doesn't know how to respond to this. She stares at her plate. But then her eyes are on Mark, watery and big.

"Yeah, it's cool here," continues Mark. "The air. The mountains."

"It's beautiful," says Vanessa, carefully spooning some of her own macaroni salad into her mouth. Mark bites into his chicken leg. A fragment falls into his lap. He's trying to find it when an audience member appears behind him. She wants to talk to Mark but he doesn't see her. Finally Vanessa touches him on the shoulder and Mark looks up. "Oh, hi."

"I just wanted to respond to your talk," says a strained-looking woman.

"Oh, sure."

"I just don't see how you can call this spoken-word stuff poetry. I think it's all for effect. It's all about the person, it's just ego."

"Huh," says Mark.

"Poetry is supposed to be about beautiful language. I went to one of those poetry slams in Denver and it was like 'The Gong Show.' It was like comedy routines. And it's all 'me, me, me, I did this, I did that.' I just don't see what the connection is to what we think of as great poetry."

"It's part of an oral tradition," says Vanessa.

"Well, so are dirty jokes," says the woman. "But that's not poetry."

"But it's evolving," says Vanessa. "Just because it isn't always good doesn't mean it's not valid."

Mark turns around to better see the woman. "I think it's the wrong direction," she says to Vanessa. "And all this complaining about academic poetry, I don't think you should criticize something if you have nothing comparable to offer."

Sarah Colbert is hearing this. "I think spoken word is more than comparable," she says. "It's accessible. Rock music wasn't taken seriously at first. Neither was film."

Mark goes back to his chicken. The woman moves over to where Sarah is and continues her conversation. "Thanks," Mark whispers to Vanessa.

"For what?"

"For talking to that woman."

"I didn't do that for you," says Vanessa.

"Yeah, I know, but thanks anyway."

Vanessa doesn't say anything. Mark eats his chicken. "So what have you done here so far?" he asks her.

"Nothing. I just got here yesterday."

"What did you do?"

"I unpacked. And did some laundry."

"You did some laundry?"

"I just rinsed out some things."

Mark speaks without looking at her: "I know I'm not your teacher anymore. I mean, I never really was. But can I give you a word of advice?"

"Maybe."

"You gotta do stuff."

"Like what?"

"Anything. Not your laundry."

Vanessa eats her macaroni. "I do stuff."

"I met this guy Burt," says Mark. "He's the one who took me to the rave. He seems to know what's going on. Give me your number and if I see him again I'll call you."

"Okay."

"I mean, if you want to do something."

"I do. Why do you think I came here?"

"Good. I'll call you."

"Good. Call me."

19

There's another Naropa function that night. Mark doesn't want to go, he doesn't like the Naropa people, but Bill seems to think it imperative he attend. Mark sits sullenly in the back of Bill's car as he and Alice drive to the Naropa campus. But as soon as they pull into the parking lot Mark can feel a buzz. They get out of the car and walk toward the party. There are people everywhere. And it's a different-looking crowd than the last two days. There are kids here now, cool kids, art student types, and a lot more adults. In the hallway of the main building they discover the cause of this new excitement. Anne Waldman is here. And Gregory Corso. And Allen Ginsberg.

Bill goes into a panic. He can't believe he left his Ginsberg books at home. Why didn't he see this coming? Alice is not as impressed. She's met Ginsberg before, he shows up at Naropa periodically. Mark, for his part, is stunned by the crowd. Where did all these cute girls come from? Why weren't they at the panel discussion? Inside, the main room is like a good night at Steel. Tight clusters of people.

A sharp buzz in the air. Everyone chattering, gossiping, looking over each other's shoulders. Mark separates from Alice and Bill. He wants to check this out on his own. He finds his way to the drink table. He waits in line and surveys the room. He spots Anne Waldman immediately. She's talking to the head person of Naropa. Behind her is another clump of Naropa big shots. But the other side of the room is where the real action is. That's where the biggest crowd of people is pressed around Ginsberg.

Mark turns back to the drink table line. A young man ahead of him is telling his friend: "He'll love you, man. You're just his type. I'll bet he hits on you. I bet he will."

A woman from the panel discussion is standing near Mark. "All the stars are out tonight!" he jokes with her. But she looks at him sideways and walks away. Mark gets to the front of the line. He orders a vodka tonic and smiles at the girl bartender. She ignores him. He's beginning to wish he'd stuck with Bill and Alice. When he turns back around he spots Sarah Colbert. He walks over to her and her friend. "Hey, you guys," he says.

But the friend looks anxious and agitated.

"Thanks for helping me with that woman at lunch," Mark tells Sarah.

"No problem—"

"Is that her?" the friend interrupts. She's nodding toward Anne Waldman.

"I think so," says Sarah.

"That can't be her."

"I think it is."

"Anne Waldman?" says Mark. "Yeah, that's her."

Sarah's friend scowls at him.

"Is that what you were asking?" says Mark, confused.

"Just go talk to her," counsels Sarah.

"What do I say?" Sarah's friend demands.

"Just tell her you like her work. And you write. Just act natural."

"Do you think she's really that good? I mean, is it worth it?"

"You're the one who wants to talk to her," says Sarah.

"I can't do it," says the friend, drinking from her cup and looking extremely upset.

Mark is not enjoying this and he moves away, bumping into a tight group of people that includes a small animated man, Gregory Corso. Mark moves around them, glancing back at the group surrounding Corso. "I think you're just marvelous," he hears someone say. He cringes and reaches for his cigarettes. They had celebrity parties at Steel all the time. It's not like he's never seen what goes on. What's bothering him is that these people are what he is. This is the top rung of the ladder that he's on.

Mark goes outside. The air is fresh and fragrant. Mark lights a cigarette and wanders the green lawn for a moment and then remembers Vanessa. He finds a phone booth and calls her. He asks her what she's doing.

"I was going to that party at Naropa."

"That's where I'm calling from."

"Is it good?"

"Yeah, it's pretty good. Allen Ginsberg is here. And Anne Waldman."

"Are you kidding? Are you serious?"

"I kid you not. They're here and the feeding frenzy is on."

"What feeding frenzy?"

"Just, you know, all the wannabes."

"Is Allen Ginsberg really there?"

"He really is."

"Okay, I'm coming. Right now."

But it takes her twenty minutes to get there and by then the party has abruptly ended. Ginsberg has left. The rumor is he's gone to take a hot tub with some students. Fortunately Alice knows where the party after the party is going to be. Ginsberg will be there. Bill is still in a panic. Alice is mildly excited. Mark would rather go looking for Agnes but he has no choice. They're standing in the parking lot when Vanessa pulls up. "That's Vanessa," Mark tells Bill, who's too overwhelmed to care.

Mark goes to her car and grabs Vanessa. "Listen, we're going to some other party. Come with us."

Vanessa is locking her car door. "But what about this party?"

"It's over. Come on. Come with us."

"But what about Allen Ginsberg?"

"He's gone. But he's going to this other party. Which is where we're going. So come on."

"But maybe I should drive."

"Don't drive, just come with us."

"But how will I get home?"

"Do you want to come or not?"

"Well, yeah."

"Then come on."

The new party is far up a mountain road. Bill drives and chatters like an idiot. Apparently he couldn't think of anything to say to Ginsberg but now he remembers hearing about a forgotten manuscript of Kerouac's found in somebody's basement in Sausalito. He'll ask Allen about that. He's rehearsing the conversation with Alice. Vanessa sits silently beside Mark. She's nervous about being away from her car. Mark is bored. And agitated. He stares out the window, at the black trees moving past in the darkness.

Alice directs them to the house and leads them inside. It's a modern mountain cabin, all wood and glass and track lighting. The crowd is similar to the Naropa party but Mark sticks with his own group this time. The four of them stand around the fireplace in the living room. But Bill is still obsessing over Ginsberg. And Mark needs a drink. So he walks around. He finds the kitchen and pours himself a Johnnie Walker on the rocks. Then he stands next to Vanessa.

"Want a taste?" he asks her, offering her his glass.

"No, I'm fine."

"Are you even old enough to drink?"

"Of course. I'm almost twenty-two, you know."

"I didn't know," says Mark, swirling the ice in his glass and then taking a sip. "Sure you don't want a taste?" he says, handing her the glass.

She takes it. She takes a tiny sip.

"Go on, it's a party, it'll relax you."

Vanessa takes another tiny sip. This one seems to register. She makes a choking face and hands it back.

"Geez," she says, coughing and patting her chest.

Mark enjoys her discomfort. He watches a new group of people come in. Vanessa regains her composure. "So did you talk to Allen Ginsberg?" she asks Mark.

"No."

"I suppose you're too cool to talk to him."

"No, I just . . . I found the whole thing sort of stupid."

"Stupid because you wish you were him."

"Stupid because I wish people would be more . . . I don't know. Not so . . . ."

"You're just jealous."

"I'm not jealous. What would I be jealous of?"

"He's famous. You're not."

Mark shrugs.

"He's a great poet. You're not."

Mark sips his drink. "Thanks for reminding me," he says. Then he walks away. If she's so smart he'll let her fend for herself.

But where to? Mark decides to tour the house. He climbs the stairs to the second floor where there's a bedroom, a fancy bathroom, an office full of computers, fax machines, etc. On the third floor is a sort of library/sitting room. It's mostly empty, unfinished, but there's a big cushy chair to sit in while you're enjoying the view, which must be spectacular. Mark shuts the door and turns off the light, so that the room is completely dark. He sits in the chair. As his eyes adjust he can begin to make out the view: treetops in the foreground, and then mountaintops, like little bumps, for miles beyond. He remembers the Kerouac book, the one where Kerouac lives in the fire tower in the mountains. Mark sips his drink and thinks about the Beat aesthetic: the celebration of nature, of the soul, of solitude. Kerouac got his solitude. Living with Mom in the trailer park. Dead at forty-seven of alcoholism and having too gentle a soul. Ginsberg, apparently the more world-ready of the two, ends up in the hot tub with the rich-kid groupies. Himself, Mark West, waiting his turn, to go which way? And that's even if he gets to the place where the paths diverge. Mark rocks the chair and thinks about Howard. Specifically when he asked him why Mark wanted to be a poet. What an excellent question. The scary thing is not that Mark doesn't know, but that at some point he must have thought he did.

20

Mark sits at the Penny Lane Cafe, at a table outside. He's got sunglasses on. He's got an iced tea. He smokes and writes in his notebook:

Dreams die hard
    They die in the desert
They die at some desk
    At some company
They die in the treetops
    At the mouths of rivers
The dreamless walk among us
    They know
The worst thing that can
    Happen happens
They do not kid themselves
    They have no illusions
They wait for the other
    Shoe to drop

E x i l e

Mark smokes. The hot sun is roasting the street but he's under the awning. The table he's writing on is wobbling so he tears out this first page, folds it up and slides it under one of the legs until the table is steady. Then he tries again:

Girls
They're fun to
Kiss
Fun to chase
Around
Fun to get in
Feminist arguments

But then you get old and you don't care anymore
You care about money and material things
Maybe buy a prostitute
No time now to chase and beg
But when you reach this stage
You know you're weakening
You know you're halfway done
The young come up behind you
With murder in their eyes
Which is why you get smarter
Why nature makes you smarter
Why you have memory and reasoning powers
Because now you're money grubbing and weak and
If you weren't smart the young
Would kill you, eat you
Fuck you dead
Their pure will against yours
You ugly old fuck
Let them win

Go down and be happy to take your polluted self
Off the pretty planet

girl on the street
girl walking with head up
girl with the sun in her hair
girl with her eyes to the sky
girl with her shoes
and her dress
and her purse on a
string

Fuck you I don't
care about you God
I didn't ask to be put here God
I didn't request time in this place God
Nature is your whore your person
who fires problem employees
your mean streak in action
God

God is not in today
God can not see you now
God will take your number and call you back
God is good
God is great
And we thank him for
Our short brutal miserable lives
(Oh but for the bracing goodness of hatred
The bracing positive of being so fucking
Furious the world blurs, rages, rips back at you)

Why I became a poet:
Because I thought I had something to say
Because I was bored
Because I thought it was something different
Because I thought girls would appreciate
    my sense of sacrifice and give me blowjobs
    but it doesn't work that way in fact
    exactly the opposite
Because I can't play guitar
Because I was a weird child and people
    said I was creative because I was embarrassing
    my family in front of the neighbors
Because I'm a pussy faggot
Because I'm not that smart and no one
    can tell good poetry from bad poetry
Because God thought it would be funny
    to watch one talentless stupid ass fuck
    hurl himself against a pointless
    artform but you know what
    god I'm not so dead as
    I look that's right you
    thought I'd amuse you but now you're
    going to amuse me you fuck I don't know how
    I don't know when but I'm going to
    make you pay make you regret
    the day you put
    breath in my body
    I will not be
    fucked over
    held down
    fucked
    by you

god
you're not fucking worth it

Dear Howard,

What's up? I'm chilling here in Boulder. It's pretty cool. Thanks for setting this up, it's really been fun. Bill Masters and I drove out. Everyone here speaks very highly of you.

Last night we went to a party with Allen Ginsberg. I felt weirdly unconcerned about this though everyone else was having major conniption fits. Sarah Colbert is here but I haven't really talked to her. There's a girl here who was a student of mine and she's pretty into it. She actually sort of blossomed in my class—not that I had anything to do with it—but it happened. (Tell the grant people, make up some inspirational story about it.)

Man, it's hot. But it's a dry heat! I miss the Yankees and the sweet smell of rotting garbage!

When the species is done
When the game is over

Dear Cynthia,

How's the big city? You'll never guess where I am. Boulder, Colorado at the Naropa Institute's Jack Kerouac School of Disembodied Poetics. Check it out: I met Allen Ginsberg. No I didn't really but I went to two parties where he was. I sort of stood next to him. It is so beautiful here. And I met some cool people one night and lots of older poetry pros at the school.

How's Damian? You guys are probably married by now. And what happened to Virginia? She's not a big

star yet obviously, at least not here in the hinterlands.
Maybe she's working on it. Or maybe she's married to
some yuppie asshole which is exactly what she
deserves, that fucking bitch.

standing in the cool summer grass
smoke a cigarette and wish to
float away into
night sky—
    Then creaky stairs
back into
the basement

Of course I love you
Look how hard my dick is

summer sun
to be a man who
stands straight
and knows himself—
    Strong women
strong life
never having the earth reach up
and slap you senseless

    Dear Mom,
    Sorry I haven't written in a while. I'm out in
Colorado now. It's sort of related to my job in Oregon
but mostly it's just a little vacation that comes with the
job. I think I'll have some money when this is all over.
I'm saving part of my salary since my rent is paid for
and I get a lot of free meals and stuff. It's still very
weird. Not really a career (teaching) I would want to

go into but maybe. It's really the only way to make a
living in the poetry business. I guess I should feel lucky.
I guess I should try to get used to it. God, it's sure
cushy enough.

energy and will and power
that's what it is
that's what you're selling
that's what you run out of
that's why some win and some lose
talent, skill, irregardless, nothing
is the same after that first burst of
exposure
every corner of your soul
those unknown corners of my soul
your soul anyone's soul
so very interesting at
first
but once they've seen it
once the light is upon it
it is just more human squirm
more human bullshit
going in and
then out and then into the earth forever—
    Vain and so well dressed is the young man
so emptied and finished is the
old man, full of narcotics and whatever
last drops of mystery he can
squeeze out

Mark leans back in his seat and sucks up the last of his
tea with his straw. He stirs the ice cubes and then lights
another cigarette. Then he tears out all that he's written,

E x i l e

wads it into a ball and shoots it basketball-style at the garbage can at the curb. He misses. The ball rolls into the street. Mark turns to the next page in his notebook and writes:

Screenplay

First scene: Two black guys are smoking crack in a burned-out basement. Suddenly an ominous light appears above them. At first they think it's the cops but they are hypnotized by the light. They stare straight at it and then, zombie-like, stand and walk up the burned-out stairway to the roof where they enter the alien space craft . . .

21

On Friday there is another panel discussion and another lunch. It is here that Mark learns that Vanessa is not going back to Portland, she's going to San Francisco. Mark becomes suddenly attentive when he hears this. He's never been to San Francisco.

"What are you going to do there?" asks Mark, poking at his potato salad.

"Go visit my friend. She goes to San Francisco State."

"You're going by yourself?"

She nods.

"Wow, so do you need gas money or anything?"

"I have money."

"Wouldn't you want company though? It'd get awful boring."

"I like being by myself."

"Well, let me see," says Mark. "Maybe I can be less subtle. Can I come with you to San Francisco?"

Vanessa looks shocked.

"What?" says Mark. "I'll pay for gas. I'll be there if you break down."

"You'll be there when I go to sleep."

"So what? We won't even have to sleep if there's two of us. We can drive straight through."

Vanessa looks into her plate, then sneaks a sideways look at Mark.

"Where did you sleep when you drove out here?" asks Mark.

"In my car."

"Where, like in a campground?"

"In a parking lot. Of Safeway."

"Huh," says Mark. "Well, okay. So we'll, uh . . . we'll stay in a hotel and I'll pay for it. How's that?"

"Why do you want to go to San Francisco?"

"I've never been there."

"But where are you going to stay when you get there?"

"Where are you going to stay?"

"With my friend."

"I'll stay there too," says Mark. "We'll tell your friend that I'm your new boyfriend."

"Fat chance."

"Tell her I'm just hanging out."

"Aren't you a little old to be 'just hanging out'? Or telling people you're my boyfriend?"

"I'm not that old," says Mark.

"You went out with that girl Samantha, didn't you?"

Mark quickly looks around to see where Bill is, but he's farther down the table, engrossed in conversation.

"And she was like a *freshman*," says Vanessa.

"She was not a freshman. She was a . . . I don't know what she was. But she was old enough. It was perfectly legal."

"There's no way I'm taking you to San Francisco."

"Okay. Don't."

"If we stayed in a hotel how would we sleep? What sort of bed?"

"There's two beds. You go to a cheap place, it's like thirty bucks. I think. I don't know. It's not like I've been to a million of them."

"Did you go to one with Samantha?"

"Listen," says Mark quietly. "Before you start judging Samantha just remember, not everyone is as prissy as you."

"I'm not *prissy*."

"Samantha knew what she liked. And she wasn't afraid to go get it."

"I am so totally not prissy. I can't believe you said that!" She stabs at her watermelon. "There's a difference between being a slut and being prissy, you know."

Mark sits back in his chair. "Free hotel room for a night. Someone to talk to. In San Francisco I'll sleep on the floor and never hang out with you. We'll tell your friend the truth. I'm just some poetry guy who wants to see San Francisco. I will literally leave in the morning and not come back until it's time to sleep. How long were you going to be there?"

"A couple days."

"Perfect. And I can help with the driving and I'll be there in case of emergencies . . ."

Vanessa looks at him. Then she looks back at her plate.

But by Sunday Mark has prevailed. Vanessa has agreed to take him along. Bill leaves earlier that morning. Mark bids him goodbye and then retreats into his basement room. He's gathering his stuff when Alice appears. She sits on the stairs and watches him pack. Mark has hardly said a word

158

to her throughout his visit and he's a bit confused by her
presence now. But he tries to be polite. Alice talks to him
about writing. She's a poet herself. She seems to want
advice. She seems to think Mark knows some secret that
will help her focus and reach the high artistic level that he
has reached. Those are her words. Mark laughs at the
"high artistic level" part. He tells her the truth: he hates his
work, is embarrassed by his life, and he's writing a screenplay about aliens who get addicted to crack cocaine.

Alice goes upstairs. He's probably offended her. Whatever. He snaps shut his suitcase and says goodbye to Paul,
who is watering the lawn. Then he walks under the hot
summer sun to Penny Lane, where he's supposed to meet
Vanessa at noon. It's eleven-forty when he gets there. He
orders an iced coffee from the teenage boy who's grown
accustomed to Mark's face. Mark tips him a dollar. He sits
outside, under the awning. He finds a bit of yesterday's
Rocky Mountain News and spreads it on the table. He
lights a cigarette and squints up the street where Vanessa's
car will hopefully appear.

Vanessa is late but she gets there. Mark is on his best
behavior. He hops up from the table and walks around to
the passenger side of Vanessa's station wagon. He lays his
suitcase in the back seat and takes out a book and several
magazines so that they won't have to talk too much.

Vanessa for her part seems more accepting of his coming than she was originally. She's gracious and helps him
position his suitcase so he can reach it from the front seat.
When everything's ready they put on their seat belts and
Vanessa steers them west, into the mountains. They're taking the scenic route.

And it is scenic. Estes Park is incredible. Mark has never

seen anything like it. At several points they get out and look down into huge ravines or out over a seemingly endless horizon of mountaintops. Later the scenery is less grand but driving through the mountain forests has its own intimate charm. The car fills with the sharp smell of dust and mountain earth, pine needles and bark. Shards of sunlight sparkle down through the tree cover. Mark enjoys it immensely. He wears his sunglasses and hangs his arm out the window, holding his palm against the force of the oncoming air.

In the afternoon they stop at a country store and buy sandwiches which they eat at outdoor tables. Here they have an amusing conversation with a married couple on vacation from Minnesota. Back in the car, Mark turns up the radio and hums to himself, tapping his fingers on the outside of the car door. Tourists drive by, families, kids, hippies in buses. "Man, this is cool," Mark tells Vanessa.

"It is."

But the scenic route has its disadvantages. Mainly that they aren't even to Salt Lake City when the sun begins to hover on the horizon. They discuss it and decide to pass through Salt Lake City and find a hotel on the opposite side. But it's nearly eleven when they get clear of the city and then there aren't any hotels anyway. At 2:00 A.M. they pull into a rest stop and Vanessa suggests they sleep in the station wagon for a couple hours. This works out easily enough. Vanessa lowers the backseat and they spread out her sleeping bag over a space equal to a small bed. Vanessa brushes her teeth in the rest-stop bathroom and crawls into the back in her shorts and T-shirt. Mark brushes his teeth too. Then he sits on a bench in front of the car and smokes, watching the moonlight on the Utah desert.

Vanessa appears to be asleep when he climbs in beside

her. She's left him space on one side. She has her back to it. He avoids touching her when he lies down. It's reasonably comfortable and there's plenty of room. But he's still not sure he's going to be able to sleep.

"You smell like cigarettes," says Vanessa's voice from her side of the car.

"I thought you were asleep."

"No."

"Are you comfortable?"

"Yeah, are you?"

"Yeah," says Mark, looking up at the roof.

"Pull the other blanket up if you get cold," Vanessa tells him.

"Okay."

"Good night."

"Good night."

The next night, after driving for twelve hours, they cross the Bay Bridge and enter San Francisco. Mark is sitting in the passenger seat, his feet up on the dash, his hand out the window. It's nine o'clock at night and the cool marine air is suddenly chilly enough that Mark has to roll up the window. But he still gawks as they approach the city. It looks like a space ship or a futuristic island outpost in a science fiction movie.

"Wow," says Mark.

"There's a map in the glove box," says Vanessa. "You'd better get it out."

Vanessa's friend Jennifer lives in the Lower Haight section of San Francisco. As they look for it, Mark stares out the window at the few scattered pedestrians. It's August but it's cold in San Francisco. A light rain begins to fall. Vanessa turns on the windshield wipers.

They find the address. Jennifer lives in a basement apartment of a large Victorian house. Jennifer is older than Vanessa. She seems a bit burdened by her visitors or maybe it's the inclusion of Mark she doesn't like. But she's got plenty of room. She shows her two guests to a room recently vacated. It has a bed and a large couch which Mark volunteers to sleep on. He sets his suitcase on the floor and tries it out. It's not very comfortable but it'll work. When Vanessa and Jennifer go into the kitchen Mark stays where he is and a few minutes later he's fast asleep.

22

Mark is good on his word. By ten o'clock the next morning he's sitting outside a coffee shop on Haight Street, reading the *San Francisco Chronicle*. He lights a cigarette and enjoys his pleasant first cigarette buzz. It's sunny outside. Mark wears sunglasses and shorts though the occasional ocean breeze reminds him of how cold it could be if the sun weren't shining.

After coffee, Mark climbs the hill to upper Haight Street. This is a predictably trendy strip, but there is something peculiar about it, something windswept and oceanic—or maybe it's the history: the drugs, the music, the Summer of Love. Whichever, there's a weird gloom to it. Even with the sun shining.

Mark smokes while he walks. He passes Deadheads, yuppies, skateboarders, and then punks and street people as he nears the end of the strip. He continues into Golden Gate Park. Which is not much different from Central Park. Except for the citrus smell. And the palm trees. And the two hippy kids shooting up in the bushes.

When he's done in the Haight, Mark takes a bus down-town to the legendary City Lights Bookstore. Inside he's surprised how small it is. But how can he not love it when they have his first two books, *Exile* and *City of Situations*? Here in San Francisco, in the context of City Lights, his books look more literary, they feel weightier in his hands. He randomly selects a poem from *City:*

The Day After

The day after
It's not even
A day
It's a dream
It's nothing
It's cars on the street
People walking
Conversations
At other tables
Proud of yourself?
No
Regrets? Shame?
Nothing
Boats on the river
The wind cries
In the wires
Grey water
Grey sky
The day is
Gone

But as he finishes the poem he is unsure what the point of it is. Or what it's about. Then he remembers: *Cynthia.*

He wrote this the day after they first slept together. How strange it took so long to register. Could it be that some-day he might read this and not remember the situation that inspired it? That he might read any of his poems and not know what they're about, or even worse, not care? It seems completely possible. It seems inevitable. Mark hastily puts the book back and tries to clear the thought from his mind: not only will the world forget him, he will forget himself.

He looks at the other books. They've got all the classic City Lights stuff: Ginsberg, Burroughs, Kerouac. Middle-era stuff, *Motel Chronicles* by Sam Shepard. New stuff: a woman named El Loco. A new Gary Snyder title. Several books by Anne Waldman. But he's still thinking about "In the Wires." Do these other people forget their poems? He picks up the *Collected Allen Ginsberg*. Nobody has forgot-ten "Howl." That's different though. It has the beatnik connection. But Mark knows it wasn't just that. "Howl" was legendary the day it was written. From Ginsberg's pen straight into the textbooks.

Mark buys postcards and goes next door to Vesuvio's, a bar he's heard of but isn't sure why. It must also have beat-nik connections. He buys a cup of coffee and sits by the window. He writes postcards to Howard, Cynthia, his par-ents. Then he lights a cigarette and watches the people walking outside. He thought at one time that another Beat-like scene might emerge from New York. And that he would be a part of it. He and Alex. The energy around No Se No those first years, it certainly seemed possible. But whatever was supposed to happen didn't. The scene went in another direction: became more multicultural, more feminist, more political. Alex retreated into journalism, and when Mark finally hooked up with Howard it all seemed like too little too late. But the books are still there, he just saw it for himself, maybe it's not too late. Maybe there's still time.

Mark spends the rest of the afternoon in the artsy SOMA district of downtown San Francisco. He finds an avant-garde bookstore on the top floor of a warehouse building. Large skylights let in so much light that Mark has to wear sunglasses to browse. But it's worth it. They have *Exile*. They have everything. Mark finds a used copy of Henry Rollins's obscure and out-of-print *Hallucinations of Grandeur*. He also finds Howard's first-ever Free City Press book, *Myths and Rituals* by David Friedrich. The poetry's still terrible but the cover looks good, dated now but interestingly so. Mark buys an old chapbook by Exene Cervenka and a photo of Patti Smith and Robert Mapplethorpe that is slightly bent and so only costs fifty cents. He finds in that same box a picture of Jean Michel Basquiat which he buys as well. Finally, he finds a local poetry calendar, listing the various local readings. He sees there's an open mike going on tonight, at Club Paradise, which is just down the street.

He goes there. It's a huge club with multiple levels. He follows the signs upstairs to the "poetry lounge." This is a cozy room with a small stage and old wooden tables. He finds a pay phone and calls Vanessa. "Wanna go to a poetry reading?" he asks her.

"Where is it?"

"Club Paradise. In the upstairs. I'll sign you up if you want to read."

"Read?"

"Yeah, it's an open mike."

"I don't . . . are you going to?"

"Sure. It's fun."

She hesitates. "Okay."

Mark gives her the address. Then he goes back to the bar and studies the sign-up sheet. He considers the available spots and puts Vanessa eighth on the list, himself twelfth. Then he orders a beer and waits for the other poets to show up.

When Vanessa arrives, the room is full. Mark is sitting at a back table, drinking his third beer, observing the competition. There's a gang of scenesters sitting at the front table. Some cute girls are along the far wall. The MC, a young guy in a ratty sweater and penny loafers, is working the room, chatting with people. The whole scene is a lot like New York. Mark wonders if anyone is going to recognize his name or know who he is. It seems possible. In fact there's an older woman he thinks he recognizes from several years ago at No Se No. But she's old and Mark can't remember her name. He avoids looking at her.

"There's so many people," says Vanessa, squeezing in beside him at the table. She's got her pack and her notebooks. Mark remembers the notebooks from his poetry class.

"Yeah, it's a good crowd," says Mark. He reaches for his cigarettes. He lights one and Vanessa frowns and starts waving at the air. This is going to be difficult, Mark can tell already. He has a definite way of acting in situations where he is going to perform. Silent, aloof, chain-smoking—he doesn't like to have anyone else around, least of all someone like Vanessa.

The reading starts. The MC is funny. A couple of the girl poets are cute. The rest of it is typical open mike stuff. Mark fidgets and drinks his beer. Vanessa, though, is interested in every reader. She sits silently beside him, carefully absorbing every word. Mark finds this annoying. He fidgets more. He drinks.

When the seventh reader goes on, Mark begins to feel anxious for Vanessa. She shows no outward signs of nerves but when the reader finishes, she begins fumbling with her papers. Mark takes her pack and Vanessa waits for the MC to say her name. When he does, she takes a deep breath and makes her way forward.

Onstage, Vanessa stands awkwardly at the microphone. She reads her first poem. Mark lights a cigarette. He drinks from his fourth beer and looks around at the crowd. They seem to like young Vanessa. And she certainly does look young. Her voice squeaks and falters but she bravely pushes on. Her first poem doesn't seem to work but the second gets a quick sharp laugh from the crowd—which surprises and flusters Vanessa—but that just works to her advantage. The crowd is charmed. Mark orders his fifth beer and watches Vanessa. She's getting the best response of anyone so far. But of course Mark hasn't had his turn yet.

Mark is halfway through his sixth beer when his name is called. He's too drunk, he knows that immediately. Also, he can feel a smugness in his body, a snideness toward the crowd that will destroy him if he lets it show. Onstage, he makes every humble gesture he can think of. He fakes being nervous, fakes fumbling with his papers. He was going to read something out of Exene's chapbook which would work if the audience knew who he was, if they saw it as a gesture from one established poet to another. But they don't know him. He's got to read something of his own. Since he doesn't have his books he's written out a couple of his better poems on one of Vanessa's notebook pages. He reads those. But his voice is terrible. He's too drunk and his throat is croaking dry. The crowd senses something is up. They watch him suspiciously as his fake fumbling becomes real fumbling. He would stop and light a cigarette. But he's left his pack at the table.

"This last poem is called 'Exile,'" he says quickly. He holds the same paper that has the other poems written on it and recites "Exile" from memory, or tries to. Halfway through he gets mixed up and forgets the lines. He skips to the ending, which doesn't make sense. He cuts his losses. He nods at the crowd and slips quickly off the stage.

"All right, that was Mark Most," says the MC as Mark collapses into the seat beside Vanessa.

"They got your name wrong," says Vanessa, tugging on his sleeve. "Tell them your name."

But Mark waves her off, the MC moves on, the next reader tells a funny story and everyone is having fun again.

23

When the reading is over Mark follows Vanessa down the stairs to the street. It was hot in the upstairs room but the San Francisco night is wet and cold. Vanessa has brought Mark a sweater. He puts it on as they stand with the rest of the crowd on the sidewalk. The other people all seem to know each other. Vanessa watches them. Mark does too.

"Hey," says a guy, passing behind Vanessa. "I liked your thing."

Vanessa doesn't realize he's talking to her.

Mark pokes her and points to the guy.

"Oh, *my* thing!" says Vanessa, gushing with embarrassment.

"Yeah, it was good," says the guy, smiling for a moment and then moving on.

Vanessa tries to act casual as she absorbs the compliment. Mark lights a cigarette and leans against a parking meter.

Vanessa, emboldened now, begins to look around at

specific people. A girl approaches her. "That was really funny," says the girl. "That part about your cat."

"I liked your poem," says Vanessa quickly. "I'm from Portland."

"Really," says the girl. She looks at Mark.

"We were at Naropa. I mean," she gestures to Mark, "not together, but we . . . he was there and I was coming out here so he came with me."

"Huh," says the girl, looking at Mark.

"We just wanted to check everything out," says Vanessa.

"Club Paradise is the best place to read. I think," says the girl. She begins to move away but Vanessa doesn't want her to. "What's your name?" asks Vanessa.

"Amber," says the girl. "You guys should come to Monty's. That's where everyone goes afterward."

"Where is it?" says Vanessa.

"It's a couple blocks that way. Do you know where Hamburger Mary's is?"

"We don't know anything," says Vanessa.

The girl looks around for her friends.

"Why don't we go with you?" says Mark.

They drive in Amber's car with two other poets to Monty's. Vanessa makes small talk, Mark says nothing. Monty's is only five blocks away. It's a neighborhood bar. Mark and Vanessa and Amber and her friends all get beers at the bar. When Amber drifts off, Vanessa talks to Mark about her performance, how she didn't know the crowd was going to laugh.

"But that's why they liked you," he tells her. "Because you were so surprised. You were so genuine."

"I guess. I was just afraid they were going to laugh at other stuff too. But they didn't. Fortunately."

BLAKE NELSON

The MC comes in. He's still wearing his ratty sweater and old penny loafers. Mark watches Vanessa watch him.

"He's *cute*," says Vanessa.

"You should go for him," says Mark. "Tonight's your night."

Vanessa turns back to the bar. "I don't mean like that!"

"But you should. Go talk to him. He's looking over here."

Vanessa sneaks a look. "No he's not!"

"He is."

Vanessa looks again. "He's talking to those girls."

Mark shrugs. Vanessa drinks her beer.

"That was fun," says Vanessa, staring at herself in the mirror behind the bar.

"You were good."

"That was really fun," repeats Vanessa.

"It's addicting," says Mark.

The next day Vanessa drives Jennifer to San Francisco State. They have coffee before Jennifer's class but it's difficult for Vanessa to not talk about her success at the reading the night before. That's all she wants to think about. After coffee she drops Jennifer off and drives to North Beach. She goes to City Lights and pokes through their poetry section. She could be here someday. She could have a book. The response at Club Paradise demonstrated that. She should stop worrying about the academic side of things and get more directly to the people. That's what Mark does. It was obvious that the Club Paradise scene was more of where he came from. And he wasn't even that good. She was much better than he was and he has books. There's no reason she couldn't also.

She walks up the street to the Trieste Cafe, which Jen-

172

nifer recommended. It's full of interesting people, artistic types, eccentric older people. She gets a coffee and sits at a corner table. She thinks about Brendon. What would he have thought if he'd been there last night? She can't wait to get back. She'll go to some open mikes in Portland, she knows they have them, it just never occurred to her to go. Now she will. She'll go to one at Cafe Omega, or anywhere that Brendon might see her. Since that night at Cafe Omega she's seen Brendon a couple times, including one day when they almost went to a matinee movie together. But Vanessa had a class. And was afraid to anyway. Brendon being too cool, too intimidating in his quiet way. Now Vanessa sees her entrance into Brendon's world of cool people, cool cafes, cool parties. She's going to be a poet. Not a student poet, a real poet. She can't wait to see him again. She wishes he was here now—in San Francisco!— he'd love it. She'll find him when she gets back. It's the first thing she'll do. She'll call him, she'll go to that matinee, she's ready now.

Across town, Mark rides a bus. He watches the city out the window and thinks about Vanessa. He talks to her in his head, explaining what went wrong at Club Paradise, giving her tips about how to handle a reading gone sour, using himself as the obvious example. He says other things too. Vague, things about the two of them: why it would never work, how she doesn't understand him, how much harder everything becomes once the newness has worn off, once you're committed.

He gets off in the seedy Tenderloin district. He wants to buy pot. He talks to one guy who tries to sell him a bag of oregano. Another guy has real pot but then tries to switch it with something else. Mark almost gets in a fight with a

third guy. He gives up and heads downtown to the Embar-
cadero Fountain. Here, after all his trouble, some tourist
kids give him a joint. He walks down a side street, smoking it as he walks. But then two speeding Rollerbladers
come flying at him from around a corner. Mark tries to
move but he's not fast enough. He bumps one of the
Rollerbladers and sends him crashing onto the pavement.
Mark rushes to apologize and help him up. But he doesn't
want Mark's help. He's pissed. Mark apologizes more,
lamely trying to hide the joint. The other Rollerblader
sneers at him. They skate away. Mark keeps walking. But
back on Market Street, he has more problems. He can't get
the groove of the crowded sidewalk, he keeps running into
people, getting in the way. There's just something *off*
about everything he does. "Bad gigs breed bad karma," a
musician friend once told him. He had a bad gig and here
comes the shit.

That night Jennifer helps Vanessa pack. Mark buys a six-
pack at the corner grocery store and drinks it by himself
on the front steps. The next morning they have breakfast
with Jennifer and then drive her to her class. On the way
out of town Vanessa wants to stop and have her picture
taken on the Golden Gate Bridge. Mark obliges her, following her onto the walkway where he takes her picture.
She looks great through the viewfinder: young, confident,
on the verge of something. She holds her blowing hair out
of her face while the blue Pacific churns in the distance.

"Do you know who Brendon is?" Vanessa asks Mark as
they speed north on Interstate Five. They are several hours
north of the city and it's now so hot that even with all the
windows down Mark is sweating.

"I don't think so."

"In Portland? He plays in a band? He hangs out downtown a lot?"

"Doesn't ring a bell."

"He wears old suits and stuff. He dyes his hair."

"Oh, yeah. That guy," Mark remembers. "I met him once at Coffee Star. He wanted to be a writer. I told him to go to New York."

Vanessa drives.

Mark looks over at her. "What about him? Do you know him?"

"I've met him a couple times."

"What's his deal? He seemed like, I don't know, the village idiot or something."

Vanessa makes a scoffing noise.

"What?" says Mark.

"He's not exactly a *village idiot.*"

"Well, what is he?"

"He's only the coolest boy in Portland."

"Really?" says Mark, impressed. He looks over at Vanessa. "So you like him?"

But she won't say anything more about it.

Whatever hopes they had of getting to Portland in one day are dashed when they stop at a restaurant along the highway. Vanessa suddenly wants to write something. She won't say what it is, though Mark suspects it has something to do with Brendon. But Mark doesn't mind the stop. He has nowhere to be, he's content to hang out in the booth and read his Exene Cervenka book. Vanessa scribbles madly for an hour and then they're off again. Vanessa drives. Mark's still got a bit of the joint from yesterday in his pocket which he pulls out. Vanessa doesn't protest, she even rolls up her window so he can light it. Then she watches him while he smokes.

"You sure like to do drugs and stuff, don't you?"

"I sure do."

"Brendon smokes pot . . ."

Mark sucks on his joint. But he's not getting anything. He looks to see if it's burning.

". . . But he doesn't act all weird about it."

"What do you mean?" says Mark.

"Just having an attitude. Like *I'm so cool, I do drugs.*"

"I don't do that."

"The thing about Brendon, he's not trying to be cooler than everyone else. He wants everyone to be cool. He's very generous that way."

Mark thinks back to his own conversation with Brendon. But all he can remember is the kid smoked all his cigarettes.

"Do you think I'm cute?" says Vanessa suddenly.

Mark turns and looks at her. The wind is twisting her black hair around her face. "You're cuter than you were last spring."

"Really? I wasn't cute last spring?"

"You weren't *not* cute, you were just . . ."

"Just what?"

"I don't know."

"What, my hair? My clothes?"

"You're more confident now," says Mark.

"Really? Does it make a difference?"

"Are you kidding?" says Mark. He's fiddling with the joint, trying to loosen the drawing end. "It makes *all* the difference."

24

At eleven o'clock that night they're still driving, they're still in the mountains, they're still three hundred miles from Portland. Mark's at the wheel now. He's tired and says so and then repeats his earlier offer to pay for a hotel room. When Vanessa doesn't object, he pulls into the first Econo Lodge he sees. The two check in and drag their bags inside. There are two double beds. Mark flops on the nearest one and turns on the TV with the remote. Vanessa opens her suitcase on her bed and eventually disappears into the shower.

Mark channel-surfs and settles on the local news. He thought the Portland newscasters looked strange, the news people in the local mountain town are all either bizarrely misshapen or still in their teens. But it's kind of fascinating. One of the stories is about a pig who escaped from somebody's truck and is shown running down Main Street, which apparently has no traffic.

Vanessa finishes her shower. Mark listens to her blow-drying her hair in the bathroom. When she's done she comes out in a T-shirt with a towel wrapped around her waist. She stands at her bed with her back to Mark. She drops the towel, revealing her pantied hips and skinny legs for a moment before she can pull her shorts back on. Mark notices her panties are old and frayed along the waistband.

"Are you looking at me?" says Vanessa, her back still to him.

Mark looks back at the TV. "No."

Before bed, Mark smokes a last cigarette in the parking lot. Trucks drive by on the highway. Crickets chirp. The night smells of evergreen trees and the high-altitude mountain air.

Back inside, Vanessa's in bed, the lights are off. Mark gets in bed too. But he's not going to be able to sleep. He lies there anyway, staring at the ceiling.

In the bed across from him Vanessa shifts violently in her own covers.

"Is it hot in here?" she says in the darkness.

"Yeah," says Mark.

Neither speaks. Outside the crickets chirp. Vanessa flops violently again.

"I can't sleep," she says.

"Me neither," says Mark.

They both stare at the ceiling.

"It's my fault," says Mark. "We should have kept driving."

"We already paid for the room," says Vanessa.

Mark leans over, pulls his cigarettes out of his shorts and puts one in his mouth.

"You sure smoke a lot."

"I sure do," says Mark.

"Doesn't it gross out your girlfriends?"

"They all smoke too."

"Really? You only go out with women who smoke?"

Mark doesn't answer. He lights the cigarette. He should have brought something to drink.

"Do you want to play cards?" says Vanessa.

Mark looks over at her. Her head is up, she's looking over at him.

"No," he says, smoking.

"Are you sure?"

"What do you want to play?"

"Gin rummy."

"I don't know how to play it," says Mark. "Maybe we should watch TV."

"I hate TV," says Vanessa.

Mark finishes his cigarette but doesn't get up. Vanessa doesn't say anything. After a few minutes he turns over again and shuts his eyes. But Vanessa's still awake, she turns on the light and gets up. Mark listens. She's doing something with her suitcase. Then his bed bounces. She's on it with him. He turns over slowly. She's sitting on his bed in her underwear and T-shirt. She's got cards.

"C'mon, let's play gin, I'll teach you."

They play. Vanessa seems giddy, she grins continuously. Mark finds the sight of her skinny body, her rail-thin legs, alarming. Also a bit of pubic hair is sticking out of her underpants.

He loses at gin. This seems to please Vanessa. He begins to complain. "Let's play something different."

"Like what?"

"Like strip poker," he says.

"No way, I don't have any clothes on."

"I know," says Mark. "And it's not fair."

"Why not?"

"It's distracting."

"Do you think I have a good body?" says Vanessa, joking, sort of.

"All women have good bodies," grumbles Mark.

"Brendon's girlfriend is so skinny. Or actually she's his old girlfriend. He doesn't have a girlfriend now. That's what Jill said. Do you know Jill, Samantha's friend?"

"When did you get involved with these people?" asks Mark, discarding a seven. They're still playing gin. Vanessa scoops up his card and lays down three sevens.

"I'm not involved with them. The thing is. About Brendon. His last girlfriend was totally hot. They were doing it constantly, according to Jill."

"Yeah, so?"

"I mean, it's just like, if I kissed him or made out with him or whatever I know he'd want sex."

"So?"

"But I've never done it."

"You haven't?"

"I mean, I did once. My freshman year. But it sort of didn't work. It was his fault. I mean, technically we did it but it wasn't really like *doing* it."

Mark stares at his cards.

"Not that it really matters. I mean, I want to do it. It was just never the right person. But with Brendon . . . I mean, can guys tell?"

"Tell what?"

"If you haven't done it?"

"I don't know. I guess so."

"How do they tell, just by, when they actually do it?"

"Or maybe how the person reacts."

"Like what if you were a real prude but you had done it before, could you really be sure?"

"What?" says Mark. "You're going to lie?" He's put a

cigarette in his mouth, unlit, it bobs as he talks. "Hell, tell him you're a virgin. He'll probably like it. Virgin prosti- tutes get top dollar."

"And you'd probably pay it," says Vanessa.

"You don't know anything about me," says Mark.

"But I thought guys want girls with experience. Espe- cially if they're like Brendon. They don't want to screw around with some dumb girl who's never done anything."

Mark looks at his cards.

"Who's the first virgin you ever slept with?"

"Myself," jokes Mark. Vanessa actually laughs. "I don't think I've ever been with a virgin," says Mark.

Vanessa discards but something about the way she sets the card down makes Mark look up. Something's hap- pened, something's clicked in her mind, she suddenly looks stunned, scared.

"What's the matter?" he asks her.

"Nothing."

"No," says Mark, "your face, it just totally changed."

"No it didn't."

"Yes it did," says Mark calmly. He takes a card.

"Can I get under the covers with you?" says Vanessa.

Mark looks up. Vanessa's watery eyes are staring straight at him.

"Are you sure you want to?"

She nods once and then scoops up the cards and throws them on her own bed. She grabs for the light and turns it off. Then she slides her skinny body into the bed beside Mark. For a moment she stays on her side but then she slides over and touches Mark, clumsily gripping his arm and letting one of her legs bump against his.

"Geez, Vanessa, this is kind of sudden, isn't it?" says Mark.

Vanessa immediately releases him, pulls away, she's getting out of the bed but Mark catches her wrist, pulls her back. "Come on, I was just kidding."

Vanessa lets herself be pulled back. Their bodies seem to find each other, they are wrapped tightly around one another almost as soon as they make contact.

"Don't make fun of me," whispers Vanessa.

"You insult me constantly."

"But this is different."

Mark tries kissing her on the forehead. She doesn't seem to mind. And he likes the taste of her. "I just want to make sure you know what you're doing."

She answers by kissing him on the mouth, a rushed frantic kiss that Mark has to stop. "No," he breathes, "slow, like this."

They kiss. They slowly lose their shirts and underpants. Mark gets a condom, and when the time seems right he tries to push inside her as gently as he can. But Vanessa reacts against him, it's as if she's trying to squeeze him out. He has to hold her steady. He keeps up the pressure and waits for her body to relax. Finally it does. She breathes out. She receives him. Mark pushes forward, then back out, then in again. She makes a tiny whispery noise as she lifts herself up. She's trying to meet him, trying to move with him.

"Slow," counsels Mark. But now he's forgetting himself. It feels incredible to be inside her, even with a condom. He stops for a minute. He lets his weight rest on her chest.

"How's that?" he whispers.

Vanessa nods.

"Doesn't hurt?"

Vanessa bites her lip and shakes her head no. She closes her eyes as he begins to move again. He falls into a rhythm.

Again, the sensation is incredible. He's losing himself in the simple motion of it. But then Vanessa begins to squirm beneath him. She's arching herself awkwardly against him. It brings Mark back to himself. It gives him an idea.

"Here," says Mark, sliding out of her, "turn over."

"Why?" says Vanessa.

"So we can do it the other way."

Vanessa reluctantly lets herself be rolled over. The sight of her bare back, the curve of her hips, Mark almost comes just looking at her.

"Lift up," says Mark. He tries to position her but she doesn't really get it.

"I don't like this," says Vanessa. "This is doggy style."

But it's too late. He's in. He begins to fuck her. He grips her hips. His eyes close. He breathes a low moan.

"What? What?" says Vanessa from the pillow.

Mark doesn't answer. He's going faster and then, before he can stop himself, he's coming. He grips her harder, fucks her harder, and then he's gone, his consciousness collapsing into blackness. He releases his hold and tips forward, his forehead landing in Vanessa's back.

"What are you doing?" she says. "Is it over?"

Mark says nothing. He falls off her to one side, his dick sliding out of her.

"Is that it?" she asks.

Mark says nothing. He rolls onto his back, his face sweating, his brain shut off, his heart beating smooth and fast in his chest.

25

In the morning Vanessa is sprawled awkwardly on her side of the bed. Mark watches her sleep. She doesn't look so sexy now. Also she's snoring, quietly but snoring all the same. Nonetheless the sight of her attracts him so intensely he can't help but scoot closer. He strokes her tangled hair. He kisses her once lightly on the cheek but her breath smells terrible. He avoids her mouth and tries to move his face into her chest. But she grunts and rolls away from him. So he gets up. He finds his underwear and puts on his pants. He slips on his shoes and a T-shirt and goes outside.

The morning sky is a brilliant blue. He lights a cigarette and stares at a mountain peak in the distance. He walks down the road to a food mart/gas station. It's open but there's no one at the food counter. Mark pours himself a cup of coffee and leaves fifty cents on the counter. He sits on the steps outside, smoking and sipping from his cup. He watches a scruffy kid pump gas. When Mark finishes his cigarette he goes back inside. An old woman is there now and he buys another coffee for Vanessa. He also picks out a couple of the least crusty-looking donuts they have in a display. The woman puts the donuts in a bag and Mark walks back to the Econo Lodge, at one point dodging the wake of dust and hot wind when a logging truck drives by.

Back in the motel, Vanessa is in the shower. Mark sits on the bed, then lies on it, then rolls over to the spot where Vanessa slept. He breathes in the smell of her. It's not like Samantha, who was so sweet, so ripe-smelling. Vanessa is slightly sour, more human, more animal. Mark's dick begins to swell. He looks at the bathroom door. He sneaks across the room and tries the knob. It's locked. He goes back to the bed and sits with his coffee. He looks at Vanessa's coffee, cooling now, it'll be cold by the time she gets to it. And the donuts: pathetic fare. He feels a sudden pang in his chest. Regret, sadness, boredom. Nothing in particular. *The day after, it's not even a day,* he says, quoting himself.

When Vanessa comes out of the bathroom, Mark is sitting on their bed. He wants her the instant she's in the room. The steam and smell of the bathroom only make it worse. She goes to her bed, where her suitcase is, and digs through her clothes. Mark watches her, his whole body aching to be with her again.

But she doesn't like being watched. "Do you mind?" she says.

Mark looks away.

She drops her towel and puts on her underpants.

Mark looks back at her while she puts on her bra. Her back, her skinny shoulders, her narrow hips––he can hardly stand it.

"I got some coffee here, and some donuts," he says.

"I'm not hungry."

Mark sips his own coffee.

Vanessa struggles with the latch of her bra. "This stupid thing," she says.

"Just so you know," says Mark, "for that Brendon guy or whoever, the preferred way for girls to act after sex is sort of gushy and cheerful."

"I don't feel cheerful."

"Yeah, obviously."

"And I'm not a girl."

"Not anymore," mutters Mark, under his breath.

"And this bra doesn't work," says Vanessa loudly.

"Let me do it."

"I can do it," says Vanessa. And she does. She puts on her shirt.

Mark drinks his coffee. He stares at the wall in front of him.

He'll just ignore her, he decides. And in six hours he'll be home.

In the car, though, he tries vainly to think of something to talk to her about. At one point he makes a joke about their night together. Vanessa's silence is brutal. He asks her about Brendon. But now that he's expressing interest, she doesn't want to talk about it. Mark can see she's thinking about Brendon though. She's impatient to get home. Mark gives up on conversation and puts his feet up on the dash. He lights a cigarette and tries to enjoy the scenery. He's on the road. He's having adventures. He's getting laid. Like Kerouac. Like Ginsberg. But different.

It's still light out when they reach Portland. Silently, sullenly, Mark pulls his stuff out of the backseat of Vanessa's car. He wants to kiss her goodbye at least but she sees it coming. She gives him a snappy "See you" and speeds away. Mark drags his stuff up the steps of his apartment building. He gets his mail on his way in. He dumps everything on the floor of his living room. It's dark in the apartment, the air is stale, he pushes open a window and opens the refrigerator. The milk has spoiled but there's a beer which he opens. He flops on the couch and shuffles through the envelopes. There's nothing interesting, a phone bill, an academic memo that doesn't concern him. But then there's a letter from Howard. Mark's heart is cheered. He opens it.

Dear Mark,

I've got some great news. The Exile *review in the* London Times *was better than anyone could have imagined. It's a rave. I'll get Nigel to fax it to Bill Masters's office. We're not even on the shelves yet and Nigel is going back for a second printing.*

And there's more. The Japanese deal is back on. There's real money and we're already seeing a bit of the domino effect. We've got a deal in Korea that is no money but sounds interesting. There will be a little money, however, from Brazil, where I'm talking to Lagos & Glaucia. I'm also talking to the German company that does Charles Bukowski's books. I've also gotten phone calls in the last week from a Dutch publisher and an Italian rep.

Also Ellen Singer from the NEA was asking about you. I knew if you gave people a chance to miss you, your reputation would rebound.

I'm a little overwhelmed as you can imagine. But I can't tell you how excited I am and happy for you and

proud for us both. This is really what it's all about.
Call me if you have any questions. Hope you're
working and that all is well.

All best, Howard

Mark lets the letter fall into his lap. He looks around at his dusty, greying apartment. He lifts the letter and reads it again, this time skipping around, Japan . . . Brazil . . . Germany. Does this mean he'll be able to go there? Probably not. But his books will. And that's good. That's worth a real drink. He gets up and goes to the kitchen, pours himself a whiskey on the rocks. He drinks a bit of it. Outside the kitchen window is the usual formation of wires and branches. Mark wishes he could tell Vanessa about this. But it wouldn't help. She wouldn't be impressed. She's not going to care that three of his books are in the back of a bookstore in Tokyo. He imagines Vanessa at home, taking a shower, doing her laundry, washing her faded panties. She'll buy new ones for Brendon, no doubt. It must be nice to be obsessed like that, to walk around with your head full of a person. A person you had a chance for at least. In Mark's case it's not a pleasant sensation at all. He drinks his drink. He can feel the work ahead of him. Somehow he must put Vanessa out of his mind.

PART FOUR

fall

26

When everyone is seated at the fall semester's first English Department faculty meeting, Jane Hanson surveys the room. There's one person she's looking for in particular and she spots him immediately. Mark West is the one slouched in the very back of the room. He wears a white oxford shirt and a too-obvious tweed blazer that doesn't quite match his face, which has an unwell paleness to it. He's sitting in the back, by the window, his feet up on the chair in front of him. In her first six weeks at Willamette, Jane has heard a lot of complaints about Mr. West. Most of them from younger faculty members, people who have to work for a living. They don't think the young poet is earning his money, is not as publicly visible as an artist-in-residence is supposed to be. Also, there is talk of aloofness and an air of superiority as there often is when Willamette faculty members are faced with anything eastern. Jane should know. She came from Columbia University, in New York, a fact that never seems to be forgotten by her associates. Never mind that she's only twenty-eight and stuck teaching English comp. It's as if she were vying for the presidency of the university the way some of the faculty members react to her.

Jane sneaks another look at Mark. He must have an oral fixation, he is both chewing gum and picking at his teeth with one of the wooden stir straws from Coffee Star. Also there is a copy of the trendy *Flash* magazine falling out of his blazer pocket. He is obviously not paying the slightest attention to the discussion, but his obliviousness seems natural enough. He does not seem to mind being there. He is looking out the window, picking his teeth, occasionally glancing over at Mary Anne. He even smiles at her once. It was Mary Anne who told Jane about Mark. She was smart enough not to offer him as a relationship possibility but instead recommended Mark as an amusing eccentric who might help Jane pass her time here at Willamette. She even suggested a dinner party, to get them together. Jane sneaks one more look at Mark, who is now scratching at his ankle with a pen. Then she focuses dutifully on Bill Masters, decides that she will take Mary Anne up on her offer.

Later that same afternoon, Mark is at the Coffee Star downtown. Mark prefers this Coffee Star to the one near campus. This one is closer to the bus mall and attracts a more populist element: school kids, secretaries, an occasional crazy person talking to himself at one of the window seats. This is also the place he first met Brendon, where Brendon interrupted his work to get the advice he never took. Still, Mark remembers the encounter fondly. He can't help but respect the guy. Mark could never just start talking to someone out of the blue like that. He can barely talk to anyone these days. The continuing foreign success of *Exile,* instead of making him more socially confident, has had the opposite effect. He's quieter now than ever. He can sometimes barely raise his voice loud enough to order coffee properly.

Which is the problem he is having now. He wanted the counter guy to leave room in his cup for cream but he didn't say it loud enough. Now he must pour some of the coffee into the garbage can by the condiment bar. But it doesn't pour cleanly. It drips down the side, burning his hand and then dribbling onto his shoes. He sees he's also got a spot of it on the new white shirt that he was trying so hard to preserve.

Mark hurriedly puts down the coffee cup and grabs a napkin. He licks it and scrubs at the brown spot on his shirt. In this, his last semester at Willamette, he is making a genuine effort to be an effective and presentable poet-in-residence. His concerns about the position not being appropriate for a "real poet" are gone now. It's an easy life, it's free money. Not that Mark has any post-Willamette prospects. But just in case, he is now doing everything he can to be a model of residential artistry.

When Mark's got most of the coffee spot out he takes a seat by the window. He's going to work but first he reads Alex's latest article in *Flash* magazine. "Does She or Doesn't She: How to Tell If Your Lover Is Faking Orgasm." For the last several years Mark has disapproved of Alex's magazine writing but he can't help smiling over this title. His mood matches the light comedy of the piece and Mark finds himself chuckling often and laughing out loud twice. When he finishes the article he flips to the front of the magazine to read Alex's bio. He smiles when it says, "Alex Wright is a veteran of the New York spoken-word underground." Such a claim would have infuriated Mark before but today it seems oddly satisfying. Unlike Mark, who always went for the crushing emotional statement in his work, Alex's best stuff was always subtle and funny. More commentary than attack. Mark sees, for the first time, that Alex's jump to the magazine business is fitting, it works, it's a natural progression. Alex is going to be big. Not in the way they originally imagined, but in a mainstream way that will no doubt eclipse Mark's more purist but ultimately fringe poetry work. Alex is going to be an American humorist. He'll end up writing columns for *Esquire*. Mark will be admired by handfuls of people in cities he's never been to. And will support himself by sleeping with ungrateful undergraduates.

"He definitely looks the part," says Jane. "Or tries to. He's so pale though. Is he sick or something?"

"I don't think so," says Mary Anne. The two of them are eating a late lunch at a restaurant downtown.

"Do you think I should read his book?"

"Sure."

"What's it like?"

"I found it to be sort of crude. But it's being translated into eight languages. Someone must think it's good."

"His ego must be huge."

Mary Anne shrugs. "He's always nice to me."

"He probably likes you."

"I doubt that."

"I bet he does. The way he smiles at you."

Mary Anne lets this go.

"So how many of his students has he slept with?" asks Jane.

"A couple. I'm not sure."

"And nobody has done anything about it?"

"Well, nobody's actually come forward or anything. I mean, it's not public knowledge."

"How do you know about it?"

"He asked me."

"He asked you what?"

"If it was against the rules."

"And what did you say?"

"I said that no, technically it wasn't."

"Mary Anne," protests Jane. "You can't encourage that sort of thing."

"Well, obviously not. But look at him, he's awfully young. He looks more like the students than the faculty."

"That's no excuse."

"Not to us."

"Where did he go to college?"

"I don't think he did."

"He didn't go to college? And he's a poet?"

"That's part of his whole shtick. You know, he's *street-wise* or whatever."

"He didn't look very streetwise to me. He looked sort of clueless. He looks like his mother dressed him."

"Well, if you don't want to meet him, you certainly don't have to."

"His ego must be huge."

"He's really not that bad."

"That's why he's not interested in women his own age. He knows they'll put him in his place."

"It's possible," says Mary Anne. "But somehow I don't think so."

Mark is coming up blank at Coffee Star. After an hour he packs up his notebooks and goes for a walk. He ends up downtown at the Alchemy Bar. He goes in and orders a beer. On the TV are highlights of last weekend's football games. He looks around at the booths. He can't really come here without thinking about Samantha. She lives in Seattle now, with a guy, or so he heard. Mark hasn't been with anyone since Vanessa. It would be nice, a warm body in his bed. Someone to curl up with. Someone like Cynthia. Or Mary Anne. He smiles at the bartendress who smiles back but it's a professional smile. Still it warms the slight chill Mark is feeling. Today was suddenly cold, the first day it's been fall-like in Portland.

Later, when he gets home, there's a message on his machine. It's Mary Anne, inviting him to dinner with some other people. He listens to the message twice. He's not very good at dinner parties. But it's something to do. It'll fill up an evening. And Mary Anne will be there.

27

Mark arrives early at the Simmons' for dinner on Friday. He's wearing Howard's herringbone blazer, his now partially stained white shirt. He makes himself a large gin and tonic and sits at the table while Mary Anne and David make the final preparations. Mark asks about the other guests and is told that Jane Hanson is a rising star in the academic world, a Columbia Ph.D., probably not long for puny Willamette. The other couple, Carl and Maureen, are married and teach at the University of Washington.

Mark has taken in this information along with most of his drink when Carl and Maureen arrive. They are bland but Mark is experienced at shaking hands, nodding, making polite inquiries. Carl is short and round and has a beard. He's involved in some sort of high-tech biochemistry project. Maureen is an anthropologist. Mark thought anthropology was the study of chimps and dinosaurs but apparently Maureen is a linguist, a language specialist. It sounds confusing. Mark makes himself another drink.

Jane is forty-five minutes late and Mark is drunk and in

need of food when she finally shows up. Mark recognizes her from the faculty meeting two days before but is not prepared for the energy she brings to the small gathering. She seems to fill the entire space with her big-toothed smile. She's not obviously pretty but there's a deadly alertness to her face. At first Mark is overwhelmed. As they all stand in the living room being introduced, he can barely meet her eye.

To make matters worse, when they sit down Mark finds himself at the end of the table, flanked by Jane, whom he's afraid of, and Maureen, whom he doesn't understand. At least Mary Anne is opposite him. At least he can see her face.

The food is served and Mark puts his napkin in his lap. His only real experience at dinner parties is with Howard, who in the first years of their association would occasionally have him over with some of his other writers, usually older poets or intellectuals. Mark did not enjoy those get-togethers. He tended to get bored and then drunk and would either lapse into total silence or make youthful pronouncements that would make Howard's other guests nervous. The best dinner party he ever attended was with Alex, with some young professional types Alex knew. Mark got thrown out of that party after a short wrestling match with a young stockbroker who thought Mark was staring at his date. He and Alex out on the street afterward: laughing, kicking garbage cans, yelling up at the windows of the offended hosts, and then collapsing into a cab in their coats and ties. Mark ripped his tie off, threw it out the cab window, has not owned one since. Not until he came here.

"So Mary Anne tells me you write," says Jane to Mark, as he struggles with an unmanageably large piece of lettuce.

Mark nods, gets most of the leaf in his mouth.

"What sort of things do you write?"

"You write poetry," says Maureen, helpfully.

Mark nods again. Maureen is a plain woman but may be more useful than she looks.

"Yeah, I write poetry. I'm the artist-in-residence," he says to Jane, not trying to brag, but he is.

"Oh, so you're the new person I've been hearing about."

"I'm not really new," says Mark, mildly confused. "Didn't you see me at the meeting on Wednesday?"

"I don't think I did."

"I saw you."

Jane smiles a big toothy smile. "That must be exciting, being an artist-in-residence," says Jane. "Your students must be very impressed."

Mark doesn't like the tone in her voice. He looks down the table at Mary Anne and shrugs. "Not really. It's sort of boring actually."

"Boring?" says Jane. "I would think it would be . . . well, having everyone think of you as a famous poet, from *New York*."

"I'm from Baltimore actually," Mark says to Maureen.

"Have you met Henry Tillman?" asks Maureen. "I love his work."

"I did meet him," says Mark. "He was great. *Conversations with Nature*."

"I love that book," says Maureen cheerfully.

"Me, too," says Mark, grinning at her.

Jane perseveres. "So what's it like writing poetry nowadays? Does anybody read it?"

"No," says Mark, smiling again at Maureen.

"I do," says Maureen.

"What do you write about?" Jane asks Mark.

"Not much. Mary Anne has my book. It's just boring poetry. Well, not boring. I try to make it not boring. That's the key at this point. Just try to be as unboring as possible."

"And hope somebody cares," says Jane.

"Exactly," says Mark.

After the main course, the group moves into the living room. Coffee is served. Mark, sobered by the food, has another large gin and tonic. He sits on the couch and then Jane sits down next to him. This makes Mark nervous and he takes a large chug of his drink. It makes him drunk again but this second wave of drunkenness is harder, heavier. It dulls Mark to the point that he remains silent for the rest of the evening. Jane, though, is funny and entertaining. Mark finds himself laughing and smiling with everyone else as she dominates the conversation. He begins to warm to her. She's attractive too, he sees, through his gin bleariness, and sitting so close to her he gets an occasional whiff of what must be some subtle, tasteful perfume. When she sits forward on the couch her slender back and shoulders remind him of a grown-up Vanessa. For a moment Mark feels a physical pull, an actual magnetic tug toward her. But they are in company. This is a dinner party. Mark crosses his legs in an adult manner, sips his drink, smiles at the warm mellowness of it all. This is how grown-ups party. He likes it. It's fun.

The party continues for another hour and then everyone suddenly stands up. Mark stands too. He's very drunk. The party is over. He says his goodbyes, catching a look of concern on Mary Anne's face as he kisses her sloppily on the cheek. He shakes hands with David. He can't quite focus on Carl but catches Maureen's face, she looks nervous, scared of him. Mark doesn't know why. Nor does he

Exile

care. He is told to follow Jane, who leads him to her car.
Jane is apparently his designated driver. They both get in
and Mark is instructed to put on his seat belt. But he has
trouble locating it. He pulls at several of the black straps
around him but then Jane helps him, touching his chest
and shoulders in the process. When he's all strapped in she
starts the car.

They drive downhill, back toward campus where
Mark's apartment is. But Mark doesn't want to go home.
He directs Jane instead toward the twenty-four-hour
Denny's down the hill from the university.

"You're going to Denny's?" says Jane, when she sees
where he wants to be let off.

Mark hesitates. He doesn't really want to go to Denny's.
But he doesn't want to go home. He needs fluids, tea.
Somehow he communicates this to Jane and the next thing
he knows he's in an alien doorway, walking up carpeted
stairs, bright white walls on either side of him. He's in
Jane's apartment.

It smells strange here. He stands next to an expensive-
looking couch and watches Jane go into the kitchen. He
should have gone to Denny's. He forces himself to sit. But
the walls seem to squeeze in on him. There are too many
books on the shelves. Too much nice stuff.

"Man, did I fuck up," says Mark, as if using the *f* word
might create a little space for himself.

"How?" says Jane from the kitchen. She's putting water
on the stove.

"Just everything," says Mark, reaching for a magazine
on the coffee table in front of him. It's *The New Yorker*.
Mark opens it and flips pages until he finds a poem. Generally he likes the poems in *The New Yorker*. But this one
is running down the page. Like water, it seems to wash in

and out of focus. When he holds it closer to his face, Mark can smell his own breath between the folds of white pages. He smells like an old drunk. He redoubles his concentration and tries to read the poem. It's called "Symphony" or maybe "Sympathy." It's by Charles Simic. Why doesn't he know people like Charles Simic? Why isn't he in *The New Yorker*? His poems are as good as this. Probably. He can't tell for sure because he can't focus enough to read it.

"What did you *fuck up?*" says Jane, putting the tea on the table in front of him.

Mark shakes his head. He stares at the tea. "Thank you," he says quietly. He puts down the magazine and attempts to lift the teacup. But it wobbles in his hand. He's too drunk. "Do you have any cream?"

"I have milk," says Jane. She gets it.

Mark sits back on the couch. The tea sits safely on the coffee table.

Jane pours some milk into it. "How's that?"

"Great," says Mark. He sits forward. He has to get some of it inside him. He grips the cup and gets it to his mouth. It's strong but hot and good. He slurps it twice, three times, gets a good throatful and sets it down. "God, I'm sorry," he says, looking around the apartment. "I don't know how I got so drunk."

"Gin and tonics," says Jane. "That'll do it." She's made herself some tea as well and now comes and sits on the couch several feet from Mark.

"Thanks for letting me come over," says Mark. "Jesus, I hate my apartment. Don't tell David and Mary Anne. It's not the apartment really, it's just, you know . . ."

"It's free, isn't it?"

"It *is* free, I should be grateful," says Mark, and for the first time he looks over at Jane. She's been watching him but now she turns away. He keeps looking at her and she lifts her hand and touches the back of her neck. It is a charming gesture, it's intended to charm. Mark smiles at the thought of it.

"So did you enjoy the dinner?" Jane finally asks.

"Fuck, yes," says Mark, sounding cruder than he wanted to. "I love Mary Anne. I mean, not, you know, I like her as a friend."

"Well, I'm glad I finally got to meet you. And hear about your book. That must be very satisfying."

Even drunk Mark is wary of this subject. He smiles blandly at Jane, who sits up and goes back to the kitchen. Mark picks up another magazine, *Ms.* There's a baby on the cover, a headline about the dangers of male children.

Jane goes into another room and is gone for several minutes. When she returns, she rinses out her teacup. She's got to go to bed. "You know," she says in the direction of Mark and the couch, "you could sleep here if you want. If you think you'd be comfortable."

But when she looks, she sees she's too late. Mark's head is back on the couch. His mouth is open. His eyes are closed. *Ms.* magazine lies open on his lap.

28

Mark wakes up a couple hours later. There's a blanket over him, a thin flannel thing that is not keeping him warm. He feels around for his blazer which is on the floor beneath him. He puts that over the blanket and lays his head back down. He closes his eyes but doesn't sleep. Birds are chirping outside. When he opens his eyes again he sees that the first faint light of morning has lit the kitchen area through a window. Where is Jane? In a bedroom somewhere. Could he just leave? The couch, expensive as it is, is not particularly comfortable. He can't stretch his legs out. He turns and faces the opposite way. This doesn't help and just constricts his legs further. Also, he now feels the dull throb in his head, the raspy dryness in his throat. His neck begins to ache and he turns over again, so that he's facing the room, which is a little lighter than before. His eyes aren't going to close this time. His head hangs off the couch. The greenish carpet, the dull grey light, the growing sickness in his stomach . . . he forces himself upright and sits back on the couch. He looks at his feet. One of his black dress socks is half off, the other is torn, his big toe is sticking out. He wants to stand up but he's suddenly drowsy again, weak, he feels like he's been physically beaten.

A cigarette would help. Mark separates his coat from the blanket and digs his Marlboros out of the breast pocket. He puts one in his mouth and stands up. He pats his pockets for his lighter as his white oxford shirt, pulled around on one shoulder, falls back into place on his body. For a moment his body rewards this physical movement with a strange postalcohol euphoria. A little rush of endorphins. Mark finds his lighter and makes his way down the stairwell to the front door. It's locked but he gently opens the bolt. Outside the air is wet and cold. The skies are grey. Mark steps across the damp porch boards in his stocking feet. He lights his cigarette. He's in the woodsy northwest section of town, a generally upscale neighborhood, but Jane is a little too near the freeway. The building across the street is run-down. On the corner there's a bum with a shopping cart rummaging through a Dumpster. Mark takes a seat on the porch and smokes. Behind him the door is ajar and up those stairs is an accomplished woman, an important woman, a Columbia Ph.D. He is all that is between her and this street, the bum, the big bad world. He is for this moment, her guard, her protector. This amuses Mark and he laughs out loud. The bum across the street waves to him.

Back upstairs, Mark raids Jane's refrigerator. He needs liquids. There's a pitcher of water, with an expensive-looking filter device inside it. He takes a long sip. Then he drinks from an orange juice carton, but just a medium sip because there isn't much left. Then he drinks some milk which seems to curdle in his mouth. He spits it into the sink.

He decides to leave. He puts on his shoes and coat. But he should leave a note. Quietly, he opens drawers until he finds a pen but before he can find paper a clock radio goes off in a room behind him. Jane's clock radio. He abandons his search. He quickly folds the flannel blanket on the couch. There's a soft noise that means Jane is upright and moving. Mark tiptoes to the stairwell and down. Again he opens the bolt, eases open the door and shuts it again. He creeps across the porch, down two of the steps, and then jumps the rest, landing in a half run on the sidewalk.

There's a light rain falling. Mark is grateful for the cool wetness. He cuts through a stand of trees to the main street. He feels inexplicably fantastic. A cafe appears on his left. Maybe he should try to write something. He's got Jane's pen but he still needs paper. There are posters for rock bands on a telephone pole. He tears through the top layers to the dry ones. He slips several of these under his coat.

In the cafe he gets a latte and sits at a table by the window. He spreads out one of the posters and writes on the back:

Alcoholic Poetry Morning #177

Wake up Jane.
It's time to eat your vegetables.
Time to drink your filtered water.

Mark crosses that out and turns the poster upside down. He chews on his pen. Outside, a tuft of fog hangs in the top of an evergreen tree.

Nature Poem #1

When animals are injured
They go into the
Woods to die

They do this because they are
Embarrassed, they'd rather
Cough themselves to death
Or otherwise disintegrate
In the privacy of a
Mountain cave or a
Forest glen or a
Field on top of mountains
Under stars

(Of course they don't enjoy the stars
They're dying)

They go into the woods
And die under a log
Their internal organs hemorrhaging
Blood flooding the various
Compartments like a punctured
Submarine

Animals go off by themselves
To die and when they're
Dead other species come and
Eat them

It is not known
What their own species think
Do animals miss each other?
Or are they glad to have
The wounded one
And his contaminating mortality
Away from the herd
Where they don't have to
Listen to him (or her)
Complain about
Lack of oxygen
The difficulty of breathing
The impossibility of fixing
Compound fractures
With your teeth

Squirrels and little chipmunks
And even household cats and
Dogs
They go off by themselves
To die
Their bodies fill with
Endorphins
To ease the pain
Their brains fill with
Insanity
Just in time

It's kind of a mess but Mark likes it. He puts that poster aside and on the back of another writes:

Nature Poem #2

Some people think
Trees feel pain
That when you cut them
Down they writhe in
Agony
The cutting hurts them
Imagine: Someone taking a chainsaw
To your ankles

Some people think that
Forests are communities
The trees all live there
In multiple generations
The grand elder trees
And the young saplings
Growing at the feet
Of their mothers
And fathers

And can you blame people
For thinking this?
Falling trees, spinning in
Slow motion
Clutching at the other trees
As they go down
Breaking branches
The loud bending snap
Of their breaking backs
Their thudding into
The earth

And then inert
Silent
Dead as men shot in
Cornfields

And then they rot
And other little trees
Start growing out of
Their remains

Some people
Live in trees
In Vermont hippies
Play flutes and wear
Flowers in their hair
The trees are their
Pets
They patronize the trees and
Humiliate their
Epic stature with their
Own nursery rhyme brains
Their hippy feet
Their mud-covered overalls

Trees would prefer
No humans
They would prefer to
War among themselves
Choking each other out
Fighting for space
For dominance for
The gold we call
Sunlight

E x i l e

This isn't as good as the first one. But Mark is happy
with it anyway. He likes them both. He sees a book, a
theme book. That's the trend now in poetry: whole books
about one subject. Marilyn Monroe. Elvis. The Civil War.
He'll do a book of nature poems. Who would expect it
from him? He can't wait to tell Howard. What fun! How
hilarious!

But even as he folds the two posters he begins to doubt
the idea. He's hung over. Whatever little rush he just had is
gone. His head hurts. He knocks into the doorway as he
leaves and then on the street he feels so sick and dizzy he
almost falls down. He sits for a moment at a bus stop
bench, lights a cigarette, waits for his stomach to settle.
Then he stands up, steadies himself, turns and begins the
long walk back to his apartment.

29

For the fall term, Mark's workshops are on Thursday nights. He has seven students. It feels too crowded after the five he had for the short six-week summer term, before he went to Boulder. Mark was amazed at how summer term worked: classes outside; students in sunglasses, shorts, halter tops; afternoon discussions during which Mark nearly fell asleep propped on one elbow in the grass. And they all got full credit for it. If Mark had known about summer school he might have gone to college himself.

But it's fall now. Real school time. This term's students are all bland and serious. Two older women. Three female undergraduates. One male graduate student who talks too much and argues. Another adolescent boy with glasses and acne who always wants to know what his grade is. There are no Vanessas in this class. Just like there were none in the summer term. The honeymoon is over. Mark is now earning his money.

Still: two hours, once a week, it's not that bad. And Mark always treats himself to a night out afterward.

Thursdays are a good night to go out in Portland. He sees bands at Sanctuary or goes to the Alchemy Bar where the ghost of Samantha keeps him company. Jill is there occasionally. Always with other women. Always talking and smoking and snubbing any undesirables who dare approach her. Mark never does.

On this last Thursday in October, though, Mark is going to the Midnight Theater across the river to see Vanessa read poetry at a cabaret event. When he first saw the flyer he shrugged it off. He's managed to avoid Vanessa most of the semester. But the flyer was well done, the event itself sounds interesting, and what's a little residual love sickness in the face of an entire Thursday night of nothing to do? Mark has a bike now too. Mary Anne gave it to him. It's an old Raleigh, a woman's three-speed. All through the late summer and fall he's used it to explore the other sections of Portland. It's become his favorite form of late-night entertainment.

Mark finds the Midnight Theater. He locks his bike to a parking meter. There's a large crowd outside. People are moving around the front-door area so Mark almost slips through without paying. But a doorman catches him. He pays his three dollars, feeling vaguely old and out of place while younger, weirder people walk in and out with complete freedom.

Mark ventures inside. The Midnight is a small, old-style movie theater, but with an ample stage which now features a band. It's three girls playing in the relatively quiet lo-fi Riot Grrrl style that Mark has read about in *Flash*. Behind the rows of seats is a standing area. At the far end there's a keg of microbrew. Mark moves through the people and waits patiently to get a beer. He looks around the room and promptly spots Jill. She's with a chattering threesome of cute Sam-like girls. Mark gets a beer. Then he sees Brendon. He's wearing an outrageous plaid blazer, goofy round glasses, his usual mop of dyed hair, tonight it's bright orange. Mark smiles at the sight of him. Brendon has emerged as the central figure in the local scene. Vanessa was right about that: Brendon's the coolest boy in Portland.

The band finishes and then there's a fashion show. Mark watches from the back wall. Brendon is the MC. Jill is part of it. So are her girlfriends. One woman is wrapped in Saran Wrap. A boy wears a dress made out of beer labels. Vanessa makes a brief appearance wearing a painted card-board box. She's a ship or a refrigerator or something. Brendon is providing commentary but there's a lot of inside jokes and the PA's not so good. Mark's not really getting it. So he gets another beer. When the fashion show is over there's a short break during which Mark settles into a seat and watches Jill and her friends gossip in the aisles.

When the show resumes, it's Vanessa's time. Brendon is suddenly serious in tone as he introduces her. The lights go down. There's warm respectful applause from a crowd that has obviously seen her before. Mark sits up in his chair. Vanessa comes onstage. She wears a vintage cocktail dress which looks affected to Mark but only because he knew her before she wore such things. The crowd apparently did not. They are rapt. Vanessa does not resort to any of the campy artiness of the other performances. She simply stands at the microphone and reads. She's very good. Her voice is clean and clear and avoids the usual poetry rhythms. Her first three poems are all simple, punchy and effective. Mark has heard none of them before. In fact, of the ten or so she reads, only one sounds familiar. But it's the usual Vanessa stuff: alienation, loneliness, disappoint-ing relationships, her cat. All of which is sprinkled with a resilient feminine strength that the crowd loves. Her last poem seems to suggest that she's through with men forever but when she's finished she grins and says something away from the mike that's directed to Brendon. All the people in the front laugh. All the people around Mark ask each other what was said. When Vanessa leaves the stage she slaps at Brendon's butt with her rolled-up poems, to thunderous applause. It's all a bit confusing to Mark, on a sexual politics level. But it worked. The crowd is won. Vanessa is a star.

After that another band plays, four boys who try desperately to hold the crowd. The singer wears a dress. His hair is in pigtails. But people talk in their seats, they walk the aisles, the line at the keg gets long again. Mark goes outside. He stands at the curb and lights a cigarette. He tries to smile at two young girls sitting on the bike rack. But it doesn't feel right. He's too old. This isn't his scene. Then there's a tap on his shoulder. It's Jill. And a friend.

"Oh, hi," says Mark, relieved to have some company.

"Do you have a couple extra cigarettes?" asks Jill, not looking at him. She's pretending she doesn't remember him. Mark is embarrassed by the awkwardness of it. He reaches into his coat pocket and again tries to smile. But she won't. She has no intention of acknowledging him in any way.

He's not sure how to respond. "So how's Sam?" he says.

"Sam?" says Jill.

"Yeah," says Mark. "Your friend Sam? My friend Sam?"

"Oh, her. She moved to Seattle," says Jill, quickly looking around as if she doesn't want to be seen talking to Mark.

But if she won't talk to him, she won't get any of his cigarettes. Mark turns his hardpack upside down in his pocket and gently shakes the remaining Marlboros out of it.

"Seattle . . . ," says Mark. He bites the cigarette in his mouth while he uses both hands to pull the hardpack from his pocket. It comes out empty. He looks at it. As does Jill and her friend. "I guess that was my last one."

Jill glares at him. Mark smiles. Jill grabs her friend and they walk away. Mark takes a last hit of his cigarette, drops it, steps on it. He hears one of the girls at the bike rack tell someone else about a party later. But when he looks at her, the girl's voice suddenly drops. This is getting embarrassing. It's time for Mark to go.

He unlocks his bike and walks it into the street. Then he rides downhill, toward the river, finding a long stretch of freshly poured blacktop which makes even the rickety three-speed ride smooth and clean. This improves his mood. Mark pedals. He coasts. The trees smell wonderful. The night air is crisp and cool. When he gets to the river he turns left and follows a jogging path along the bank. This is a bouncy ride, but worth it as a nearly full moon illuminates the river and the gleaming dirt path.

A mile or so later Mark encounters a construction site that prevents his further progress. So he drops his bike in the grass and climbs on top of a concrete slab. He gets one of the loose cigarettes out of his pocket. He lights it and smokes and quietly tortures himself with the idea that he'll never be part of a scene again. Not like he was in New York. He and Alex and the rest of them sitting on the stoop outside No Se No. He had his time. He was Brendon once. But he's got to let it go. He's got to do what Alex and Cynthia and the rest of them did: move on.

Interesting then that when he finally returns home hours later it is Alex's familiar voice on his answering machine.

30

Alex's message: He's coming to Seattle. To interview a band for *Flash*. He's going to have a day off between the interview and the concert. He was thinking of driving down to Portland. Would Mark like to have lunch? Could he maybe show him around? Alex has been told he should hike the Columbia River Gorge, has Mark been there?

Mark hasn't. He hasn't been anywhere. He plays the message again and tries to unscramble his own conflicted thoughts about his old friend. But whatever he thinks of Alex, he'll have to see him. What's he going to do? Say no?

That night he dreams the meeting in advance. In the dream Alex arrives at the airport but has no car. Mark meets him there but he doesn't have a car either. They end up walking, through swamps, through forests, through fields that never end. Time is running out. They have to get downtown. But they're lost and Alex is getting ahead and Mark's legs are caught in the mush of a muddy wheatfield . . .

In the morning Mark is severely agitated. He has to call

Alex back in New York and puts it off for several hours. When he finally dials the number he gets a voicemail box at *Flash*. He's relieved. He tells the machine that it'd be great to see Alex, to check out the Gorge. He admits in a joking voice that he's never been there, or to the mountains, or to the coast. Alex can show *him* around! As he says this last bit he wonders if he's being too self-deprecating but when the machine offers him the chance to re-record his message he hangs up.

Still agitated he walks down the street to the student cafeteria where he gets a cup of coffee and tries to write a new poem:

Nature Poem #3

at the mall
the woman talks to the man
who does not hear her
or see her
but looks instead
over her shoulder
at the other food court patrons
he sees with
crosshairs
he identifies targets
competing men who must be
destroyed
female hips legs
panty hose that must
be
penetrated
the woman tells the man

about her day while
he systematically kills off
half the mall
population

Mark frowns at the paper and drinks his coffee. Why did he call Alex back? Fuck Alex. Fuck Alex and his stupid *Flash* magazine. Fucking sellout. Fucking pretentious ass-hole. Mark remembers Alex too fondly. He forgets how Alex always scammed on his women. Alex was above picking up girls. But he wasn't above stealing the ones Mark brought around. The little fuck.

"Mark?"

His internal anger must be apparent because Mary Anne recoils slightly when she sees his face. "Oh, hi," says Mark, forcing a smile.

"Are you busy?"

"No, no, I'm just . . . sit down. What's up?"

"Not much." She reluctantly sits. She's got coffee. "How are you doing?"

"All right," says Mark.

"You know, I was worried," she says. "Jane said you slept over at her house."

"Yeah. I fell asleep on the couch."

"That's what she said. But in the morning you were gone. She was quite concerned. She was worried you might sleepwalk. That maybe you'd wandered into the street."

"No, I just went home. I was going to leave a note. I guess I forgot."

"Well, as long as you're okay. She thought it was very strange behavior."

"I'll apologize next time I see her."

"I wasn't worried myself. I was like, *I'm sure he's fine, Jane, I'm sure he just woke up and left. I think that's his style.* We were joking about it."

"That's not my style," says Mark, the specter of Alex suddenly back, suddenly irritating him again.

"We were just joking. You know Jane sort of liked you."

"Yeah?" says Mark.

"You didn't like her?"

"She was all right."

"I think she's going back east next year. I didn't think she'd last long out here. Did you know she's writing a book?"

"No."

"It's about Hannah Arendt and Mary McCarthy. And it's not just some academic thing, she's got a real publisher. She's going to be a big deal in the academic world."

Mark says nothing.

"You're not impressed?"

"Sure I am. Sounds great."

"You didn't like her though."

"I got the feeling she was probing."

"Probing for what?"

"Weakness."

"Oh, don't be silly," says Mary Anne, turning motherly on him. Mark likes it when she does this. He begins to relax. He pulls a cigarette out of his pack and puts it in his mouth. "This old friend of mine from New York is coming to town."

"Yeah?"

"He's on assignment for *Flash* magazine."

"*Flash* magazine? Wow. That's a big magazine."

"You think so?"

"Oh, sure. Isn't it the hot new thing? I mean, I know I'm not that up on things."

Mark likes this too. How easily she dismisses the whole world of coolness. How stable she is. How cheerfully unhip. A lot of good it does him, understanding what's cool and what's not, especially now that he's a boring old poetry teacher.

Mary Anne finishes her coffee. She's got to go. "Well, I was going to play matchmaker with you and Jane but I guess that's a no-go?"

"What did you have in mind?"

"Nothing really. The thing is, you and she might cross paths again. It seems possible. It would be a pity if you didn't at least get to know each other."

"You mean cross paths again teaching?"

"Well, yeah."

"I don't know how much more teaching I'm going to do."

"Why? What are you going to do instead?"

That's an excellent question and Mark has no answer. But with Alex heavy on his mind he is reluctant to give up Mary Anne's company. He goes outside with her, lights his cigarette and walks with her to her class. They don't talk once they're outside. The grounds look nice. But fall in Portland is unsatisfying. It's late coming and then oddly temperate. Also the leaves don't really change, at least not all at once. And there are so many evergreens, the trees that do turn colors end up being isolated cases, all by themselves, surrounded by their own solitary rings of red or yellow leaves.

With Mary Anne safely deposited at her class, Mark heads downtown. He stops at a local bookstore and spots Henry Tillman's *Conversations with Nature*. God, what a terrible title. Again he looks at the picture on the back. Henry is sagging around the eyes, his hair is white and thinning. And yet there is something in his expression, an ease, a contentment. For the first time it occurs to Mark that Henry might know something he doesn't. Henry Tillman may be miles ahead of him.

Mark carries *Conversations* around with him as he looks at other things and then can't part with it at the check stand. For the first time in his life, Mark pays full price for a poetry book. He proceeds to Coffee Star, where he sits by the window and struggles to read the first poem. But he can make no sense of it. And it's full of nature words. How is Mark supposed to know what a "hydrangea" is, or what a row of "kohlrabi" looks like? Probably he's just stupid. He should have gone to college. Alex had a degree in something or other. American Studies was it? It's so true about education. It sets you up for life. Alex will work his way up among the other college types in the magazine business and Mark will end up fired from his teaching job and living with people like the lady sitting across from him who wears three coats and mumbles into her cup of steaming water . . .

31

On the night before Alex arrives Mark is so agitated he can barely contain himself. He goes to the Alchemy Bar and drinks three thick pints of Black Porter Ale. He drinks them fast. When he leaves he's so drunk he's wobbling. He goes to Sanctuary. A terrible band is playing too loud. He has a drunken screaming conversation with a guy he's sitting next to. It dries his throat. He drinks more beer. When he leaves he's so drunk he's sick. He lurches down the street and throws up in a doorway. That feels better. He wipes his drooling chin on his sleeve. But it's late. He's got to go home.

It's a long walk back to his apartment. He moves through downtown on the side streets, avoiding the police cars that prowl the empty city, bored, looking for someone to bother, someone like Mark. Sure enough, Mark isn't halfway home when a squad car falls in behind him and follows him for most of a block. Mark is more afraid of the crew-cut, bodybuilding Portland police than he ever was of their New York counterparts. He concentrates and manages to walk straight. Apparently he passes the test. The cop car turns away at an intersection. Mark breathes easier, the air is clearing his head, he dares to light a cigarette, which also helps stabilize his alcohol-soaked equilibrium.

But in his apartment building he is blind-drunk again. He falls on the stairs, drops his keys, finally pushes into his apartment. But he hates it here. He hates the table, the chairs, the TV that gets one channel. He lights a cigarette. He needs liquids. He goes into the kitchen, yanks open the refrigerator, grabs a can of Sprite and promptly breaks the tab off before it's open. He slams it on the counter, his cigarette falls from his mouth, the dishes collapse in the dishrack. He picks up his cigarette and sucks on it until it's going again. Then he goes back to the Sprite can. The broken tab. He gets out his pocketknife and tries to push the tab down with the screwdriver. It won't go. So he opens the small blade and stabs at the top of the can. But the blade folds up and cuts into the side of his hand. Mark ignores the blood that immediately appears around his fingers. He reopens the blade, stabs again. This time it goes in. Sprite shoots everywhere, it sprays Mark, gets in his eyes, stings and burns. In a blind rage, Mark grabs the Sprite can and throws it across the room where it explodes against the wall, gushing and ricocheting, spinning in place where it lands on the floor.

Mark yanks open the refrigerator and gets another one. This time the tab opens. He takes a long drink and then, winding up like a pitcher, slams the can as hard as he can into the opposite wall. It thuds, fizzes, rolls back toward him. Mark kicks it across the room and goes for a third. This one he shakes violently. Blood is now mixing with the general mess. When the can's about to burst Mark sets it on the counter, picks up his knife again and stabs wildly at the top until it explodes in a vicious gush of sticky burning fizziness. He steps back from the gushing Sprite can and sees the blood all over everything. He looks down at his knife hand. It's covered with blood and is dripping on the floor. Mark wraps his bleeding hand in the tail of his shirt. With his other hand he manages to light a new cigarette. Then he leans against the blood-splattered door of the refrigerator. He smokes, his heart pounding, his knees shaking. He lets his knees collapse and his back slide down the smooth white refrigerator door until he's crouched on the floor, his knees up, his bleeding hand cradled in his lap.

Alex Wright leaves MCA Record's Seattle publicity office and drives his rented Mercury Cougar back to his hotel. It's raining and he runs through the parking lot to the lobby. He is now regretting his arrangement to drive to Portland. He wasn't really sure he wanted to see Mark and he especially doesn't want to drive all the way to Portland in the rain just to have one awkward lunch. But he already called. Mark already called back. He's committed. Who knows, it might be fun. He takes a shower and then repacks his day bag with a rain slicker, an extra pair of socks, his hiking shoes.

But he still feels tired as he steers his car onto the I-5 freeway. When Alex first got involved in journalism he loved the idea of getting paid to travel, to talk to interesting people, to see free concerts, movies, etc. But what a trap that is. And how completely he's fallen into it. His editors run him ragged. Most of what he writes is complete shit. And the minute he hesitates, they'll just find some other starving writer with journalistic stars in his eyes.

⠿ ⠿ ⠿

Mark is sitting on his living room couch when the phone rings that afternoon. He's dressed and ready to go. He's got a makeshift bandage on his right hand. He's gone through an entire package of gauze pads trying to stop the bleeding but the knife wound has finally closed. With his left hand he lifts the phone to his ear. "Hello?"

"Hello? Mark?"

"Hi, Alex," says Mark.

"Mark, hey! How's it going?"

"Great, Alex. How are you?"

"Great. Great."

"Where are you?"

"The Hilton, downtown. Where are you?"

"I'm just up the hill."

"I see. I see."

Mark isn't sure how to proceed. "So are you still thinking of hiking in the Gorge?"

Alex laughs nervously. "I was going to ask you. You're the native. Can you do it in the rain?"

"I kind of doubt it. But I'm sure you could drive around."

"It sounds like you're really taking to this outdoor lifestyle," jokes Alex.

Mark smiles at the voice of his friend. "You know how it is."

"I do, I do. Well, we might as well get something to eat. Let me take you to lunch."

They arrange to meet. Mark hangs up and goes to the mirror. He straightens his collar, brushes the hair out of his face. He looks terrible: tired, pale, sunken. But it's just Alex. He's got to remember that. It's just Alex.

⋕   ⋕   ⋕

Alex looks great: healthy, clean, new clothes. They meet in the lobby and take the elevator to the top-floor restaurant where they are shown a table by the window. For the first few moments, Mark can only stare at the city beneath them. It looks enormous, much more far-reaching than the tiny grid of streets he lives on. When the white-jacketed busboy brings water, Mark feels self-conscious. He has to remind himself that he is an artist-in-residence, at Willamette University. Alex checks the menu matter-of-factly. Mark guesses Alex must eat every day in restaurants like this one. Mark takes up his menu too.

"Are you still a vegetarian?" Mark asks. Alex had taken up vegetarianism shortly after he started at *Flash*.

"I am," says Alex. "I am."

Mark doesn't like how he keeps repeating things. Maybe that's how they talk in the magazine business. What a world that must be. Beautiful women everywhere no doubt. Everyone slick and clean and smart as shit.

Mark will have the chicken. He puts his menu down and waits for Alex, who continues to look at his. While he waits Mark drinks his water and looks down at the grey rain-soaked city below.

After the waitress takes their order Alex launches into all the great things he's heard about Mark's books. This doesn't turn out to be much though. Mostly it's what Howard told him when he called to get Mark's number.

"But that's amazing," says Alex. "To be translated. To be published abroad. Who would have thought of something like that back at No Se No?"

"No one," laughs Mark, who is not immune to this flattery. For the few minutes they talk about it, Mark warms himself in the praise of his friend.

"You made it," concludes Alex. "You were the one who made it pay."

"But it's all sort of too late, you know? It just seems like too little too late."

"Everything is like that," says Alex. "That's how it is at *Flash*. You get to do everything you wanted to do when you were twenty-five. But now you're thirty-five and you couldn't care less."

Mark appreciates this bit of understanding and for a while they are old friends, having lunch. Alex eats and drinks his Perrier. Mark chews his chicken and drinks his Coke.

"What happened to your hand?" asks Alex after a long silence.

"I cut it," says Mark, looking at it. "I was trying to open a Sprite can."

"Did you have to have stitches?"

"Nah," says Mark. He looks at the bandage. There's a thin brown line running down the center of the gauze pad. He's seeping.

"Maybe you could sue them."

Mark shrugs.

Alex eats.

"So what band did you interview?" Mark asks.

Alex tells him. He describes the interview. The conversation lags.

But when the busboy clears their table Alex begins to grin. He wipes his mouth with his napkin and fingers the stem of his water glass. "You know I actually have some serious news," he says.

"Yeah?" says Mark.

Alex nods several times. And then: "I'm getting married."

"No shit," says Mark. His eyes immediately fly back to

the window, hover over the river, the bridges, the flimsy West Coast architecture.

"Her name's Christine," says Alex. "She works at the magazine."

"Wow," says Mark. He forces himself to look Alex in the eye. But Alex feels as awkward as Mark does and they both stare at the crumpled napkins between them.

"She's amazing," says Alex.

"She must be."

"It just seems like the right time and you know . . . if you meet someone . . . and at this point, it's not like time just goes on indefinitely."

"I know what you mean," says Mark.

"So I just thought, she's great, I'm completely happy, this must be the time."

Mark nods his agreement. "Yeah, I hang around with some married people on campus—"

"You? Married?" says Alex, chuckling.

"No," says Mark. "I said I *hang around* with some married people."

"Right, right," says Alex, suddenly embarrassed. "I didn't mean that to sound—"

"No, you're right," admits Mark. "You're the one who should do it. I'll let you see what it's like."

"Well, it's scary is what it is so far. But great though. Christine . . . I just can't say enough . . . she's fantastic."

"I'm sure you'll be really happy," says Mark.

"I just hope I can handle it."

"I'm sure you will," says Mark, letting his eyes drift back to the window.

32

In spite of the awkward lunch, or maybe because of it, the two friends decide to drive the scenic Columbia Gorge. In the rain. They get stuck in traffic just outside the city. In the strained silence Mark fiddles with the radio. He finds the alternative music station, which reminds Alex of something. "So have you heard Virginia Taylor's new record?"

"No," says Mark.

"She's on Warner Brothers. It's kind of a big deal. The first single's pretty good."

"I haven't heard it."

"You will from the sounds of things. They're really pushing it. I think someone said Cynthia did the cover photo."

"Cynthia? My Cynthia?"

"I think she's seeing Damian. Remember him?"

"Uh-huh," says Mark. A song he likes has come on the radio. He turns it up and hums the melody softly to himself.

"So what's up with you? Do you have a girlfriend?" asks Alex.

"No," says Mark.

"Not even any prospects?"

"I slept with Virginia Taylor. Right before I left New York."

"Really? Wow."

"Yeah, I fuck all the stars."

"Well, it's a start."

"A start to what?"

"I don't know," shrugs Alex, changing lanes. Alex has gained weight, Mark notices. His face looks sort of flabby.

The Columbia Gorge is the place where the Columbia River cuts through the Cascade mountain range on its way to the ocean. Mark is not finding it very interesting though. He's also remembering Alex's aversion to cigarette smoke and so denies himself the cigarette that would make the ride a bit more tolerable. The two talk intermittently. Alex's conversation, Mark notices, is divided like the sections of a magazine: music, books, movies, people.

After an hour they come to Multnomah Falls. Someone has told Alex about this and he wants to stop. Mark feels weird following Alex through the parking lot. Most of the people there are families or young couples. He and Alex look like gay tourists. Especially with Alex wearing his Ralph Lauren rain poncho or whatever the hell it is. Mark lights a cigarette. At least it's stopped raining.

Multnomah Falls is spectacular. Mark follows Alex along a forest path to the pool beneath the cascading water. There are trails leading up the steep cliff and Mark worries Alex is going to want to climb to the top. But he doesn't. Instead, the two men stand on a cement platform and stare at the falling water. The mist wets both their faces.

"It's so lush," says Alex, admiring the dense greenery. "This is rain-forest country."

Alex is getting that stupid look he gets when he's impressed by something. "So what do you think of this area?" he asks Mark. "Would you want to stay here?"

Mark takes a drag of his cigarette. "No, not really."

"Seattle's pretty urban. But down here . . ."

"If you were married and having kids maybe," says Mark.

Alex continues to admire his surroundings. Mark's cigarette is going out. It's too wet here. He holds it behind his back, away from the airborne moisture.

Finally Alex tires of the falls and they retreat to the small tourist lodge. Alex buys some postcards, encouraging Mark to do the same. They buy coffees and sit at a greasy plastic table. Alex writes a postcard to his fiancée and his magazine editor. Mark writes to Howard and then, for fun, to Mary Anne, because her box is beneath his at the English Department.

"So Virginia Taylor got a record deal," says Mark, when he's finished his cards. "That bitch."

Alex shifts uncomfortably in his chair.

"She was going to put me on the guest list to this dumb show she did and then I walk all the way down there . . ."

Alex says nothing. He's rewriting the postcard to his fiancée. Mark reaches for his cigarettes. There's a no-smoking sign directly above Alex's head but Mark lights one anyway. He gets two good drags off it before an old woman yells at him from across the room. Mark takes another drag and puts it out.

"Still smoking those butts," says Alex, shaking his head. But then he goes back to Christine's postcard, the happy dream he is creating on that tiny space with his pen and hand.

Back in Portland, Alex drops Mark off in front of his apartment building. It's raining lightly. It's dark.

"Well, hey," says Alex, "it was great to see you."

"It was," says Mark. "Good luck with everything. And good luck with Christina."

"It's just Christine. No *a*."

"Oh, right."

"Listen, I'll send you an invitation."

"Send it to Howard. I'll be back in New York, I don't know, mid-January."

"Great," says Alex.

"Okay," says Mark.

Back in his apartment Mark puts away his wet coat, dries his hair, puts on dry pants and shoes. The bandage on his hand is coming undone. He peels it off. The wound is turning purple. He washes it as best he can but then it starts bleeding again. He uses a towel to stop the flow. Then he rewraps it with paper towels, since he's out of gauze.

In the living room Mark turns on his TV. But it still gets only one channel. He looks in his refrigerator for something to eat or drink. There's nothing. He looks around his apartment. He hates it here. His coat is still wet. He puts it on anyway. Then he goes out.

His first stop is the Alchemy. The bartendress remembers him from last night. She brings him a pint of the same Black Porter Ale he was drinking then but when he gets out his wallet he's down to his last dollar. He starts to explain but the bartendress gives him the beer and takes the dollar as a tip. He calls out "Thanks!" and drinks from the pint glass. He lights a cigarette. That feels better. He watches the bartendress talk to someone on the other end of the bar. She's about his age. He needs someone his own age. Someone who smiles like she smiles. He thinks back to the night before, he talked to her a bit then, could she maybe like him? Mark can't imagine anyone liking him.

But it doesn't matter because when his first pint is gone he's broke. He leaves and walks through the rain to a cash machine a couple blocks away. Then he's close to Sanctuary and decides to find Chuck, the drug dealer. But the cover is ten bucks. And the door girl won't let him look in. He starts to argue but that doesn't help. His days of bluffing or overpowering Portlanders are over. He's been here too long. He's become one of them.

He leaves. He walks to Maggie's Place, a strip bar farther down the block. Here he orders a double whiskey with a beer chaser. He sits at the end of the bar and lights a cigarette. But he's in the way of the people playing pool, redneck locals with cowboy hats. He moves to another section of the bar but now he's in the place where the dancers sit. When he finally settles in the middle of the bar one of the dancers is staring at him. She wants to talk. Could he buy her a drink? Mark is tempted but he's drunk now and he feels vulnerable. He'd better move on. He downs the whiskey, downs the beer, walks past the dancer to the door.

The rain has momentarily stopped when Mark returns to the Willamette campus. He stumbles up the hill toward his apartment. It's only ten-thirty, there are still night-class students around. Mark avoids them. But when he gets to his apartment building he can't bear to go in. He keeps walking and finally collapses on the the wet steps of the library building. He can feel his pants soaking through but he can't be bothered to get up. He gets out a cigarette. But then, before he can light it, he hears something. A laugh. A ringing female voice. It's Mary Anne. Mark stands up. He looks across the lawn. He sees her, she's saying goodbye to . . . Jane. Now Mary Anne is walking down the hill. Mark does the same, moving parallel to her for a while, then cutting across the wet grass to intercept her.

"Hey, Mary Anne," Mark calls out, softly, quietly. He's surprised by how calm and sensible he sounds.

"Oh, Mark," says Mary Anne, happy to hear his voice, but not quite able to see him. He comes toward her from the trees, from the dripping black branches.

"Where are you going?" asks Mark.

"Well, home, obviously. Where are you going?"

"Nowhere. I was just . . ." She's waiting for him. As he approaches, she looks him over. "Avoiding going home."

"You're just standing in the rain?" she says. She sees the homemade bandage on his hand. "What's that?"

"Oh, I cut my hand," says Mark. The bandage is falling off again. He tries to stick it back in place. But then they both see that his hand is dripping blood.

"It's bleeding," says Mary Anne. "What are you doing out here? Mark, you're soaking wet."

"I've been wet all day. I went to Multnomah Falls."

"Are you drunk?"

"A little."

"Do you need stitches in that? When did you do it?"

But Mark is losing his ability to speak. He looks at his hand. He can't answer.

"Do you want to come over? Do you want me to look at that?"

Mark nods his head yes.

33

David's not home. Mary Anne takes off her coat while Mark stands unsteadily in the hallway. He's got to pull himself together. He takes off his own coat. Mary Anne throws him a towel, for his head, he didn't notice how wet he was.

Mary Anne is all business. She takes Mark into the bathroom, holds his hand under the light and peels away the bandage. "This needs stitches. And it's getting infected."

"It already closed once," says Mark. His voice is hollow and weak. "It'll close again."

"I don't know if I have anything," says Mary Anne. She's not going to argue with him, thank God. She leaves the room. Mark checks himself in the mirror. He looks like he's dead.

Mary Anne comes back with iodine. And soap. "All right, we'll wash it out and soak it in iodine and if it gets infected and your hand falls off, that's your problem."

Mark nods. "Where's David?"

"Seattle."

"What's he doing up there?"

"Visiting some friends."

Mark winces when Mary Anne forces his hand under the tap.

"Is that too hot?"

Mark shakes his head.

"It has to be hot."

"I know, I know," says Mark, imitating Alex.

"How did you do this?"

"Trying to open a Sprite can."

"It's cut right down to the—"

"My friend told me to sue."

"Your friend from New York?"

"Uh-huh," says Mark. He glances once at where she's scrubbing his hand.

"How did that go?"

"Okay. He's getting married." Mark grimaces. "That's what he wanted to tell me, I guess. I don't know why."

"Well, you're an old friend."

"He kind of hit me with it. Kind of stuck it in my face. Then he laughed at me and said I'd never get married."

"Is that true?"

"I don't know. Who cares? It's not for him to say, the little prick."

"So it didn't go that well."

"And then I sucked up to him. That was the worst part. He had the car, though. What could I do?"

"You could have gone to a hospital and got this sewn up. What a mess."

"Sorry." He watches her in the mirror, her wide face, her meaty hands. When she puts the iodine on he watches, wondering why it doesn't hurt. Then it hurts. Bad. He practically jumps out of his skin. "Jesus Christ!"

Mary Anne grips his wrist. "Don't move!"

"Ahhhhhhhhhhh," cries Mark, sucking air violently through his teeth.

"I have to. It's getting infected." She turns her back to him, tucks his forearm into her armpit and grips it firmly. Then she must pour the whole bottle of iodine directly into the cut because Mark nearly faints from the vicious burning that follows. He grips her shoulder with his good hand and his chin bumps the back of her head. "Ahhh Jesus, ahhhh fuck!" he says. He loops his good arm around her neck.

She slips out of his grip. But she holds his wrist. His red-stained hand looks like a prosthesis. He opens his hand slightly but that just makes it hurt worse.

"Now don't move. I'll see if I've got anything we can put over it."

Mark sits on the toilet seat. He stares at his hand. He watches the hall for Mary Anne. He wants her to stay physically near him. He wants to be able to see her.

She comes back with a large Band-Aid. At first it doesn't stick but she reinforces it with masking tape.

"All right," says Mark, when it's done. "Now all I need is some whiskey to dull the pain."

"How about some herbal tea to dull the pain?" says Mary Anne.

Mark will take it. He follows her into the kitchen and sits at the kitchen table. Mary Anne puts water on. Then she disappears and comes back in sweatpants, a sweater, wool socks.

"You've probably got to go to bed," says Mark.

"I can stay up. It's kind of nice without David. Having the run of the place."

Mark nods. "Is it fun to be married?"

"Fun isn't the right word."

When the tea is ready they both sit at the kitchen table. Cleanly bandaged, still a little drunk, in the presence of his favorite female, Mark is quiet and content. Mary Anne doesn't say much either. They both sip their tea.

"Do you want to watch TV or something?" Mark finally says.

"Do you?"

"If you don't have to go to bed."

They go into the living room. Mark sits on the couch while Mary Anne turns on the TV. When she joins him on the couch, Mark wants to touch her, wants to sit next to her. He scoots toward her, then away.

"What are you doing?" she says.

"I don't know," he says, honestly enough. He scoots back toward her. He puts his arm around her, but it doesn't feel right, so he takes it back.

She looks at him.

He looks back. "Do you want a back rub or something?"

"A *back rub?*" she says.

"I don't know. I just want to . . . touch you."

"I'm *married.*"

"I know."

She looks at the TV. "I guess I wouldn't mind a little neck massage."

Mark has to get up and move to the other side of her. So he can use his good hand. But that doesn't work. He suggests she sit on the floor, which she reluctantly does. She sits against the couch. Mark kicks one of his legs over her head so he's straddling her. "There, how's that?"

"This is weird, Mark."

"I know." But as he massages her neck she begins to

239

relax. The TV plays. Her head dips forward. Mark kneads the muscles in her shoulders.

"Your hair smells nice," Mark tells her. He moves up her neck to the base of her skull.

"That feels good," says Mary Anne quietly.

Mark keeps doing it. He pauses to sip his tea, gripping it carefully with his bandaged hand. Then he reaches down and kisses Mary Anne's neck. The skin is cold. He kisses it again on the other side. But it's hard, bending over so far. He kicks his leg back over her head and slides himself down onto the floor beside her.

"Now what are you doing?" asks Mary Anne, her face hidden under her mussed hair.

"I'm going to kiss you."

"You are?"

"Yes." It's difficult though. She won't really turn toward him. He kisses the side of her neck and then tries to dig through her hair for her face.

"I don't . . . ," says Mary Anne.

But Mark has found her face. He kisses her on the cheekbone. He gets himself turned around so he's facing her, but it's hard, with only one hand, trying to maneuver.

He finds her mouth. She tastes like herbal tea. At first her lips won't respond. He doesn't push. He pecks gently once, twice, then tries to open her lips with his.

She opens. She kisses him back. The inside of her mouth is warm. But their mouths are out of sync. He wants so badly for it to be good but they aren't finding a rhythm.

"I'm going to turn off the TV," she says.

Mark sits back.

Mary Anne lifts herself off the floor and switches off the TV. Mark gets off the floor and sits on the couch. Mary

Anne sits beside him. She stares straight ahead. "I feel like I'm in high school," she says.

"I know. Me too."

"Do you think we should stop?"

"No. At least not until we get it right."

"Get what right?"

"Kissing."

"Aren't I doing it right?"

"No, you're . . . you're great," he says, kissing her again. "You're beautiful," he says softly. This time she's more into it. She touches his face. His tongue slips into her mouth. She's delicious. They roll over to one side. Mark lets his thigh ease up and gently press against her crotch bone. She likes it, she moves with it. Mark becomes dizzy with arousal.

"Do you want to go to the bedroom?" she finally gasps. He does.

They go there. She slips off her sweater and helps Mark remove his pants. He marvels at how matter-of-fact she becomes once it's clear they're going to have sex. It occurs to Mark how much more sexual married life is than single life. In bed, he hands her a condom and she puts it on him. She gives him a bit of expert head and then crawls on top of him and puts his dick inside her. Mark is stunned by how fast it all happens. He lies passively on his back, his bandaged hand extended out to his right, where it won't be disturbed. Mary Ann knows what she's doing. She hunches over him, making her stout shortness even more so. Her breasts hang and flop as she works her way easily to orgasm.

Mark is having trouble enjoying it. He's wanted her for so long. But now he's just getting his dick fucked. Finally he gets her around the neck with his left hand and clumsily rolls her over. But he can't quite get himself set in the missionary position either. It's the sheets, they're too slick, his knees slip, he can't get any traction. Meanwhile she's pushing against him, she's trying to come again. Mark struggles to meet her thrusting hips. Finally he gives up on protecting his bad hand and uses it to grip the top of the bed. Once he's anchored he can press back against her. Which is just what she wants. She gasps. Her middle-aged face turns upward, her back arches, she's coming, and then he does too, slipping below consciousness so that for one instant his only sensation is the dull ache in the fleshy part of his fist.

34

"Mark . . . hey, Mark!"

Mark returns from a pleasant dream. Mary Anne is tapping him on the sternum.

"Wake up. You can't sleep over. You have to go."

Mark slips his sore right hand around her neck and pulls her head down to his chest. Her soft hair mingles with the wisps of hair on his own chest. He wants to kiss her but she's not sleepy and endorphinized like he is. She's awake. She's concerned. She wants him out.

"What? Is it David?"

"Well, yeah," she says. "Obviously."

"When's he coming back?"

"Tomorrow. But I don't want . . . I want you to leave now. I want to wash the sheets."

Mark wants to kiss her. He loves her. He wants a wife of his own. "Okay. I'll get up." He tries to pull her face down to his own.

"I want you to go *now*."

"Well, just kiss me then."

She turns her face to his and pecks him once on the mouth. But she sees that isn't going to be enough so she kisses him with her mouth open. She does it fast and he tries to slow her down. He's getting hard again. He tries to kiss her neck, tries to roll her over.

"What are you doing?" says Mary Anne.

Mark doesn't answer. Instead he takes her hand and guides it to his dick.

"Please, Mark," she says. But she's holding it, she squeezes it once. He rolls her onto her back, gets between her legs, rubs himself against her scratchy pubic hair.

"Mark, Mark!" she pleads with him. "Can I please just get a condom?"

She does. Mark is so hard it hurts. But she hesitates before putting it on. "You promise you will leave after this?"

Mark nods. She puts it on. He gets on top of her. She's not really wet enough but he gets it in anyway. She seems to know how to do this: fuck without actually wanting to. Mark gets farther inside her. She begins to coo. It sounds fake. Mark chews on her neck, her shoulder, her ear. He drives both hands under her hips, tearing the bandage loose in the process. When he's got her firmly in both his hands he lifts her slightly, tilts her toward him. Mary Anne's cooing sounds a little more real but Mark isn't paying attention. He's gone. He's somewhere else. His hand burns and aches and still he grips her harder. His teeth clench as his chin digs into her shoulder. Then he straightens up. He grips Mary Anne around the middle and lifts her with him until he is on his knees and she is airborne, arched backwards. He fucks her this way, grimacing, using all his strength to hold the position. It's heavenly and cruel and he finds himself grunting, crying out.

"Shhh! Mark! Be quiet!"

Mark sucks his voice back into himself. When he comes he collapses forward. Mary Anne immediately tries to squirm out from under him but he's bigger than she is, taller, he won't release her. He mashes down on her, holds her, tries to bury his face between her neck and shoulder. But she's frantically twisting her head away. "You have to go now. You promised!"

"I know," says Mark, out of the hazy blackness engulfing his consciousness.

"Now! Come on," whispers Mary Anne. She's out from under him. She's escaped. The lights come on.

Pushed out the door at four in the morning, it's as if Mark never woke up, as if the dream were just moving to a new location, this one being the quiet lawns and paths of the Willamette campus. His body tingles with sleepiness. His brain remains pleasantly fogged. He walks on unsteady knees toward his apartment but then reconsiders and heads downhill to Denny's.

Denny's is relatively quiet. There are a few cabdrivers sitting at the counter. Mark sits away from them, in the smoking section. The waitress comes. She looks at the homemade bandage on his hand. It's mangled, it's falling off, it's a mess. Mark orders coffee and flips open the plastic menu. He considers the pictures of food. It all looks pretty good in the pictures but down the counter the breakfast one man is eating looks disgusting. He'll order it anyway. He lights a cigarette. It's warm in the Denny's. Mark shivers for a moment. But then his vision blurs, he lapses. He almost falls out of the chair which rotates too easily, it's constantly twisting an inch or two in either direction, it's making him sick. He moves over one chair closer to the cabbies. The waitress comes back with his coffee. She's a large unpleasant woman. She doesn't like the fact that he's moved. Fuck her. Mark takes the coffee. It's full right to the top, he pours cream in anyway, it spills. Mark pours sugar into it, stirs it, more spills. There's no napkins. And what happened to the waitress? He wants to order. Here she comes. She's got a towel. "Is there a problem here, sir?" she asks.

"No," says Mark. "I just spilled some coffee."

"That place not good enough for you?" She indicates the fact that he moved.

"It spins too much," says Mark. But the one he's sitting on does the same thing.

"Let's just try to keep the coffee in the cup."

"You're the one who filled it so full," says Mark as she strides away. She must weigh three hundred pounds. Denny's is starting to irritate him. And this woman. They don't have angry black people in Portland. They have mean overweight white people.

Mark is still thinking about this when a new overweight white person approaches him from behind the counter. It's the manager. "Sir, we're going to have to ask you to leave."

Mark looks at him.

The manager scoops away his coffee cup which seems to finalize the situation. Now there really is no real reason for Mark to be here.

"Okay," says Mark.

"We need you to leave now, sir. Albert will show you out." A black man appears at his side. In a fake police uniform.

Mark has trouble getting out of his seat. That's why they're kicking him out. They think he's drunk. Maybe he is.

Outside he's shaking again. His knees feel like they're about to collapse. He coughs a raspy cough and then leans on the low brick wall outside the restaurant. He lights a cigarette. The first drag clears out whatever it was in his chest. But then the manager is there again. Coming down the sidewalk toward him. He's got the black guy with him.

"Sir, if you don't leave the premises immediately we will have you arrested for trespassing."

"Wow," says Mark, amazed at the manager's tenacity. The black man behind him, Albert, stands with his hands on his belt. On his face there is no expression. None whatsoever. It must be weird to be a black person in Portland.

"Sir, this is Denny's property and we want you off it. *Now.*"

Mark considers letting himself be arrested. It might be easier than hiking the twelve blocks back to his apartment. It's nice being arrested, being totally under someone else's control. No decisions. No thinking required. They might even sew up his hand.

But he's afraid of the Portland police. Who knows what they'd do to him. He flicks his cigarette into the street. "I'm sorry," he tells the manager. "I didn't mean to fuck up your night. I really didn't."

"Albert, will you accompany this gentleman off the premises?" asks the manager, who then scurries back into the building. Mark has no idea why he's so pissed. But he's going to obey the poor man. He waves Albert away and manages to stagger down the street. And then up toward his apartment. Twelve blocks. When he's halfway there, it starts to rain.

The next morning the phone rings. Mark is asleep on the couch, still dressed in his wet clothes from last night. He isn't going to answer but then hears Mary Anne on the answering machine. He manages to find the phone where it rests on a cardboard box. "Hello?"

"Mark? Are you awake?"

"No."

"Listen, I have to talk to you about last night."

Mark wipes the crust from his eyes.

"Okay," says Mary Anne. "First of all. I'm sorry about throwing you out like that. Did you get home all right?"

"Yes."

"Well, I just . . . the truth is . . . I've never done anything like that. I mean, I've never had sex with someone since I was married . . ."

Mark sits up. He rubs his aching temples.

"It's nothing about you, Mark. I really like you and I've enjoyed hanging out and everything . . ."

"Could we have this conversation later? I don't feel too good."

"No. David will be home."

"So what?"

"That's why I'm calling. Because I'm not like you. I can't just do something like this and then forget it. This is going to be very hard for me. It's already hard. I've never been able to keep things from David."

"You're going to tell him?"

"I'm going to try to *not* tell him. For his sake." Her voice suddenly breaks. "Oh, God. I can't believe I did this."

"Listen, Mary Anne, I know this is weird. But you can't freak out."

"I know. I'm sorry. But you have to understand. I'm not like you. And I don't want you to think I can continue anything with you because I can't."

"That's what I mean," says Mark. "You don't have to *continue anything.* I don't expect anything."

"I don't even think I can talk to you anymore."

"Mary Anne, come on. That's absurd. We'll just be friends. Like we were before. Christ, I love talking to you. You're the only—"

"But I *can't!* You have to understand. There's only a month left in the term. That's what I want from you. I want you to promise me . . ."

"What?"

"I think we should avoid each other. Completely. It would be the best thing for both of us."

A hardness comes into Mark's voice: "And why should I do that? Why should I give up the only thing that brings me even the tiniest amount of pleasure in this stupid place?"

There's a pause. "Because you care about me?"

"Well, of course I care about you. Jesus Christ, you're the only—" But now he's losing it. He closes his eyes.

"I've made a terrible mistake," continues Mary Anne. "And now I've hurt you. And David. And myself. I know that. I blame myself, Mark. It's all my fault. But I still need your help. I need for you to do this one last thing for me . . ."

35

Mark does as he is told. When he sees Mary Anne on campus he nods, waves, keeps walking. She pretends to wave or nod back but she doesn't really. She won't ever meet his eyes. He's thinking he might still chat with Jane but the embargo on Mark West seems to include her also. She doesn't even pretend to wave. At English Department meetings Mary Anne and Jane sit together, as far away from Mark as they can get. At the last faculty party they arrive late and leave early.

David, when Mark sees him, remains his bland self. At first Mark considers befriending him but that would probably just upset Mary Anne and it's not like David and Mark ever had anything to say to each other. So Mark avoids him.

Bill Masters remains the one Willamette person Mark feels somewhat comfortable with. But even with him there is a growing distance. Perhaps Mark didn't live up to his billing. Or maybe Bill had something different in mind when he hired the young poet. Anyway, Mark's time at

Willamette is almost over. When Bill invites Mark to lunch
one day an embarrassed silence comes over them. There's
just nothing left to say.

Thanksgiving comes. Mark continues working on his
nature poems, though more and more the poems stray
away from nature and toward sex. Mark assures himself that
sex is nature too. It's really the best part of nature. His
favorite place to work is still the downtown Coffee Star. The
same babbling crazy woman is there almost every day. One
day Brendon is there with his friends. Mark says nothing to
him and Brendon doesn't notice Mark back in his corner.

One night he sees Jill at the Alchemy. She's ordering a
beer at the bar. Mark asks her about Samantha. This time
Jill is reasonably civil to him. Sam is working at a hair
salon in Seattle. Does Mark have a cigarette? He does this
time. Jill doesn't thank him for it. When her beer comes
she leaves. She's got people she's got to talk to.

Sanctuary is still loud and cold and dark the couple of
times Mark strays inside. Bad bands, bad beer, white-trash
drug dealers. Mark has accomplished one thing since he
left New York. He is almost completely drug-free. If he
doesn't count caffeine, nicotine or alcohol.

As Mark wanders the rainy streets on the last night of
November he remembers his initial impressions of Portland. How superior he felt. How easy it was going to be: to
write, to meet people. In general none of the potential of
the place has been realized for Mark. Poetry-wise he got
nothing, maybe three or four savable poems. The nature
theme he still likes, but if he gets a book out of it, he'll
have to write most of it in New York. But he likes that idea
too. Writing your nature book in New York City. He'll
make a trip to the Bronx Zoo to insure authenticity.

⁜ ⁜ ⁜

The days are at their wettest, shortest and greyest when Bill Masters calls Mark and invites him to Henry Tillman's mountain home. Bill explains that there might be snow, they may have to put on chains. Mark, who is watching "Oprah," agrees instantly to the adventure. Anything to get out of the house.

The next day Bill picks up Mark. It's raining when they begin. It turns to snow as they rise into the mountains. They drive for an hour and then stop at a truckstop for gas. Mark goes into the log-cabin-style minimart and gets a coffee. He stands outside and watches two truckers chatting in the snow while a third measures his tire chains against his tires. The air smells of diesel fuel and the minty winter forest. Mark enjoys the entire scene. Thank God for Bill Masters and his road trips.

The roads are clear until they get to Henry Tillman's long driveway. This is a sloppy mixture of snow and mud and makes for some slippery driving. Fortunately it's mostly flat and they make it to the house without incident. As Bill shuts off the engine Mark can see he's nervous about bringing Mark and the older poet together again. "It'll be fine," Mark assures his boss.

And it is. Henry welcomes them in his gruff grumbling way. Mark enjoys the sight of him. His hair is snow-white and sticks out at several different points on his head. He wears a large flannel shirt with suspenders, thick wool pants, red socks and slippers. Bill and the older man greet each other warmly. Mark hangs back until Bill reintroduces them.

"Nice to see you, sir," says Mark, smiling into the man's face. Henry's expression sours slightly at the sight of him. But he shakes Mark's hand. They all go inside.

Henry is apparently a bachelor. Or maybe his wife died. Mark should have asked Bill earlier. The three of them sit at Henry's kitchen table and drink coffee. Bill and Henry talk about people Mark doesn't know. At one point an old dog enters the room. He comes to the table and is scratched by Henry and then Mark. He is very old. His eyes are red and watery. Mark can almost feel the pain in his legs. He moves slowly away from the humans to his bed, a large wicker basket. Mark watches him settle himself. The dog falls asleep instantly. And then is absolutely motionless.

The conversation has turned to plumbing, a water pump, Mark isn't paying attention. But whatever it is, it's broken and Bill wants to look at it. They all get up and walk into a back room that is full of canvas raincoats, thick boots, down parkas. It's a muddy, dog-haired room but Mark follows the other two, putting on a coat and slipping his feet out of his leather shoes and into thick rubber boots. Then they go out, into the forest, into the snow.

Henry leads the way. Though snow is no longer falling from the sky, it is still falling from the tree branches. Miniature avalanches of white dust collapse periodically around them. Mark is last in line behind Henry and Bill. They move downhill, along a path, to a creek that is still running despite the snow. They pause to rest for a moment.

Mark watches the trickling water. "Wow," he says. "That water must be cold."

Henry and Bill exchange amused looks. They continue across the creek and proceed along its opposite bank. The path, smooth and white in front of Henry, is muddy and stomped down behind Mark, from just the three of them walking on it. A fragile thing, this nature.

Fifty yards later they arrive at their destination. It's a dam, a beautiful man-made pool of ice-tinged water. Apparently there is a water pump here that is malfunctioning. Mark can see the pipe and the small wooden box it's connected to. Bill and Henry tromp over to the box and lift the top off. They inspect the problem. Henry's got a large wrench in his pocket and he whacks at something metallic inside the box. The blows ring and echo down the hill, down the creek bed. For the first time Mark realizes how isolated they are. The creek no doubt finds its way back to the road, but above them there is nothing. Trees, snow, air, nothing.

"Does anything live up here?" Mark wonders out loud.

Henry stops what he's doing and looks at him. He's got the wrench in his gloved hand. Bill also looks at him.

Henry speaks: "There's some deer that have been coming down out of the mountains the last couple weeks."

Mark nods at this.

"They're starving to death."

Mark nods some more. He can't quite look at Henry so he gazes into the trees. It's getting dimmer out. It's late afternoon. Ever so subtly, the darkness has begun.

Henry and Bill go back to their work. Mark scoops up a handful of snow and makes a snowball. But to throw it might offend—they're working, he's playing—so he lets it drop into the whiteness at his feet.

When they're done in the box, Bill trudges through the snow to the opposite side of the pool. Apparently he helped in the construction of it. Mark walks around to Bill's side to get a different view of the woods. He looks up the hill and tries to imagine the deer working their way down toward civilization. Like dazed soldiers, lost in the battlefield: the deer don't care that there are cars and deadly humans waiting below. They don't care because they're dying anyway. They come out of hiding because they've got nothing to lose.

Henry and Bill finish their repairs. The three of them head back to the house. The strange gloom that hangs in the trees inspires Mark to speech. "So these deer," he asks Henry, from behind Bill. "What happens when they get down to where the people are?"

"They eat garbage. They make a nuisance of themselves."

"Do people kill them?"

Bill laughs nervously at this question.

"Not this time of year," says Henry.

"Hunting season's in the fall," Bill explains quietly. "It's illegal to kill them now."

But Mark wanted to hear it from Henry. As the day is ending, he now wants something from this man who is so unlike himself. He doesn't know what it is exactly but if he could probe around, ask stupid questions long enough, maybe it would come out.

But twilight has come. They are back at the house. There isn't room for all three of them in the tiny coat-and-boot room, so Mark waits outside. A soft wind blows through the trees. Snow spills from the branches. Mark stands absolutely still, absolutely quiet, and does his best to commune with the snow-filled forest. But the silence seems not to affect him. Perhaps he is not capable of absorbing such sublimity. Perhaps he's not worthy of it.

When Henry and Bill are done, Mark goes into the dog-haired room and changes into his city clothes. In the kitchen they have a last cup of coffee and then it's goodbye. Bill and Mark walk to the car. Bill shakes hands with Henry. Mark does too. He smiles into the man's face but Henry won't really look at him. Mark gets in on his side. Bill starts the engine. More waves and the car starts to move. Mark wiggles his cold toes inside his city shoes.

PART FIVE

winter

36

Mark wiggles his cold toes inside his city shoes. He's riding uptown on the subway. He's coked up and chewing savagely on a piece of gum. The back of his head is pressed hard against the window so that the vibration of the train is rattling his brain, his entire consciousness. There's something tight and aggressive about every muscle in his body. And it's not just the coke. He's going uptown to Cynthia's engagement party. Cynthia's marrying Damian.

Mark has been back in New York for three weeks now. The apartment Howard found for him is across the hall from a successful young video-making couple named Peter and Claire. So young and successful are Peter and Claire that they have kept Mark coked out of his brain for most of the time he's been back. Consequently he hasn't seen anyone. He hasn't been out. He's done nothing but snort coke and write. After a year of nonproductiveness, he has produced a thick book's worth of aggressive, edgy, fucked up and—Mark is convinced—totally brilliant nature poems.

But now he's got his old life to deal with. Cynthia. Damian. Alex. Virginia Taylor might even be there. The train stops at Ninety-sixth Street and Mark explodes out of his seat, nearly flattening an old woman as he pushes out of the subway car. He runs up the stairs to the street. Aboveground it's cold and clear, the end of January. Mark spits out his gum and begins a fast march to Ninety-third. He slaps at his pockets for his cigarettes. He has to duck inside a furniture store to light one. The proprietor protests, Mark ignores him, puffs his cigarette, walks.

Damian's apartment building is nice. His father is rich. Of course Cynthia's going to marry him, she's not stupid. Mark nods at the doorman as he walks in. He rides up in the elevator. He's wearing his teaching outfit, a sweater over his oxford shirt, grey pants, his black overcoat. When he gets to Damian's floor he pauses at a mirror in the hallway. He looks like shit. But his clothes look good. And anyway, he's been an artist-in-residence. What can they say? Any idiot can get married. Mark has earned his new status in society. Willamette paid him *just to exist*. He marches confidently to Damian's door and pushes the buzzer. But as he releases it he feels the terrible, sickening slippage of the coke. His elation, his confidence takes a wild staggering dip. He'll have to do more when he gets inside.

Damian answers the door. He looks glad to see Mark. Mark does his best to seem positive also. "Congratulations," he tells his rival.

"Thanks," says Damian. But there's something strange about the way he looks at Mark.

"Everybody's getting married nowadays," jokes Mark. Damian continues to look at him in a quizzical way. Mark ignores it. He can't concern himself with any awkwardness between Damian and himself. He's the old boyfriend, Damian's the new husband, yeah yeah, so what.

He's barely inside when Alex appears. Alex approaches him so fast that Mark has to shake his hand with his coat still hanging off his shoulder.

"It's good to see you, Mark," says Alex, with a weird earnestness. He's probably trying to make up for being so snotty back in Portland. It's probably occurred to Alex that Mark is going to do just fine. *Exile* is doing well overseas, and Alex, as a journalist, is probably eager to keep on the good side of a potentially major American poet.

"How are you?" says Alex, as Damian takes Mark's coat.

For a moment it seems everyone in the room is watching them.

"I'm great, Alex," says Mark, allowing a slight sarcasm to enter his voice. "How the hell are you?"

Alex mutters something and Mark smiles around at the room. The coke is slipping, but even without it Mark can't help but bask in this attention. Obviously the word is out. Of all the people in their little group, Mark is the only one who held on, who didn't sell out. And he made it. All these people, the ones who wanted to write or make films or play music, they caved in. They got married. They got normal jobs. And now they look at him. Finally, Mark is the star.

Cynthia appears. She hugs him. The admiration in her eyes is obvious. All of this is too much. Mark has got to do more coke.

"You look great," says Cynthia. "Can I get you anything?"

Mark is stunned by the love in her face. Cynthia doesn't want to marry Damian. She wants to marry Mark! It's so obvious. Isn't she afraid Damian will see?

"You know, I'd really love a drink," says Mark. "I know it's early. I drank too much coffee this morning. I've kind of got the shakes."

With Alex sticking close to him Mark follows Cynthia to the kitchen and makes himself a vodka and grapefruit juice.

"So how was Portland?" says Cynthia. "I got your post-card. I'm sorry I didn't get a chance to write you back."

Mark waves his hand. "Don't worry about it. You were busy. You're getting married, for Christ's sakes."

Cynthia is embarrassed. She smiles weakly.

"Yeah," continues Mark. "Portland was cool. I mean it's just starting to come now, the artistic payoff. I'm doing this nature poem thing. It's like a goof but it's not. The critics will call it postmodern, I'm sure."

Cynthia carefully pulls a strand of hair out of her face. "Have you seen Howard?"

"Fucking Howard," laughs Mark. He sips his drink. "Yeah, Howard was right about getting out of town. It worked. I can't wait to show him this new stuff. He's going to freak."

Cynthia looks at Alex. There's something tight in her face.

Mark takes another sip of his drink. He gulps it this time. The alcohol is working. It's warming the coldness of the fast-declining coke high. Still, Mark has to get to the bathroom.

"So you haven't seen him?" says Alex.

"Who, Howard? Nah," says Mark. "I mean he found me an apartment. Fucking nice too. Christ, I'm making him money now. I guess he *better* look out for me." Mark intends this as a joke but it doesn't come out right. He's got to learn how to deal with this sort of thing. Give credit to the "little people" as it were. "Yeah, Howard's the great-est," he says. "I love the guy."

Alex smiles and nods at this. Cynthia too.

"Christ," blurts Mark. "I gotta go to the bathroom."

Mark takes his drink with him. He goes into the bath-room and locks the door. The only flat surface in the room is the back of the toilet. He lowers the seat top and sits on it backward. He dumps the coke on the top of the porce-lain tank. It's not very much. He'll do it, finish his drink and get out of here before things get too weird. He runs the water to cover the sound of a few perfunctory chops. Then he shapes the white powder into lines and snorts them up. When it's gone, he licks the toilet top. Then he takes another large gulp of his drink, flushes the toilet, takes a long deep breath. His skin tingles with the pleasant rush of the drugs. Peter and Claire, now those are real friends.

He unlocks the door and opens it. Alex is standing just outside the door. Cynthia is behind him. They're waiting for him.

Mark laughs nervously at the sight of them.

They say nothing.

"What?" says Mark, looking back and forth between them.

Alex turns to Cynthia.

"Why do you guys keep looking at each other?" says Mark.

"We want to talk to you," says Cynthia.

"Why?" says Mark. He can feel his eyes narrowing. He's not going to listen to any criticism from these two. They don't know what it's like being a real artist. They don't know the pressure.

"We want to . . ." Alex again looks to Cynthia.

"Stop looking at each other!" says Mark.

Cynthia abruptly turns and leaves the hall. Alex breathes deeply. But then he can't face Mark. He looks at the floor.

Mark takes a wild slug of his drink. "Listen, if this is one of those interventions, or some sort of anti-fucking-drug thing, man I don't fucking want to hear it. You got your little gig at *Flash* and I'm doing my thing and if you don't fucking like it . . ."

Alex looks up at Mark. There's a strange pleading look in his face.

Mark continues. "Don't even fucking think about giving me some fucking lecture—"

But then Alex is right in his face, gripping his shoulders. "It's not that," says Alex. "It's nothing like that. It's Howard. Howard has AIDS. He's sick. He's dying."

Mark almost drops his drink but Alex catches it. Alex holds his drink, holds his arm as Mark tips backward into the wall behind him. Like on the subway, Mark's skull settles itself on the hard surface behind him.

"He didn't say anything," says Alex. "Nobody knew. Until just a couple months ago. And now he's bad."

Mark is trying to get his drink up to his mouth. He does, but then he can't drink it. He lets it fall back down. It spills. It pours out on his shoes.

"I'm sorry," says Alex, his voice dropping. "I didn't know how to tell you."

Cynthia's voice mingles with Alex's in the blur of Mark's consciousness. The two of them lead Mark into a dark bedroom. The coats of the other guests are there. They seat Mark on the edge of the bed.

"That's why . . . that's why he wouldn't have lunch with me," says Mark quietly.

"Probably," says Alex. He's sitting on Mark's left. Cynthia squeezes in on his right. Cynthia has tears in her eyes. Alex is choked up too. Mark stares at a place on the wall in front of him. "Oh, no," he whispers. "Oh, God, no."

Cynthia puts an arm around Mark. Alex scoots a little closer and puts his arm around Cynthia's arm. "I'm so sorry," says Cynthia in her quiet feminine voice.

Mark's body wants him to cry. And his friends want him to as well. They are there for him in a way they have never been before and will probably never be again. But it's no use. The coke, the alcohol, the unexpected anger churning up in Mark's chest: it creates an obstacle course, a maze. His grief can't find its way out and sits like a poison in a place just above his stomach, in his heart.

37

Mark walks home from Damian's. He walks the forty blocks along Central Park West toward midtown. It's late now, on a Sunday night, the streets are quiet and relatively deserted. At one point he stops to rest. He sits on a frozen park bench and lights a cigarette. Above him the skies have clouded over. He looks up into the indistinct whiteness of the New York overcast. A bus drives by. He smokes.

In midtown Mark turns left on Fifty-fourth Street. He finds a familiar coffee shop and goes inside to warm himself. He sits at the counter. He used to come here when he worked as a foot messenger during his first months in New York. His last deliveries were always at Rockefeller Center and then he'd come here. He was so broke then. And the messenger money was terrible. The other messengers were teenagers from the Bronx, Brooklyn: brash young black kids laughing about guns and shootouts and who killed whom. Mark would sit with them in the messenger office, waiting for the calls to come in. At that point Mark had little hope of making it in the big city. He was just trying to stretch out his time, so when he went home he could at least tell people he'd *lived* in New York. But then he found No Se No, the downtown scene, Alex, and eventually Howard. And as soon as you had friends, as soon as you had connections, you could get better jobs, better apartments, New York was suddenly the easiest place to live imaginable.

Mark drinks coffee and smokes. The coke is out of his system, the alcohol's worn off. Howard is dying. He's gotten used to the idea. He's thinking about himself now. Mark will have to contact Nigel and deal with the other foreign publishers. He'll have to find a new publisher at home. His personal life: he'll have to get his shit together. No more leaning on Howard for everything. Mark felt alone before. Now he really is.

When Mark gets home he creeps carefully past the door of Peter and Claire. They're the last people he wants to deal with now. He unlocks his own door and slips inside. He turns on a desk lamp in the kitchen and leaves the other lights off. He sits on the couch and lights another cigarette. A half hour goes by and there's a knock at the door. It's Peter. He can tell by the knock. Drug addicts, they always want company. Mark doesn't get up. He continues to smoke. He looks around the beautiful apartment. The owners, Nicholas and Kenneth, are in Brazil shooting a documentary about life in the barrio. When Peter is gone Mark picks up the remote and flips through the channels with the sound off. There's nothing on, though, so he goes to his desk where he looks at his latest nature poem. He can't concentrate though. He was going to wait until tomorrow to call Howard but now he thinks that's cowardly. He should call right now. He almost does too. He sits on the couch, pulls the phone into his lap, lights another cigarette. But when the cigarette's gone, Mark is tired and has tears in his eyes. He puts the phone back and lies down on the couch.

The next morning Claire knocks on the door. How can Mark feel he's alone? He opens it and there she is, eager to do something, to get together, to attach their lives to his.

"I was wondering if I could borrow a couple cigarettes," she explains modestly.

Mark gives them to her.

"Where'd you go last night?" she asks, lighting one. "We went out with a friend who's a writer."

"Oh, yeah?"

"We thought maybe you two should meet."

"Actually I sort of got some bad news. My publisher has AIDS. He's pretty sick."

"Oh, that's terrible."

"So I'm just kind of lying low. You know, trying to get used to it."

"Of course," says Claire. She's originally from down south somewhere. There's the tiniest twang still in her voice. "If there's anything we can do. Or if you want to be alone . . . your publisher, is that . . . Howard?"

Mark nods.

"Oh, my God. That's so terrible. Oh, he was . . . we just met him once. But what a wonderful man."

"Yeah."

"Did you go visit him?"

"Not yet," says Mark. "Yeah, I was going to. I don't know . . ."

"You should visit him," says Claire. "Even if you don't know what to say. Even if it seems hopeless."

Mark smiles painfully. Claire's right. Everyone's right. Everyone knows more about life than he, the great poet.

"Well, like I said. If there's anything we can do."

"I appreciate it," says Mark.

Mark shuts the door. He goes to the phone. He dials Howard's Brooklyn number. That old familiar 718. It rings twice and picks up. "Hello?"

"Hello? Is Howard there?"

"No, he's not."

"Uhm, do you know where . . . do you know when he'll be back?"

"He might be back Wednesday. I'm not sure."

"Oh. Uh . . . where is he?"

"He's in the hospital," says the voice, with the faintest hint of impatience.

"Well, this is Mark West. I work with Howard. He does my books . . ."

"Uh-huh."

"Who are you?"

"I'm Robert."

"But I mean, like, who are you?"

"I'm Howard's brother."

"Oh."

"And I'm kind of busy. Can I leave a message for Howard?"

"Yeah," says Mark, standing up straight. "Yeah, my message is, I'm really pissed off, I mean *upset,* that I was not informed about Howard's condition. And I want to see him. What hospital is he in anyway?"

"You'd be better off coming here. He should be back on Wednesday."

"Yeah, and I want to be informed about his condition. Or, you know, whatever's happening."

"I'll leave the message."

"And take my number. I'm at . . ." But he's forgotten the

number and it's not written on the phone. "Uhm . . . I'm at Nicholas's. Christ, Howard got me this apartment. It's Howard's friend's Nicholas."

"Okay."

"Does Nicholas know about this?"

"I couldn't tell you."

"Well, all right. Okay. And I'm . . . I'm sorry, you know, I didn't mean to sound, I just—"

"Okay. 'Bye."

Mark holds the phone against his chest when it hangs up. The world is just too big for him. It's too brutal. He is not strong enough. He calls Alex.

"Alex!"

"Hello? Mark?"

"Alex, what are you doing on Wednesday?"

"I don't know. Why?"

"You gotta come visit Howard with me."

"I'm going to be in the office."

"Afterward."

"I think I'm going to Christine's sister's for dinner."

"Well, how about Thursday."

Alex sighs. "Uh, Mark?"

"Yeah?"

"I'm not going to come with you to Howard's."

"Why not?"

"Because you're going to have to deal with this yourself."

"But he's your friend too."

"I've already visited him. And I'll visit him again. And I'll come with you sometime if it works out. But I'm not going to come and hold your hand."

"But he didn't tell me he was sick. He hid it from me."

"He hid it from everyone. You're just going to have to deal with it."

"But I can't. I'll . . . I'll freak out. If Howard dies I won't have anyone."

"Maybe that's why you should go yourself."

"What does he look like? Is he all . . . skinny and everything?"

"He is."

"I'll die. Alex, you know I'll fucking *die*."

Alex sighs again. "You know, Mark, I don't know what happened to you. You used to be——"

"Oh, fuck you, Alex. Fuck you."

"Listen, Mark. Just go over there. He knows how hard it is for people to see him. He's still Howard. He still understands."

"Oh, God," says Mark, his voice breaking.

"Act like a grown-up, Mark. Deal with it."

They hang up. Mark smokes a cigarette at the window. He goes back to the phone. He dials.

"Cynthia?"

"Oh, hi, Mark."

"Listen, I was thinking of stopping by Howard's on Wednesday. I was wondering if you might want to come along."

"I don't think I can on Wednesday."

"How about Thursday?"

"I could maybe do that. Have you talked to him yet?"

"No, I talked to his brother."

"Oh, Robert. He's sweet."

"So what time on Thursday?"

"You know, actually, I can't on Thursday. I can maybe do it on Friday, if Damian isn't busy. Maybe the three of us could go."

"Yeah," says Mark. "The three of us."

"Maybe on Friday."

"Let's plan on it."

"We can't plan on it, Mark. I'll have to talk to Damian."

"Okay, call me back."

"Listen, don't wait on us."

"No, no, I'm not, I'm . . . I'm going on Wednesday. I just thought all of us could . . ."

"Well, maybe we can. Maybe Friday. But in the meantime, go see him yourself."

"Yeah, no, I mean . . . that's what I was going to do."

38

Wednesday is February first. The bright eastern sky hurts Mark's eyes as he walks to the subway stop. But otherwise it's a relief to be back on the New York streets. Especially today: he hasn't slept, his clothes are dirty, his eyes are red and swollen. Streams of people pass him on the street. He doesn't see them. They don't see him. The big city. The big empty.

On the subway he reads an abandoned issue of the *Daily News*. He reads an unfunny cartoon and bursts into a loud laugh. The other riders watch him warily. Mark sounds insane, he can hear it in his own voice. He coughs to cover another chuckle. Then he throws the paper aside, a little more dramatically than he needed to. More sideways glances. A small Hasidic boy stares at him. Mark leans his head back, lets it rest against the rattling window.

Brooklyn is quiet as usual. A nice, sedate place. Mark should move out here. He will when he gets older. When he gets married. But who's he going to marry? Alex was right, it's beyond Mark's capabilities. Maybe if he totally lost it he could get one of those mothering types. Women who like fuck-ups. Mark isn't quite fucked up enough though. More drugs, more alcohol. But really how much worse could he get? And anyway he doesn't like those types: hysterical girlfriends trying to drag their drunken artist boyfriends out of Steel, he's seen it, the screaming, the sobbing, the police lights in the street.

Mark stops. He's at Howard's. He turns to face the steps but can't move. He breathes deeply but there's a choking sensation in his throat. He blinks and his eyes burn. He digs a paper napkin out of his coat pocket and dabs at his face. Then he steps up to the door and buzzes Howard's apartment.

Robert is there and lets Mark in. Howard is in the kitchen and comes out immediately. He doesn't look nearly as bad as Mark expected. And anyway, they haven't seen each other in a year. Howard introduces Mark to Robert. Everyone smiles and shakes hands. Does Mark want tea? Sure. He sits down on the familiar sofa. Robert goes back to Howard's office. Howard makes the tea.

"So tell me about Portland," Howard says, placing the steaming cup in front of Mark.

Mark does. "It was great. I mean, I didn't really take full advantage of it. I never went hiking or anything. But it was still really fun. And I met some nice people. And like you said: it was good to get away."

"How'd you like the other faculty?" asks Howard.

"They were great. They were really nice, really solid down-to-earth types. Bill Masters was great. And everyone was very impressed about my books and being associated with you and everything."

Howard smiles. Mark smiles back. Mark is noticing Howard's face. It didn't look much different when Mark first came in. It looks skinnier from this angle. His arms look different too. But the worst part are Howard's legs. Even through his pants, they look like sticks. His ankles look like they could just break. Mark looks into his cup.

"And I taught. I guess I wrote you that. Teaching the workshops. It was okay. Not too bad. Not too distracting from my . . . from my own stuff." Tears begin to well in Mark's eyes.

"I'm glad to hear it."

"The whole thing was really . . . positive . . ." Mark's voice trails off.

Silence fills the room.

"Howard?" says Mark.

"Yes?"

"Why didn't you tell me, you know, about being sick?" Mark begins to break down. A tear streams down his face.

"I didn't know, for one thing," Howard's voice says. "And then when I did know, well, what am I going to say? What do you say to people?"

Mark wipes his face with his sleeve. He takes deep breaths until he can talk again.

"I'm sorry," says Mark, a new determination in his voice. "That's probably why you don't want to say anything, so you don't have to sit around watching people cry all day."

"In a way, it is."

"Thanks for doing all that stuff for me while I was away," whispers Mark, struggling to keep the hardness in his voice.

"I was glad to do it. It's been very exciting. In fact I have some stuff for you here. I just talked to Nigel last week . . ."

Howard struggles to get out of his chair. Mark jumps up to help him but it's too late, Howard is up. Mark follows him into his office. Robert is sitting on the floor, with a huge box of papers. Mark nods and smiles at him. But Robert, who looked fine when he opened the door, now looks shell-shocked, distraught, destroyed.

Howard has trouble with the heavy file cabinets. Mark wants to help, he hesitates and then grips the cabinet. Howard gets it open and then looks inside. Mark can't help but catch the confusion on the older man's gaunt face. He looks like he doesn't know what he's doing.

"What is it, Howard?" says Mark.

"It's the Italian edition."

"That's all right, Howard, we don't have to get it now."

"But it's here, it's beautiful. I want you to see it."

"Really, Howard," says Mark. "I could care less."

Howard looks at him with a strange intensity. "Of course you care," he says. "It's your book."

"Okay," says Mark quietly, "let's have a look."

Robert gets up from the floor. "I think I mailed that actually," he tells his brother.

"Where?" asks Howard.

"To Oregon? I think that was the address in your Rolodex."

"Oh, great," says Howard.

"It's all right," Mark tells Robert. "I'll call them. I was meaning to call Bill anyway."

Back in the living room Howard has to take some pills. Then Robert wants Howard to rest but Howard doesn't want to. This little altercation is hard for Mark to watch. The two brothers are both so exhausted, so strained to their limits.

"Listen, I gotta go," says Mark.

This brings an exasperated silence from Howard. Robert must win all these arguments. Mark wonders if the best thing he could do for Howard is side with him against his brother. But no, the best thing he can do is leave. At least that's what he wants to do.

"Hey, uh, Cynthia and Damian, they were thinking of maybe coming by later in the week. Maybe Friday. I was going to come too. Is that cool?"

"Of course. Call first. Talk to Robert if I'm not here."

Howard offers his hand to shake and Mark takes it. But then he attempts to hug his publisher. It's an awkward motion, Mark has never touched him like this before. And then when Mark feels how small he is, when he thinks he can feel his ribs through his shirt and sweater, Mark's heart nearly stops in his chest.

"Thanks for coming by, Mark," says Howard.

Mark has trouble raising his eyes and when he does Howard isn't looking at him anyway. Mark is not so big a part of Howard's life as Howard is of his. And anyway what difference does it make? Nothing matters now.

Mark gets one block away from Howard's before he starts crying. He walks and cries and smokes. This goes on for a while and when he finally looks up at a street sign, he's totally lost. It's almost a relief. He hasn't eaten yet today and walks into a corner pizza shop. He gets a soggy slice and sits at the window. A couple bites and he's had enough. He lights a cigarette. He's all cried out now and for the first time in a long time he feels pleasantly removed from himself. He smokes and sits motionless on the stool, staring across the street at the apartment fronts on the opposite side. He watches a woman with a stroller struggle to get out the front door of her building. Another woman, older, walks by with a wheeled grocery basket. Finally Mark gets up. He asks the man behind the counter where the nearest subway station is. The man gives him directions. Mark thanks him and steps back onto the cold sidewalk.

39

Cynthia never calls back. Mark doesn't call her either. He's thinking he'll go see Howard on Friday regardless but on Thursday night he ends up having a drink with Peter which leads to several bong hits which leads to a coke session that goes late into the night. On Friday, Mark isn't going anywhere.

But then on Saturday Mark's phone rings. "Is this Mark West?"

"Yes, it is."

"My name is Brenda Kassner? I'm a producer at WPNY here in New York?"

"Uh-huh."

"We're doing a show tomorrow on if poetry matters?"

"Oh. Uhm, I don't think——"

"Allen Ginsberg had a scheduling conflict so we decided to call you. The other panelists are Galway Kinnell, Richard Wilbur and Sharon Olds. This is for 'The Debra Harper Show.' It runs live, nationwide."

"Oh."

"And the reason your name came up was: we thought we needed someone younger? And we saw your *New York* magazine article?"

"Richard Wilbur," says Mark. "Didn't he win the Nobel Prize?"

"He won the Pulitzer Prize. Twice. And he was the Poet Laureate of the the United States."

"Huh," says Mark. "And you want me?"

"You got reviewed in the London *Times*, right?"

"Well, yeah."

"And you're translated in Japan?"

"Yeah, but——"

"Then we want you. We want someone younger. We do the show live tomorrow. Shall I give you the address?"

Mark writes it down. Then he hangs up and lights a cigarette. His first instinct, naturally, is to call Howard. To ask for advice, to commiserate, to brag. Instead he stands at the window and watches people walk on the street below.

That night Mark goes to a movie with Peter. They meet Claire and some other friends at the theater. Everyone is excited for Mark. None of them know much about poetry but they all know what a Pulitzer Prize is. Afterward they go to the apartment of the friends. They are also music-video makers. And cokeheads. Mark passes up several lines and sips from a vodka tonic instead. But not doing the coke is making him drink too much so he switches to straight tonic and then rewards himself by doing a line or two or three. Fortunately, the coke runs out before he gets too wired. Peter gives him a Valium anyway. And a last bit of coke, in case Mark needs a pick-me-up in the morning.

Mark sleeps reasonably well. He wakes up early and

takes a long hot shower. Then he shaves and dresses and prepares to leave. He wasn't going to bring the coke but at the last minute he stuffs it in his pocket.

He rides the D train uptown. WPNY is on West Fifty-ninth Street. It's Sunday, midday, it's surprisingly warm. Mark sweats in his sweater and black overcoat. He arrives at the address early and so kills time by walking around the block. But when he sees a pay phone, he suddenly panics. He put off calling Howard yesterday and then forgot about it last night. He's got to tell him to tune in. It's Howard's success too. What was Mark thinking? He rushes to the phone and dials Howard's number. He gets Robert on the phone. Howard's not there, he's in the hospital.

"Could you tell him I'm going to be on the radio? Like in about an hour, on WPNY."

"I'll give him the message."

"Could you call him? I think he'll be excited. There's all these famous people. Really famous. It's going national."

"I can call the hospital. That's all I can do."

Mark hesitates. Does he sound like a raving egomaniac? "I mean, you know, I just thought, if he's just sitting there, he might want to listen."

"I'll call the hospital."

Mark is now late when he arrives at the studio. In the hallway he meets and shakes hands with Brenda Kassner and meets, very briefly, Sharon Olds. Then Mark dashes into a restroom and finishes off his coke. He doesn't meet Richard Wilbur and Galway Kinnell until he's sitting with them at a large table in Studio C. Another woman, not Brenda, introduces him to the two older poets, who are polite and reserved. Anyway, conversation is difficult as headphones are being passed out, microphones arranged, tape recorders readied. Mark puts on his headphones and finds the utter silence reassuring. The coke has energized him physically but the adrenaline in his bloodstream seems to be slowing his brain. For instance, he can think of nothing whatsoever to say to the other poets, who, for their own part, aren't saying much anyway.

"Hello? Can you hear me?" someone says in the headphones.

Mark wants to say yes, but who does he say it to? A woman's hand touches his back and then pulls his microphone closer to him. He manages to smile across the table at Sharon Olds, who returns his sheepish expression with a dazzling grin. She oozes presence. She and the other two. Down the table Richard Wilbur is wearing a beautiful Brooks Brothers suit. Galway Kinnell looks like a movie star. These are the great men and women of American letters. Mark swallows a hard, coke-dried swallow.

"Uh," says Mark, ripping off his headphones. "Excuse me!" He manages to catch the attention of the female assistant. "I need water."

Mark's frantic request is then duplicated. All the guests want water. Richard Wilbur and Galway Kinnell chuckle at something between them. Then Wilbur smiles over at Mark. Mark tries to swallow but his throat is so dry it won't go down. He forces a weak smile but the older man has turned his attention to Sharon Olds. The water comes and Mark gulps it. Then the symposium begins.

The first question is, Does poetry matter in the age of television, computers, the Internet?

Richard Wilbur thinks it does. His voice is deep, rich, resonant. Mark watches him touch his chin and consider his remarks. He looks like a duke or a count. His face is impossibly smooth and clean: facials.

Galway Kinnell is more earthy. But he too thinks poetry matters. He thinks it's part of a general meditative tradition.

Sharon Olds wants to rephrase the question. But yes, of course poetry matters. She enjoys the Internet and thinks that poetry is never afraid of the future. Instead it meets the advances of civilization and colludes with them.

Mark thinks poetry matters too. "Like when I first came to New York. I didn't really know anyone. And then I started hanging out at these open mikes. And it was this cool scene. And it brought me together, you know, with other people that I could relate to."

Debra Harper stops the conversation there to introduce everyone. She does the three established poets first. Mark is gulping water. He's sweating now, and dizzy. The water doesn't seem to quench the thirst in his throat and upper chest. When Debra Harper gets to Mark she seems to hesitate. At first Mark thinks she's trying to justify his presence on the panel. Did he sound that stupid? But then he sees that in fact she's gushing, she's introducing him to America.

Meanwhile, Richard Wilbur is asking one of the assistants for something else, coffee, it turns out. Galway Kinnell has removed his headphones to adjust something. Sharon Olds is doodling on a notepad.

Mark shouldn't have done the coke. It's not helping him think and it's making speech impossible. Fortunately, when Mark finishes his water, Sharon Olds slides hers over to him.

The next question is about the academization of poetry. Richard gives his opinion. Galway gives his. Then Sharon politely takes issue with Richard. Then Galway joins in. Mark is thankful to be skipped over.

The next question: Is poetry too esoteric, too inaccessible? Richard doesn't think so. Galway resists the idea, poetry is art, it has to be complicated. Sharon Olds admits there has been some commonality lost as poetry adjusts to the academic context. It looks like Mark is going to avoid this one too but Debra Harper presses him. And so he talks. "It seems like it is sometimes. I always try to make my stuff so you can easily understand it."

"How about this *underground scene* you were talking about?" asks Debra. "Is the new generation going to make poetry more accessible?"

"Yeah, sure, I mean, it's more just normal language, or whatever. More like talking. It's just more straightforward and real, I guess."

Mark sees out of the corner of his eye a grunt of impatience from Richard Wilbur. But Debra Harper keeps things moving. The last question: Does America properly support the arts, literature, poetry?

Richard talks about steps he took as Poet Laureate to strengthen the position of poetry not just in the literary world but throughout American society. Kinnell talks about the romance of being young and obscure and the inevitable alienation of success. Sharon Olds discusses the ways being a woman makes it doubly difficult to be taken seriously as an American artist. Debra rephrases the question for Mark: "Do you feel like America has overlooked you? Since your work has done so well abroad but you are virtually unknown here?"

"Not really," says Mark into the microphone.

"Do you think neglect hinders your development as an artist?"

"No," says Mark. "It's probably for the best. I mean, it would be sort of insulting if they liked what you were doing. I mean, America is so, you know, sort of stupid.

Who cares what they think? I hate America. I mean, not like I really hate it, but just . . . I just wish there was something to watch on TV. Or something to read. It's just so boring. I'm scared to go to Europe. What if it's just as bad? Then there'd be no hope at all."

Mark can sense there is some sort of commotion at the end of the table. Galway is saying something to Richard. Mark can hear it vaguely in his headphones. He hears Sharon Olds clear her throat.

Then Richard bursts in with that wonderful voice of his. Mark reaches for his water, he isn't hearing what Richard is saying, he's just listening for any breaks, any more questions. Time's almost up. Sharon is now saying something. Mark's face is hot. He can feel the sweat dripping down his forehead. When he looks up from his water, Galway is staring at him. Mark tries to smile. Then he sees Richard Wilbur glaring at him, in mid-sentence. Richard is talking *to him*. Mark clutches the sides of his headphones but all he catches is Debra desperately explaining that they're out of time. Mark missed something. But it doesn't matter. He just wants to get out of here. He's dying for a cigarette.

40

The next day Mark meets with the new manager of Steel. He's a short, weasely man. "We do things a little differently here now," Mark is told as they tour the club. But that's obvious. For one thing they have redesigned the place. It's trendier now, brighter, the old back room is now officially a VIP room. Also the money is different. They pay you now. With the taxes taken out. Which means you'll have to report your tips. Which means you'll lose half your money. The new manager shows Mark the new cash registers. He points out the surveillance cameras above each one. He grins at Mark. There'll be no free lunch now that he's in charge. Mark doesn't know what to say.

But he remains polite. He lights a cigarette and waits patiently while the manager runs upstairs to take a call. Mark's only regret: he listed Howard in his references. He shouldn't have. He doesn't want to expose Howard to this man. Nor does he want Howard to think of him working at Steel, of him sliding back into his old ways. Mark smokes his cigarette, looks around his old workplace, says goodbye to it.

The new manager promises to call as he leads Mark out. Mark thanks him and is happy to be outside, out on busy West Broadway. He walks to Canal Street, to a diner where he gets a fried-egg sandwich and coffee and flips open an abandoned *New York Post*. But he feels a weird electricity the minute he touches the paper. There's something in it, something that relates to him. Mark flips slowly through the first couple pages and there it is, in a page-six gossip item:

> *The literary world is all abuzz on Monday following a rare moment of generational conflict. Ex Poet Laureate and Pulitzer Prize–winner* **Richard Wilbur** *took young poet* **Mark West** *to task on National Public Radio last Sunday. Mr. West apparently hates American culture, and considers modern poetry "boring and stupid." Mr. Wilbur wasted no time letting his junior know what he thought of his inflammatory comments, much to the delight of host* **Debra Harper.** *"We don't usually get such drama from the poets," said Deb. "It was refreshing." Mr. West, to his credit, enjoys profound critical appreciation in Japan and Europe but is apparently known only in subterranean "spoken word" circles here in the Big Apple.*

Mark reads the item again as he chews his sandwich. He sips his coffee. He reads it one more time. As usual his first impulse is to call Howard and confer, how will this play, who will see it, will it help, hurt, advance his career? But he can't do that. Instead he shuts the paper. He's going to leave it but he can't do that either. What if Howard misses it? If nothing else it'd be something for them to talk about during his next visit. He removes the page from the paper, folds it carefully and slips it into his pocket.

Outside he lights a cigarette and takes a deep breath. Now he feels the tingles of excitement. He pulls out the page, unfolds it, reads it again, grins to himself. Maybe he should go see Howard right now. He returns the page to his pocket and starts walking. He must be smiling because on the next block a young woman smiles back at him. Sex, he hasn't even thought about it. He turns to watch the girl, sucking hard on his cigarette, which even for its calming qualities is having no effect on the excitement rising in Mark's chest.

Back in his apartment there are several messages on his answering machine. The first is from Cynthia. By total coincidence she was listening to "The Debra Harper Show." And then this morning she saw the item in the *Post*. The second message is from the guy at Steel. He'd like to talk to Mark about possible shifts. The third is from a reporter at *Newsweek*. He's doing a story on the new "spoken word" phenomenon and he wants to ask Mark some questions. Then someone from *Flash* comes on. Would Mark like to do an "Up & Comers" profile? It has to be low-keyed, more humor-oriented. They try to avoid politics. The next message is from Robert. Howard had a stroke. He's in a coma. They don't think he's going to come out of it.

Mark doesn't like hospitals. Especially hospitals in New York. They're too small, too crowded, too full of human suffering. Howard's room is full of flowers. It's a small private room: Howard's family money coming through when it counts. Howard lies motionless on the bed. Robert stands beside him with another woman who is too distraught to talk. Mark stands beside them, then retreats to the back wall. He doesn't feel right here. There is something about his relationship with Howard: Mark's immaturity, his attitude, the idea that he was somehow doing Howard a favor to work with him. All of that is somehow palpable in this room. Mark is guilty here. Guilty of not appreciating a wonderful man.

When Robert finally leads the sobbing woman away, Mark breathes a deep sigh. But alone in the room, he doesn't know what to do with himself. He slides around the foot of the bed to get to the window. But the view is of an air duct and a brick wall not two feet beyond the glass. So Mark sits in the small chair by the bed. He tries to look at Howard but can't quite lift his eyes that high. Instead he pulls one of the flowers out of the vase on the windowsill. He holds it by the stem and looks into the top of it, into the soft folds of the petals. He sniffs it. It smells flowery, musky, not sweet. Mark puts it back. He looks at his hands. He looks at the brick wall. Finally he looks at Howard. The man's face is like a skull now, but without the pleasing hardness of bone. The skin is still there, too much skin, it hangs. Mark can't look. He tries to speak. He considers holding Howard's hand, maybe he can sense the contact, the warmth, probably not. Mark tries to speak. "Howard?" he starts. It occurs to him to get out the *Post* article. It's still in his pocket. He'll read it to Howard. That would be nice, wouldn't it? But what if someone came in? To be caught reading his own press clippings to a man in a coma. Jesus. He leaves the paper in his pocket.

"Howard, you fucked up," he whispers to the inert body. "I needed you to teach me how to deal with things like this. But look at you. How am I ever . . . going to learn anything . . . now?" He says these last words into his lap, his head down. With no particular thought in his mind, his body begins to squeeze out tears, one after another. They land in his lap, on his bare wrists where they protrude from the sleeves of Howard's herringbone blazer.

Then Robert is back. With a doctor. Mark can't speak, he just goes out. He finds his way through the hospital halls to the stairwell, which is concrete, bleak, grey. But then it releases him onto the bright street. Mark stands for a moment in the sunshine. He lights a cigarette and starts to walk. He's on Second Avenue, he heads south toward Wall Street. He walks through the East Village, across Houston, into the Lower East Side. He passes within a block of No Se No. He's got nothing better to do, he doubles back.

It's not open. Not even close. It looks so different that for a moment Mark wonders if he's even on the right street. But he is. He remembers the doorway, the stoop, the cracks in the sidewalk. There are people walking by. Mark moves to let two Puerto Rican women pass. He's going to stand there for a second, to let the sight of it sink in. But then something pushes him along, the flow of foot traffic, the wind, the sun shining down. He lets it, he walks, and then suddenly he can breathe again. He's awake again. And starving hungry. He throws down his cigarette and crosses the street, catching a glimpse of himself in a storefront window. But it doesn't look like him. It looks different. It looks like an adult. Like a grown-up. Like someone who knows what he has to do.